Join favou

Louise Allen

as she explores the tangled love-lives of

Those Scandalous Ravenhursts

First, you travelled across
war-torn Europe with
THE DANGEROUS MR RYDER

Then you accompanied Mr Ryder's sister,
THE OUTRAGEOUS LADY FELSHAM,
on her quest for a hero.

You were scandalised by
THE SHOCKING LORD STANDON

You shared dangerous, sensual adventures
with
THE DISGRACEFUL MR RAVENHURST

You were seduced and swept off your feet by
THE NOTORIOUS MR HURST

Now meet
THE PIRATICAL MISS RAVENHURST

Author Note

After five Ravenhurst love stories it is time to meet the youngest and most distant of the cousins. Clemence lives a life of privilege and comfort at the heart of Jamaican society until circumstances force her to make a choice—marriage to the despicable Lewis Naismith or flight.

Clemence has a plan—Ravenhursts always do—but it does not include running straight into the clutches of the most feared pirate in the Caribbean. There doesn't seem any way out, unless she can trust both her instincts and the enigmatic navigator Nathan Stanier.

I knew Clemence would have the courage and wits to survive on the *Sea Scorpion*, but what is a young lady to do when she is comprehensively ruined in the process?

I do hope you enjoy finding out as much as I did. I felt sad to write the last word in the chronicles of *Those Scandalous Ravenhursts*, but perhaps one day I can return to their world and explore the life and loves of some of the other characters I met along the way.

THE PIRATICAL
MISS RAVENHURST

Louise Allen

Lincolnshire
County Council

AD 04527041

Askews

£3.79

All the characters in this book have no existence outside the imagination of the author, and have no relation whatsoever to anyone bearing the same name or names. They are not even distantly inspired by any individual known or unknown to the author, and all the incidents are pure invention.

First published in Great Britain 2009
Harlequin Mills & Boon Limited,
Eton House, 18-24 Paradise Road, Richmond, Surrey TW9 1SR

© Melanie Hilton 2009

ISBN: 978 0 263 86797 8

Set in Times Roman 10½ on 12¼ pt
04-0909-79537

Harlequin Mills & Boon policy is to use papers that are natural, renewable and recyclable products and made from wood grown in sustainable forests. The logging and manufacturing process conform to the legal environmental regulations of the country of origin.

Printed and bound in Spain
by Litografia Rosés, S.A., Barcelona

For Nathan Oakman
who is sure to grow up to be a hero

Louise Allen has been immersing herself in history, real and fictional, for as long as she can remember, and finds landscapes and places evoke powerful images of the past. Louise divides her time between Bedfordshire and the Norfolk coast, where she spends as much time as possible with her husband at the cottage they are renovating. With any excuse she'll take a research trip abroad—Venice, Burgundy and the Greek islands are favourite atmospheric destinations. Please visit Louise's website—www.louiseallenregency.co.uk—for the latest news!

Recent novels by the same author:

RAVENHURST FAMILY TREE

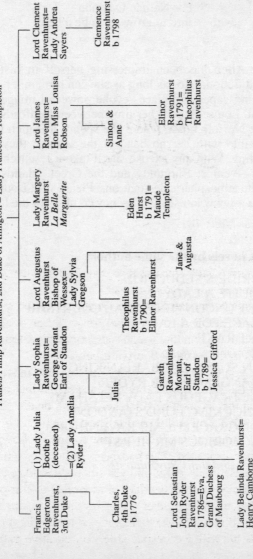

Francis Philip Ravenhurst, 2nd Duke of Allington = Lady Francesca Templeton

Francis Edgerton Ravenhurst, 3rd Duke — (1) Lady Julia Boothe (deceased) =(2) Lady Amelia Ryder

Charles, 4th Duke b 1776

Lord Sebastian John Ryder Ravenhurst b 1786=Eva, Grand Duchess of Maubourg

Lady Belinda Ravenhurst=Henry Camborne Viscount Felsham d 1814 =Major Ashe Reynard, Viscount Dereham

Lady Sophia Ravenhurst=George Morant Earl of Standon

Julia

Gareth Ravenhurst Morant, Earl of Standon b 1789= Jessica Gifford

Lord Augustus Ravenhurst Bishop of Wessex=Lady Sylvia Gregson

Theophilus Ravenhurst b 1790= Elinor Ravenhurst

Jane & Augusta

Lady Margery Ravenhurst *La Belle Marguerite*

Eden Hurst b 1791= Maude Templeton

Lord James Ravenhurst=Hon. Miss Louisa Robson

Simon & Anne

Elinor Ravenhurst b 1791= Theophilus Ravenhurst

Lord Clement Ravenhurst= Lady Andrea Sayers

Clemence Ravenhurst b 1798

Chapter One

Jamaica—June 1817

'I would sooner—'

'Sooner what?' Her uncle regarded Clemence with contempt. 'You would sooner die?'

'Sooner marry the first man I met outside the gates than *that*.' She jerked her head towards her cousin, sprawled in the window seat, his attention on the female servants in the torch-lit courtyard below.

'But you do not have any choice,' Joshua Naismith said, in the same implacably patient tone he had used to her in the six months since her father's death. 'You are my ward, you will do as I tell you.'

'My father never intended me to marry Lewis,' Clemence protested. She had been protesting with a rising sense of desperation ever since she had recovered sufficiently from her daze of mourning to comprehend that her late mother's half-brother was not the protector that her father had expected him to be when he made his will. Her respectable, conservative, rather dull Uncle Joshua was a predator, his claws reaching for her fortune.

'The intentions of the late lamented Lord Clement Ravenhurst,' Mr Naismith said, 'are of no interest to me whatsoever. The effect of his will is to place you under my control, a fitting recompense for years of listening to his idiotic political opinions and his absurd social theories.'

'My father did not believe in the institution of slavery,' Clemence retorted, angered despite her own apprehension. 'Most enlightened people feel the same. You did not have to listen to what you do not believe in—you could have attempted to counter his arguments. But then you have neither the intellectual capacity, nor the moral integrity to do so, have you, Uncle?'

'Insolent little bitch.' Lewis uncoiled himself from the seat and walked to his father's side. He frowned at her, an expression she had caught him practising in front of the mirror, no doubt in an attempt to transform his rather ordinary features into an ideal of well-bred authority. 'A pity you were not a boy—he raised you like one, he let you run wild like one and now, look at you— you might as well be one.'

Clemence hated the flush she could feel on her cheekbones, hated the fact that his words stung. It was shallow to wish she had a petite, curvaceous figure. A few months ago she had at least possessed a small bosom and the gentle swell of feminine hips, now, with the appetite of a mouse, she had lost so much weight that she might as well have been twelve again. Combined with the rangy height she had inherited from her father, Clemence was all too aware that she looked like a schoolboy dressed up to play a female role in a Shakespeare play.

Defensively her hand went to the weight of her hair, coiled and dressed simply in the heat. Its silky touch reminded her of her femininity, her one true beauty, all the colours of wheat and toffee and gilt, mixed and mingling.

'If I had been a boy, I wouldn't have to listen to your disgusting marriage plans,' she retorted. 'But you'd still be stealing my inheritance, whatever my sex, I have no doubt of that. Is money the *only* thing that is important to you?'

'We are merchants.' Uncle Joshua's high colour wattled his smooth jowls. 'We make money, we do not have it drop into our laps like your aristocratic relatives.'

'Papa was the youngest son, he worked for his fortune—'

'The youngest son of the Duke of Allington. Oh dear, what poverty, how he must have struggled.'

That was the one card she had not played in the weeks as hints had become suggestions and the suggestions, orders. 'You know my English relatives are powerful,' Clemence said. 'Do you wish to antagonise them?'

'They are a very long way away and hold no sway here in the West Indies.' Joshua's expression was smug. 'Here the ear of the Governor and one's credit with the bankers are all that matter. In time, when Lewis decides to go back to England, his marriage to you may well be of social advantage, that is true.'

'As I have no intention of marrying my cousin, he will have no advantage from me.'

'You *will* marry me.' Lewis took a long stride, seized her wrist and yanked her, off-balance, to face him. She was tall enough to stare into his eyes, refusing to flinch even as his fingers dug into the narrow bones of her wrist, although her heart seemed to bang against her ribs. 'The banns will be read for the first time next Sunday.'

'I will never consent and you cannot force me kicking and screaming to the altar—not and maintain your precious respectability.' Somehow she kept her voice steady. It was hard after nineteen years of being loved and indulged to find the strength to fight betrayal and greed, but some unexpected reserve of pride and desperation was keeping her defiant.

'True.' Her head snapped round at the smugness in her uncle's voice. Joshua smiled, confident. The chilly certainty crept over her that he had thought long and hard about this and the thought of her refusal on the altar steps did not worry him in the slightest. 'You have two choices, my dear niece. You can behave in a dutiful manner and marry Lewis when the banns have been called or he will come to your room every night until he has you with child and then, I think, you will agree.'

'And if I do not, even then?' Fainting, Clemence told herself fiercely, would not help in the slightest, even though the room swam and the temptation to just let go and slip out of this nightmare was almost overwhelming.

'There is always a market for healthy children on the islands,' Lewis said, hitching one buttock on the table edge and smiling at her. 'We will just keep going until you come to your senses.'

'You—' Clemence swallowed and tried again. 'You would sell your *own child* into slavery?'

Lewis shrugged. 'What use is an illegitimate brat? Marry me and your children will want for nothing. Refuse and what happens to them will be entirely your doing.'

'They will want for nothing save a decent father,' she snapped back, praying that her churning stomach would not betray her. 'You are a rapist, an embezzler and a blackmailer and you—' she turned furiously on her uncle '—are as bad. I cannot believe your lackwit son thought of this scheme all by himself.'

Joshua had never hit her before, no one had. Clemence did not believe the threat in her uncle's raised hand, did not flinch away until the blow caught her on the cheekbone under her right eye, spinning her off her feet to crash against the table and fall to the floor.

Somehow she managed to push herself up, then stumble to her feet, her head spinning. Joshua Naismith's voice came from a long way away, his image so shrunk he seemed to be at the wrong end of a telescope. His voice buzzed in her ears. 'Will you consent to the banns being read and agree to marry Lewis?'

'No.' *Never.*

'Then you will go to your room and stay there. Your meals will be brought to you and you will eat; your scrawny figure offends me. Lewis will visit you tomorrow. I think you are in no fit state to pay him proper heed tonight.'

Proper heed? If her cousin came within range of her and any kind of sharp weapon he would never be able to father a child again. 'Ring for Eliza,' Clemence said, lifting her hand to her throbbing face. 'I need her assistance.'

'You have a new abigail.' Joshua reached out and tugged the bell. 'That insolent girl of yours has been dismissed. Freed slaves indeed!' The woman who entered was buxom, her skin the colour of smooth coffee, her hair braided intricately. The look she shot Clemence held contempt and dislike.

'Your mistress?' She stared at Lewis. No wonder Marie Luce was looking like that: she must know the men's intentions and know that Clemence would be taking Lewis's attention away from her.

'She does as she is told,' Lewis said smoothly. 'And will be rewarded for it. Take her to her chamber, make sure she eats,' he added to the other woman. 'Lock the door and then come to my room.'

Clemence let herself be led out of the door. Here, in the long passage with its louvred windows open at each end to encourage a draught, the sound of the sea on the beach far below was a living presence. Her feet stumbled on the familiar smooth stone flags. From the white walls the darkened portraits of generations of ancestors stared blankly down, impotent to help her.

'Where is Eliza?' Thank goodness her maid was a freed woman with her own papers, not subject to the whim of the Naismiths.

Marie Luce shrugged, her dark eyes hostile as she gripped Clemence's arm, half-supporting, half-imprisoning her. 'I do not know. I do not care.' Her lilting accent made poetry out of the acid words. 'Why do you make Master Lewis angry? Marry him, then he will get you with child and forget about you.'

'I do not want him, you are welcome to him,' Clemence retorted as they reached the door of her room. 'Please fetch me some warm water to bathe my face.' The door clicked shut behind the maid and the key turned. Through the slats she could hear her heelless shoes clicking as she made her way to the back door and the kitchen wing.

Clemence sank down on the dressing-table stool, her fingers tight on the edge for support. The image that stared back at her from the mirror was not reassuring. Her right cheek was already swelling, the skin red and darkening, her eye beginning to close. It would be black tomorrow, she realised. Her left eye, wide, looked more startlingly green in contrast and her hair had slipped from its pins and lay in a heavy braid on her shoulder.

Gingerly, Clemence straightened her back, wincing at the bruises from the impact with the table. There was no padding on her bones to cushion any falls, she realised; it was mere luck she had not broken ribs. She must eat. Starving herself into a decline would not help matters, although what would?

The door opened to admit Marie Luce with one of the footmen carrying a supper tray. The man, one of the house staff she had known all her life, took a startled look at her face and then stared straight ahead, expressionless. 'Master Lewis says you are to eat,' the other woman said, putting down the water ewer she held. 'I stay until you do.'

Clemence dipped a cloth in the water and held it to her face. It stung and throbbed: she supposed she should be grateful Uncle Joshua had used his ringless right hand and the blow had not broken the skin. 'Very well.' Chicken and rice, stuffed pimentos, corn fritters, cake with syrup, milk. Her stomach roiled, but instinct told Clemence to eat, however little appetite she had and however painful it was to chew.

She knew the worst now: it was time to fight, although how, locked in her room, she had no idea. The plates scraped clean and the milk drunk, Marie Luce cleared the table and let herself out. Clemence strained to hear—the key grated in the lock. It was too much to hope that the woman would be careless about that.

She felt steadier for the food. It seemed weeks since she had eaten properly, grief turning to uneasiness, then apprehension, then fear as her uncle's domination over the household and estate and her life had tightened into a stranglehold.

It was pointless to expect help from outside; their friends and acquaintances had been told she was ill with grief, unbalanced, and the doctor had ordered complete seclusion and rest. Even her close friends Catherine Page and Laura Steeples had believed her uncle's lies and obediently kept away. She had seen their letters to him, full of shocked sympathy that she was in such a decline.

And who could she trust, in any case? She had trusted Joshua, and how wrong she had been about him!

Clemence stood and went to the full-length window, its casement open on to the fragrant heat of the night. Her father had insisted that Raven's Hold was built right on the edge of the cliff, just as the family castle in Northumberland was, and the balcony of her room jutted out into space above the sea.

When she was a child, after her mother's death, she had run wild with the sons of the local planters, borrowing their clothes, scrambling through the cane fields, hiding in the plantation buildings. Scandalised local matrons had finally persuaded her father that she should become a conformable young lady once her fourteenth birthday was past and so her days of climbing out of the window at night and up the trellis to freedom and adventures were long past.

She leaned on the balcony and smiled, her expression turning into a grimace as the bruises made themselves felt. If only it were so easy to climb away now!

But why not? Clemence straightened, tinglingly alert. If she could get out of the house, down to the harbour, then the *Raven Princess* would be there, due to sail for England with the morning light. It was the largest of her father's ships—her ships—now that pirates had captured *Raven Duchess*, the action that had precipitated her father's heart stroke and death.

But if she just ran away they would hunt her down like a fugitive slave… Clemence paced into the room, thinking furiously. Her uncle's sneer came back to her. *You would sooner die?* Let him think that, then. Somewhere, surely, were the boy's clothes she had once worn. She pulled open presses, flung up the lids of the trunks, releasing wafts of sandalwood from their interiors. Yes, here at the bottom of one full of rarely used blankets were the loose canvas breeches, the shirt and waistcoat.

She pulled off her gown and tried them on. The bottom of the trousers flapped above her ankle bones now, but the shirt and waistcoat had always been on the large side. After some thought she tore linen strips and bound her chest tightly; her bosom was unimpressive, but even so, it was better to take no chances. Clemence dug out the buckled shoes, tried them on her bare feet, then looked in the mirror. The image of a gangly youth stared back, oddly adorned by the thick braid of hair.

That was going to have to go, there was no room for regret. Clemence found the scissors, gritted her teeth and hacked. The hair went into a cloth, knotted tightly, then wrapped up into a bundle with everything she had been wearing that evening. A thought struck her and she took out the gown again to tear a thin, ragged strip from the hem. Her slippers she flung out of the window and the modest pearls and earrings she buried under the jewellery in her trinket box.

The new figure that looked back at her from the glass had ragged hair around its ears and a dramatically darkening bruise over cheek and eye. Her mind seemed to be running clearly now, as though she had pushed through a forest of fear and desperation into open air. Clemence took the pen from the standish and scrawled

I cannot bear it... On a sheet of paper. A drop of water from the washstand was an artistic and convincing teardrop to blur the shaky signature. The ink splashed on to the dressing table, over her fingers. All the better to show agitation.

She looped the bundle on to her belt and set a stool by the balcony before scrambling up on to the rail. Perched there, she snagged the strip from her gown under a splinter, then kicked the stool over. There: the perfect picture of a desperate fall to the crashing waves below. How Uncle Joshua was going to explain that was his problem.

Now all she had to do was to ignore the lethal drop below and pray that the vines and the trellis would still hold her. Clemence reached up, set her shoe on the first, distantly remembered foothold, and swung clear of the rail.

She rapidly realised just how dangerous this was, something the child that she had been had simply not considered. And five years of ladylike behaviour, culminating in weeks spent almost ill with grief and desperation, had weakened her muscles. Her dinner lurched in her stomach and her throat went dry. Teeth gritted she climbed on, trying not to think about centipedes, spiders or any of the other interesting inhabitants of the ornamental vines she was clutching. However venomous they might be, they were not threatening to rape and rob her.

The breath sobbed in her throat, but she reached the ledge that ran around the house just beneath the eaves and began to shuffle along it, clinging to the gutters. All she had to do now was to get around the corner and she could drop on to the roof of the kitchen wing. From there it was an easy slide to the ground.

A shutter banged open just below where her heels

jutted out into space. Clemence froze. 'No, I don't *want* her, how many times have I got to tell you?' It was Lewis, irritated and abrupt. 'Why would I *want* that scrawny, cantankerous little bitch? It is simply business.'

There was the sound of a woman's voice, low and seductive. Marie Luce. Lewis grunted. 'Get your clothes off, then.' Such a gallant lover, Clemence thought. Her cousin had left the shutters open, forcing her to move with exaggerated care in case her leather soles gritted on the rough stone. Then she was round, dropping on to the thick palmetto thatch, sliding down to the lean-to shed roof and clambering to the ground.

Old One-Eye, the guard dog, whined and came over stiffly to lick her hand, the links of his chain chinking. There was noise from the kitchens, the hum and chirp of insects, the chatter of a night bird. No one would hear her stealthy exit through the yard gate, despite the creaky hinge that never got oiled.

Clemence took to her heels, the bundle bouncing on her hip. Now all she had to do was to get far enough away to hide the evidence that she was still alive, and steal a horse.

It was a moonless night, the darkness of Kingston harbour thickly sprinkled with the sparks of ships' riding-lights. Clemence slid from the horse's back, slapped it on the rump and watched it gallop away, back towards the penn she had taken it from almost three hours before.

The unpaved streets were rough under her stumbling feet but she pushed on, keeping to the shadows, avoiding the clustered drinking houses and brothels that lined the way down to the harbour. It was just her luck that

Raven Princess was moored at the furthest end, Clemence thought, dodging behind some stacked barrels to avoid a group of men approaching down the centre of the street.

And when she got there, she was not at all certain that simply marching on board and demanding to be taken to England was a sensible thing to do. Captain Moorcroft could well decide to return her to Uncle Joshua, despite the fact that the ship was hers. The rights of women was not a highly regarded principle, let alone here on Jamaica in the year 1817.

The hot air held the rich mingled odours of refuse and dense vegetation, open drains, rum, wood smoke and horse dung, but Clemence ignored the familiar stench, quickening her pace into a jog trot. The next quay was the Ravenhurst moorings and the *Raven Princess*…was gone.

She stood staring, mouth open in shock, mind blank, frantically scanning the moored ships for a sight of the black-haired, golden-crowned figurehead. *It must be here!*

'What you looking for, boy?' a voice asked from behind her.

'The *Raven Princess*,' she stammered, her voice husky with shock and disbelief.

'Sailed this evening, damn them, they finished loading early. What do you want with it?'

Clemence turned, keeping her head down so the roughly chopped hair hid her face. 'Cabin boy,' she muttered. 'Cap'n Moorcroft promised me a berth.' There were five men, hard to see against the flare of light from a big tavern, its doors wide open on to the street.

'Is that so? We could do with a cabin boy, couldn't we, lads?' the slightly built figure in the centre of the group said, his voice soft. The hairs on Clemence's nape rose. The others sniggered. 'You come along with us, lad. We'll find you a berth all right.'

'No. No, thank you.' She began to edge away.

'That's "No, thank you, Cap'n",' a tall man with a tricorne hat on his head said, stepping round to block her retreat.

'Cap'n,' she repeated obediently. 'I'll just—'

'Come with us.' The tall man gave her a shove, right up to the rest of the group. The man he called Cap'n put out a hand and laid it on her shoulder. She was close enough to see him now, narrow-faced, his bony jaw obscured by a few days' stubble, his head bare. His clothes were flamboyant, antique almost; coat tails wide, the magnificent lace at his throat, soiled. The eyes that met Clemence's were brown, flat, cold. If a lizard could speak…

'What's your name, boy?'

'Clem. Cap'n.' She tried to hold the reptilian stare, but her eyes dropped, down to where the wrist of the hand that held her was bared, the lace fallen back. There was a tattoo on the back of his hand, the tail and sting of a scorpion, its head and body vanishing into his wide-cuffed sleeve. Her vision blurred.

'Come along then, Clem.'

There was nowhere to run to and the long fingers were biting into her collarbone. Clemence let herself be pushed towards the tavern. It was crowded, she told herself, inside she'd be able to give them the slip.

She knew what they were, and knew, too, that she would be safer by far with Uncle Joshua and Lewis than with these men. They were pirates, and the man who held her, unless scorpion tattoos were the latest fashion, was Red Matthew McTiernan.

They bundled her up the steps, across the porch and

into the heat and light and noise of the tavern. She let herself be pushed along, her eyes darting about the room for an escape route as the crowd shifted uneasily to let McTiernan and his men through. This was a rough place, but the customers were reacting like foxes when the wolf arrives at the kill.

A man came forward, wiping his hands on a stained apron. 'He's over there.' He jerked his head towards a table in the far corner.

The man who sat there was alone, despite the pressure for tables. He was playing hazard, left hand against right, his attention focused on the white cubes that bounced and rolled. He was tall, rangy, carrying no surplus weight. *Built for speed, like a frigate*, Clemence thought, staring at him when she should be watching for her chance. His hair was over-long, brown with sun-bleached tips, his skin very tanned, his clothes had the look of much-worn quality.

'Stanier.'

He looked up, his eyes a startling blue against his dark skin. 'Yes?'

'They tell me you want a navigator's berth.' The man called Stanier nodded. 'Are you any good?'

'I'm the best in these seas,' he said, his lips curving into what might, charitably, be called a smile. 'But you knew that, McTiernan, or you wouldn't be here.'

The bony fingers gripping her shoulder fell away, down to rest on the hilt of the sword that hung by the captain's side. As a ripple of tension ran round the small group, Clemence eased back, poised to slide into the crowd behind.

'That's Captain McTiernan to you.'

'It is if I serve with you,' Stanier said, his tone equable. 'And I will, if it is worth my while.'

'You know what I'm offering,' McTiernan snapped.

'And I want my own cabin. And a servant.'

'What do you think you are? One of his Majesty's bleeding naval officers still? They threw you out—so don't go putting on airs and graces with me.'

Stanier smiled, his eyes cold. 'More fool them. I'm just the best navigator you'll ever see, navy or no navy.'

Now. Clemence slid one foot back, then the other, half-turned and—

'Oh, no, you don't, my lad.' The big man with the tricorne spun her round, fetching her a back-handed cuff that hit her bruised face. Blinded with the sudden pain, Clemence staggered, fell and crashed into a chair in a tangle of limbs.

She put out her right hand, grasping for something to hold on to, and found she was gripping a muscular thigh. Warm, strong—somehow, she couldn't let go.

'What have we here?' She looked up, managing to focus on the interested blue eyes that were studying her hand. She looked down as the navigator lifted it from his leg, prizing the fingers open. An ink stain ran across them. 'You can write, boy?'

'Yessir.' She nodded vehemently, wanting, in that moment, only to be with him, her hand in his. Safe. Lord, how desperate was she, that this hard man represented safety?

'Can you do your figures?' He put out one long finger and just touched the bruise on her face.

'Yessir.' She forced herself not to flinch away.

'Excellent. I'll take you as my servant, then.' Stanier got to his feet, hauling Clemence up by the collar to stand at his side. 'Any objections, gentlemen?'

Chapter Two

'That's our new cabin boy.' Nathan Stanier studied the speaker. Big, of Danish descent perhaps, incongruously pin-neat from the crown of his tricorne to the tips of his polished shoes. Cutler, the first mate, the man with the washed-out blue eyes that could have belonged to a barracuda for all the warmth and humanity they held.

'And now he's mine,' Nathan said. 'I'm sure there's someone else in the crew who can carry your slops and warm a few hammocks.'

The lad stood passively by his side. Nathan thought he could detect a fine tremor running through him—whether it was fear or the pain from the blow to his face, he could not tell.

The boy looked too innocent to be aware of the main reason this crew wanted him on board. It was no part of his plans to act as bear-leader to dockside waifs and strays, but something was different with this lad. He must be getting soft, or perhaps it was years of looking out for midshipmen, so wet behind the ears they spent the first month crying for their mothers at night. Not that training the navy's up-and-coming officers was any longer a concern of his. Lord Phillips had seen to that, the old devil.

Cutler's eyes narrowed, his hand clenching on the hilt of his weapon. 'Let him keep the boy,' McTiernan said softly. 'I'm not one to interfere with a man's pleasures.' Someone pushed through the crowded room and murmured into the captain's ear. 'It seems the militia is about on the Spanish Town road. Time to leave, gentlemen.'

Nathan put his hand on the boy's shoulder. 'Don't even think about making a run for it,' he murmured. There was no response. Under his palm the narrow bones felt too fragile. The lad was painfully thin. 'What's your name?'

'C...Clem. Sir.' That odd, gruff little voice. Nerves, or not broken properly yet.

'How old are you?'

'Sixteen.'

Fourteen was more like it. Nathan gestured to one of the waiters and spun him a coin. 'Get my bags—and take care not to knock them.' He didn't want his instruments jarred out of true before he'd even begun. 'Have you got anything, Clem?'

A mute shake of the head, then, 'They just grabbed me, outside.' So there was probably a family somewhere, wondering what had happened to their son. Nathan shrugged mentally—no worse than the press-gang. He had more important things to be worrying about than one scruffy youth. Things like staying alive in this shark pool with all his limbs attached, making sure McTiernan continued to believe he was exactly what he said he was—right up to the point when he despatched the man to his richly deserved fate.

The boy scrambled down into the jolly boat, moving easily between the half-dozen rowers. He was used to small craft, at least. He huddled into the bows, arms wrapped tightly around himself as though somehow, in this heat, he was cold.

The rowers pulled away with a practised lack of fuss, sliding the boat through the maze of moored shipping, out almost to the Palisades. The sound of the surf breaking on the low sand-bar sheltering the harbour was loud.

He should have known that McTiernan would choose to drop anchor at the tip of the bar close to the remains of the infamous Port Royal. All that remained of the great pirate stronghold now after over a century of earth-quake, hurricanes and fire was a ghost of one of the wickedest places on earth, but the huts clinging to the sand inches above the water would be the natural home for McTiernan and his crew.

It was darker now, out beyond the legitimate shipping huddled together as if for mutual protection from the sea wolves. The bulk that loomed up in front of them was showing few lights, but one flashed in response to a soft hail from the jolly boat. The *Sea Scorpion* was what he had expected: ship-rigged, not much above the size of a frigate and built for speed in this sea of shallow waters and twisting channels.

He pushed the boy towards the ladder and climbed after him. 'Wot's this?' The squat man peering at them in the light of one lantern was unmistakably the bo'sun, right down to the tarred and knotted rope starter he carried to strike any seaman he caught slacking, just as a naval bo'sun would.

'*Mr* Stanier, our new navigator, and that's his boy.' McTiernan's soft voice laid mocking emphasis on the title. 'Give him the guest cabin, seeing as how we have no visitors staying with us.'

'What does he mean, guest cabin?' Clem whispered, bemused by the captain's chuckle.

'Hostages. You need to keep them in reasonable condition—the ones you expect a great deal of money for, at any rate.' And if you didn't expect money for them, you amused yourself by hacking them to pieces until the decks ran scarlet and then fed the sharks with the remains. He thought he would refrain from explaining why McTiernan was nicknamed *Red*. Time enough for the boy to realise exactly what he had got himself into.

The cabin was a good one, almost high enough for Nathan to stand upright, with a porthole, two fixed bunks and even the luxury of a miniscule compartment containing an unlovely bucket, another porthole and a ledge for a tin basin.

Clem poked his head round the door and emerged grimacing. Amused, Nathan remarked, 'Keeping that clean is part of your job. Better than the shared heads, believe me.' It seemed the lad was finicky, despite the fact he couldn't have been used to any better at home. 'Come with me, we'll find some food, locate the salt-water pump.' He lifted the lantern and hooked it on to a peg in the central beam. Clem blinked and half-turned away. 'How did your face get in that mess?'

'My uncle hit me.' There was anger vibrating under the words; perhaps the boy wasn't as passive as he seemed.

'You stay with me, as much as possible. When you are not with me, try to stay out on the open deck, or in here; don't be alone with anyone else until we know them better. You understand?' A shake of the head. Damn, an innocent who needed things spelled out.

'There are no women on the ship. For some of the crew that's a problem and you could be the answer.'

Clemence stared at him, feeling the blood ebbing away from her face. They thought she was a boy but even then they'd… Oh, God. And then they'd find she was a girl and then… 'That's what the captain meant when he said he wouldn't deprive you of your pleasures,' she said, staring appalled at her rescuer. 'He thinks you—'

'He's wrong,' Stanier said shortly and her stomach lurched back into place with relief. 'Lads hold no attraction for me whatsoever; you are quite safe here, Clem.'

She swallowed. That was an entirely new definition of *safe*. Whatever this man was, or was not, the fact remained that he was voluntarily sailing with one of the nastiest pirate crews in the West Indies. His calm confidence and size might provoke a desire to wrap her arms around him and hang on for grim life, but her judgement was clouded by fear, she knew that. When the rivers flooded you saw snakes and mice, cats and rats all clinging to a piece of floating vegetation, all too frightened of drowning to think of eating each other. Yet.

'Right.' She nodded firmly. *Concentrate*. She had to keep up this deception, please this man so she kept his protection—and watch like a hawk for a chance of escape.

'Are you hungry? No? Well, I am. Come along.' She followed him out, resisting the urge to hang on to his coat tails. As a child she'd had the run of her father's ships in port, sliding down companionways, hanging out of portholes, even climbing the rigging. This ship was not any different, she realised, as they made their way towards the smell of boiling meat, except that the crew were not well-disciplined employees, but dangerous, feral scum.

They located the galley mid-ship, the great boiler sitting on its platform of bricks, the cook looming out of the savoury steam, ladle in hand, meat cleaver stuck in his straining belt like a cutlass. 'You want any vittles, you'll wait to the morning.'

'I am Mr Stanier, navigator, and you will find food for my servant and me. Now.'

The man stared back, then nodded. 'Aye, sir.'

'And as we're in port, I assume you'll have had fresh provisions loaded. I'll have meat, bread, butter, cheese, fruit, ale. What's your name?'

'Street, sir.'

'Then get a move on, Street.' He looked at Clemence. 'Wake up, boy. Find a tray, platters. Look lively.'

Clemence staggered back to the cabin under the weight of a tray laden with enough food, in her opinion, for six, and dumped it on to the table that ran down the centre of their cabin. Stanier stood, stooping to look out of the porthole, while she set out the food and his platter, poured ale and then went to perch on the edge of the smaller bunk bed, built to follow the curve of the ship's side.

What was he staring at? She tried to retrieve some sense of direction and decided he was looking out at the wreckage of old Port Royal, although what there was to see there on a moonless night—

'Why aren't you eating?' He had turned and was frowning at her.

'I ate before…before I left.'

'Well, eat more, you are skin and bones.' She opened her mouth. 'That's an order. Get over here, sit down and eat.'

'This isn't the navy,' Clemence said, then bit her lip and did as she was told.

'No, that is true enough.' Stanier grinned, the first sign of any real amusement she had seen from him. It was not, now she came to think about it, a very warm smile. It exposed a set of excellent teeth and crinkled the skin at the corners of his eyes attractively enough, but the blue eyes were watchful. 'What's happened to *sir*?'

'Sorry, sir.' She slid on to the three-legged stool and tried to recall how her young male friends had behaved at table. Like a flock of gannets, mostly. 'I haven't got a knife, sir. Sorry.'

'Have you got a handkerchief?' Stanier enquired, then did smile, quite genuinely, when Clemence shook her head in puzzlement. With an effort she kept her mouth closed. When he smiled, he looked… She hauled some air down into her lungs and tried not to gawp like a complete looby. Thankfully he had his back to her, rummaging in one of the canvas kit bags piled in the corner of the cabin. He turned back, holding out a clasp knife and a spotted handkerchief. 'There.'

'Thank you.' She tucked the handkerchief in the neck of her shirt as a bib and unfolded the knife, trying not to imagine sitting next to him at a dinner party, both of them in evening dress, flirting a little. And then walking out on to the terrace and perhaps flirting a little more… Which was ridiculous. She never flirted, she had never wanted to.

'You should carry that knife all the time. Can you use it?' Stanier speared a thick slice of boiled mutton, laid it on a slab of bread and attacked it with concentration.

'On a man? Er…no.' Clemence thought about Lewis. 'But I probably could if I was frightened enough.'

'Good,' he said, swallowing and reaching for his ale. 'Go on, eat.'

'I thought I'd wait for you, sir. You're hungry.' He was eating like a man half-starved.

'I am. First food for forty-eight hours.' Stanier cut a wedge of cheese and pushed the rest towards her.

'Why, sir?' Clemence cut some and discovered that she could find a corner still to fill.

'Pockets to let,' he said frankly. 'If this hadn't come along, I'd have been forced to do an honest day's work.'

'Well, this certainly isn't one,' Clemence snapped before she could think.

'Indeed?' In the swaying lantern light the blue eyes were watchful over the rim of the horn beaker. 'You're very judgmental, young Clem.'

'Pirates killed my father, took his ship.' She ducked her head, tried to sound young and sullen. It wasn't hard.

'I see. And you ended up with Uncle who knocked you around, eh?' He leaned across the table and put his fingers under her chin, tilting her face up so he could see the bruises. 'Heard the expression about frying pans and fires, Clem?'

'Yessir.' She resisted the impulse to lean her aching face into his warm, calloused hand. It was only that she was tired and frightened and anxious and wanted someone to hold her, tell her it was all going to be all right. But of course it wasn't going to be all right and this man was not the one to turn to for comfort, either. Something stirred inside her, the faint hope that there might be someone, somewhere, she could trust one day. She was getting tired—beyond tired—and maudlin. All she could rely on was herself.

Stanier seemed to have stopped eating, at last.

'I'll take these plates back.'

'No, you won't. You're not wandering about this ship

at night until you know your way around.' He took the tray from her. 'Look in that bag there, you'll find sheets.'

It was a fussy pirate who carried his clean linen with him, Clemence thought, stumbling sleepily across to open the bag. But sure enough, clean sheets there were, even if they were threadbare and darned. She covered the lumpy paliasses, flapped another sheet over the top, rolled up blankets for pillows and then shut herself into the odorous little cubicle. If she did nothing else tomorrow, she was going to find a scrubbing brush and attack this.

But privacy, even smelly privacy, would perhaps save her. She couldn't imagine how she would have survived otherwise in a ship full of men. Clemence managed to wedge open the porthole to let in the smell of the sea, then emerged. Water and washing would have to wait; all she wanted now was sleep and to wake up to find this had all been an unpleasant dream.

Could she get into bed, or would Stanier want her to do anything else? She was dithering when he came back in. 'I am not, thank God,' he remarked, 'expected to stand watch tonight. Bed, young Clem.' He regarded Clemence critically. 'No soap, no toothbrush, no clean linen, either. I'll have to see what we can find you in the morning. I don't imagine going to bed unwashed and in his shirt ever troubled a boy, though.'

'No, sir.' Clemence thought longingly of her deep tub, of Castile soap and frangipani flowers floating in the cool water. Of a clean bed and deep pillows and smiling, soft-footed servants holding out a drifting nightgown of snowy lawn.

Stanier sat down on the edge of his bunk and shed his coat, then his waistcoat and began to unbutton his shirt. The air seemed to vanish from her lungs. He was going to strip off here and now and… He stood up and she bent to pull off her shoes as though someone had tugged a string.

She risked a peek up through her fringe. He was still standing there, she could see his feet. There wasn't anything else she could take off while he was there… Belt. Yes, she could unbuckle that. Out of the corner of her eye she could see him heeling off his shoes. One foot vanished, he must have put it on the bunk to roll down his stocking. Yes. A bare foot appeared, the other vanished.

'What are you doing, boy?'

'Buckle's tight,' she mumbled.

'Need any help?'

'No!' It came out as a strangled squawk. Thank goodness, he was going into the privy cupboard. As the door closed Clemence hauled off her trousers and dived under the sheet, yanking it up over her nose.

The door creaked. He was coming out. Clemence pulled the sheet up higher and pretended to be asleep. Drawn by some demon of curiosity, she opened her eyes a fraction and looked through her lashes. Stanier was stark naked, his breeches grasped in one hand. She bit her tongue as she stifled a gasp. He tossed the clothes on to a chair, then stood, running one hand through his hair, apparently deep in thought.

She should close her eyes, she knew that, but still she stared into the shifting shadows, mesmerised. Long legs, defined muscles, slim hips, flat stomach bisected by the arrow of hair running down from his chest. Clemence's eyes followed it, down to the impressively unequivocal evidence that she was sharing a cabin with a man. She had known that, she told herself. Of course she had. It was just seeing him like this, so close, so male, made it very difficult to breathe.

It was not as though she was ignorant, either. She had swum with her childhood playmates in the pools below the waterfalls, but this was no pre-pubescent boy. In a slave-owning society you saw naked adults, too, but you averted your eyes from the humiliating treatment of another human being. She shouldn't be staring now, but Stanier seemed so comfortable with his own body, so relaxed in his nudity, that she doubted he would dive for his breeches if he realised she was awake. Only, he did not know she was a woman, of course.

'Asleep, boy?' he asked softly.

Clemence screwed her eyes shut, mumbled and turned over, hunching her shoulders. Behind, she heard his amused chuckle. 'You'd better not snore.'

Nathan eyed the bunk. The lad had made it up tidily enough, but sleep did not beckon. In fact, he felt uncomfortably awake, which was a damnable nuisance, given that he was going to need to be alert and on his guard at daybreak to take *Sea Scorpion* out of harbour and on to whatever course McTiernan wanted. Knowing the man's reputation, he would set something tricky, as a test.

He found the thick notebook in his old leather satchel and climbed into bed with it. From the opposite bunk came the sound of soft breathing. And what the hell was he doing, acquiring someone else to take care of when he had his own skin to worry about?

Nathan set himself to study the notes he had made on the area a hundred miles around Jamaica. He had not been bragging when he had told McTiernan that he was the best navigator in these waters: he probably was. In theory.

He did not underestimate his own strengths, his depth of knowledge, his experience in most of the great oceans of the world. The problem was, the Caribbean was not one of them and he knew that two months spent weaving through their treacherous waters making endless notes was not enough. Not nearly enough. At which point he became aware of the nagging heaviness in his groin and finally realised just why he was so restless.

What the hell was that about? And why? He had more than enough on his mind to drive any thought of women from it, and in any case, he'd hardly seen a female all evening, so there should be no inconvenient image in the back of his mind to surface and tease him.

The flash of dark eyes and black hair, the remembered lush curves of his late wife, presented themselves irresistibly to his mind. Nathan shifted impatiently. He thought he had learned not to think about Julietta; besides, lust was no longer the emotion those thoughts brought with them.

The recollection of Clem's slim, ink-stained fingers gripping his thigh rose up to replace that of Julietta's hands caressing down his body. Nathan shifted abruptly in the bed in reflexive rejection. For God's sake! He was as bad as this crew, if that was the cause of his discomfort.

From across the cabin came an odd sound—Clem was grinding his teeth in his sleep. Nathan grinned, contemplating hefting a shoe at the sleeping boy. No, he could acquit himself of that particular inclination—it must simply be an odd reaction to finding himself in the most dangerous situation in all his thirty years. The thought of straightforward danger was somehow soothing. Nathan put the book under his pillow, extinguished the lantern and fell asleep.

Chapter Three

'Wake up!'

Clemence blinked into the gloom of the cabin, momentarily confused. Where…? Memory came back like a blow and she scrabbled at the sheet twisted around her legs. It was, thankfully, still covering her from the waist down and her shirt shrouded the rest of her.

Stanier was tucking his shirt into his breeches. She felt the colour flood up into her face at the memory of last night, then found herself watching as his bare chest vanished as he did up the buttons, long brown fingers dextrous despite his speed. As if she was not in enough trouble without finding herself physically drawn to the man! She had never felt that before, but then she had never been rescued by a tough, attractive man before either, which probably accounted for it. Whatever the explanation, it was not a comfortable sensation. Surprising areas of her insides seemed to be involved in the reaction.

'Come on, look lively!' So, now she had to get out of bed, find her breeches and get into the cubby hole, all under Stanier's, admittedly uninterested, gaze. She tugged at the shirt, which came to just above her knees, slid out from under the sheet, scooped up her trousers and edged round the table.

'You are far too thin.'

She whisked into the cupboard and shut the door. Enough light came through the porthole to see the bucket, but of course, there was still no water to wash in. 'Things were difficult since my father died,' she said through the thin panels, fumbling with the fastenings on her trousers and tightening her belt. Thinking about her father, she felt reality hit her. Pirates had taken *Raven Duchess*, killing her father as surely as if they had knifed him, and now here she was, not only in their hands, but feeling grateful to a man who was as good as one himself. She'd had some excuse last night, she had hardly been herself. Now, after a night's sleep, she should face reality.

He *was* a pirate. She had seen him accept the position with her own eyes, heard him state his terms to McTiernan. So he was just as bad as the rest of the crew and deserved a fate as severe as theirs should be. Clemence opened the door and stepped out, jaw set.

'I'm sorry about your father.' Stanier was coatless, a long jerkin, not unlike her own waistcoat, pulled on over his shirt. 'Do you know which ship it was that attacked his?'

Clemence shrugged, combing her hair into some sort of order with her fingers. They had never discovered who had been responsible. The one survivor, found clinging to a spar, was too far gone to communicate, even if his tongue had not been cut out.

Her face felt greasy, she was sticky and sweaty under the linen bindings around her chest and there was grit between her toes. 'Could have been this one for all I know,' she said, having no trouble sounding like a sulky boy.

'I hope not,' Stanier said.

'Why should you care? You're one of them,' she pointed out, too angry with him and his casual sympathy to be cautious.

'True.' She had expected anger in return, even a cuff for her insolence, but he looked merely thoughtful. 'There are degrees of piracy.'

'Like degrees of murder?' Clemence retorted. 'Anyway, you've chosen to sail with the absolute scum of the seas, so that makes it first-degree piracy.'

'You're outspoken, lad.' Stanier came round the table and took her chin in one hand, tipping up her face so he could study it. 'I wonder you dare.'

'I don't care if you *are* angry. Things can't get much worse.'

'Oh, they can, believe me,' Stanier said softly, tilting her head, his fingers hard on her jawbone. 'Is that eye paining you much?'

'Only when someone hits it,' Clemence said, contemplating struggling, then deciding it was certain to be futile. He was too close, far too close for comfort. She could smell him, his sweat. Not the rank odour of the habitually unwashed crew, but the curiously arousing scent of a man who was usually clean, but was now hot and musky from bed. Goosebumps ran up her spine.

'Well, if you want to avoid that, you can go and find me some coffee and bread.' Did he really mean it? Would he hit her if she displeased him? Of course he would, he thought her just a troublesome boy and boys were always getting beaten. 'Then bring it up on deck. It'll be dawn soon.' He picked up a telescope from the bunk and fitted it into a long pocket in his jerkin, then dropped a watch into another. 'Here, take this and remember what I said about staying out of trouble.'

Clemence caught the clasp knife that was tossed to her, fumbling the catch. Stanier frowned, his gaze sharpening. 'It's this eye,' she said defensively, recalling her playmates' jibes that she *caught like a girl.* 'I can't see out of it properly.' Then he was gone and she could hold on to the end of the table, ridiculously shaken.

Toughen up, she told herself fiercely. *Think like a boy.* Which was easier said than done, given that all her treacherous feminine instincts were telling her quite the opposite whenever Stanier was close. The knife fastened to her belt, she made her way to the galley. Instinctively, she kept her head down, trying to make herself as small and inconspicuous as possible, until she found she was being stared at curiously. Perhaps looking like a victim was not a good idea in the middle of this crew, used to preying on the weak.

Clemence arrived at the galley, head up, shoulders back, practising a swagger. She conjured up Georgy Phillips, the leader of her gang of childhood male friends. He would love this adventure. He was welcome to it.

'Mr Street? I've come for Mr Stanier's coffee. And something to eat.' There was bacon frying, she could smell it. 'Some bacon.'

'That's for the captain.' But the cook said it amiably enough, slopping a black liquid that might have been coffee into a mug.

'But there's lots of it. And Mr Stanier's to have what he wants, the captain said so.' Street was hardly likely to check, and it seemed that Stanier had got what he'd demanded as a price to sail with them.

'Did he now?' Street shoved a piece of plank with bread on it towards her. There wouldn't be any of that once they were at sea and the land-bought supplies went stale. 'Go on, then. You want some coffee, too, boy?'

'Please, sir.' Clemence was pretty certain that the cook didn't warrant a *sir*, but a bit of crawling did no harm. She carved off four thick slices of bread and slipped round behind the man to layer bacon between them, dribbling on the rich melted fat for good measure. Street let her take a pewter plate, then watched, a gap-toothed grin on his face, as she juggled two mugs of coffee and the food.

'Don't drop it, boy, you'll not wheedle any more out of me,' he warned.

'Nossir, thank you, sir.' Now she had to find her way on deck, up at least two companionways, with her hands full. At least they were still at anchor; she would soon have to do this sort of thing with the ship pitching and tossing.

She made it with the loss of half a mug of coffee when one hand made a grab for the food as she passed him and she had to duck and run. Muttering, she regarded her coffee-stained trousers with resignation, and climbed out of the hatch on to deck.

It was a scene of apparent chaos, but she had seen enough ships preparing to make sail to know this all had a purpose. The light was waxing now, she could see the length of the deck and the lamps were extinguished. With the plate clutched protectively close to her chest, Clemence negotiated the steep steps up to the poop deck and found Stanier deep in conversation with the tall, oddly neat man with the pale blue eyes. The one who had hit her. Mr Cutler, the first mate.

They had a chart spread out on the raised hatch cover

of the stern cabin and were studying it. As Clemence came up behind them, Stanier straightened. 'I agree, that's the best course if you aren't concerned about speed.'

'Are you suggesting there's a faster way?'

Stanier extended one finger and indicated something Clemence could not see. The sight of that long digit, the one that had traced a question down her bruised cheek, made her shift uncomfortably.

'That's a dangerous passage, too big a risk.' Cutler shook his head.

'Not if you hit it at just the right time.' Stanier began to roll up the chart. 'How much speed do you need? Are you chasing something or just patrolling?'

'Best pickings have got over twelve hours' start on us, there's no catching the *Raven Princess* now.' Clemence almost dropped the food. 'But if you've got the knack of that passage, then the captain will be glad to see it.'

'That's what I thought. And it brings you out in the shelter of Lizard Island. You've got good anchorage, fresh water and command of the shipping lanes through there. And you never know, *Raven Princess* might have been delayed. Too good not to check, I'd have thought.'

Bastard! 'Your coffee, Mr Stanier.' She thrust the mug into his hand, forcing him to grasp the heated metal, and was gratified by his wince as he snatched at the handle. He deserved it. That was *her* ship he was talking about capturing. 'And some bread and bacon. Sir.'

He looked at her narrowly over the rim of the mug as he blew on his coffee. 'That all for me?'

'Yessir.'

'Take your knife and cut it up. Take half and eat it.'

'You'll spoil the brat.' The mate's lip lifted in a sneer.

'He's half-starved and no use to me unless he's fit.' Stanier gave a dismissive, one-shouldered shrug. 'Clem, eat and then go and get that cabin shipshape. You can unpack everything, just don't drop the instruments.'

Clemence found a corner on the main deck and curled up with her breakfast on top of a low stack of barrels, safely out of the way of the hurrying hands. Just when she had started liking the man, he turned out to be as bad as the rest of them. She shook her head abruptly; it was a lesson not to trust any of them. Ever.

Despite her feelings, she could still enjoy the food. The bacon was good, still warm, savoury, the bread soaked with salty grease. She scrubbed the back of her hand across her mouth, then wiped her palms on her trousers without thinking. The resulting mess—smears of ink, coffee, grease and dust—was unpleasant, but she could hardly change her clothes.

Street was surprisingly helpful when she returned her crocks. 'Ship's sail-maker's over there. Doubles as tailor, for them as wants it.' He nodded towards a man sitting cross-legged on a pile of rolled hammocks. 'Hey, Gerritty! Navigator's boy needs slops.'

The tailor squinted at Clemence. 'Look in that chest, see what'll fit,' he said through a mouthful of big needles, his accent a thick Irish brogue. 'I'm not making you anything, mind, not wasting my time on boys.'

'Thank you.' The trunk held a motley collection, some of it quality, some of it sailors' gear. Clemence had the uncomfortable feeling that most of it had been taken from captives. She found two pairs of trousers that looked as though she could take them in to fit, some shirts, a jacket and a warm knitted tunic. 'May I take these?'

'Aye.' The sail-maker produced an evil-looking knife and cut some twine. 'He any good, this new navigator?'

Clemence shrugged. 'Don't know. He only took me on yesterday. Talks like he is.' The Irishman snorted at her tone. 'Where can I get a bucket and a scrubbing brush?'

She wasn't looking forward to tackling the privy cupboard, but she wasn't prepared to live with it either. She was uncomfortably aware that if life had not favoured her with the wealth to keep servants, then she would have made a very reluctant housekeeper, but some hard cleaning was preferable to squalor, any day of the week.

It took her half an hour to locate cleaning materials, dodging some rough teasing on the way. On her way down to the cabin she collected a second lantern by the simple expedient of stealing it from another cabin, then started by washing the portholes and cleaning the lamps. She made the beds, glancing with interest at the thick leather-bound notebook under Stanier's pillow, but cautiously left it untouched, unpacked his bags and set the instruments out on the table with care.

They were shiny, complex and obviously expensive. She raised the fiddles around the sides of the table in case the instruments slid about and eyed them, fascinated. Perhaps he would show her how they worked.

The rest of his gear she stowed in the lockers. It was good quality stuff, but well worn and included, she was thankful to see, a huswif with thread and needles. At least she could alter her new clothes herself.

And that just left the privy. Clemence had an idea how to deal with that.

* * *

They were out of harbour, the island receding behind them, the breeze stiff and steady, the sun on the waves, dazzling. It was a day when it felt good to be at sea, even without the relief of having piloted the ship out under the hypercritical gaze of Cutler and Captain McTiernan, who lounged with deceptive casualness against a raised hatch cover.

'What's going on down there?' Cutler craned to see where a group were clustered round the rail, peering at something in the sea. Laughter floated up.

'I'll take a look.' Nathan stretched, glad of an excuse to shake the tension out of his shoulders. 'I need to get my sextant, anyway.'

He assessed the mood of the group as he approached it. They were having fun, probably at someone's expense, but it was good humoured enough. 'What's up?' He shouldered his way to the rail, the hands dropping back, tugging forelocks when they saw who it was. McTiernan's crew were worryingly well disciplined.

Hell. 'Clem, what the devil are you doing?' The boy leant over the rail, a rope in his hands, the muscles on his slim forearms standing out with the effort. His trousers were filthy, he had bound the handkerchief Nathan had given him around his forehead and he looked a complete urchin with smudges on his face and grime up his arms.

Except that there was an elegance about the line of his back, the arched feet, braced on the deck, were small, the backside exposed by the shirt riding up was rounded and the skin below his collar was unexpectedly delicate.

Blinking away a sudden sensation of complete confusion, Nathan snapped, 'Clem!'

'Sorry, sir.' He was hauling at whatever it was now and it rose up suddenly, landed on the deck and showered them all with water. 'That bucket, sir. Seemed the easiest way to clean it.'

It was, certainly, a very clean bucket. Angry, for no reason he could determine, Nathan narrowed his eyes at the flushed, bruised face that met his gaze with a look of eager willingness that was surely false. Nathan had dealt with dumb insolence often enough to recognise it now.

'Look at the state of you, boy. I'll not have a servant that looks like a swine-herd.'

'I'll go and change, sir.'

The boy was angry, he realised with a jolt. Angry with him. Was he still brooding on Nathan's role on a pirate ship? Well, he was going to have to accept it, pretty damned quickly.

'Go,' he said with a jerk of his head, not realising until Clem and the bucket had vanished that the boy had nothing to change into. But that was not his problem—navigating this ship to place it in the best possible position for some fat merchantman to sail right into its jaws was. That was his job.

When he came down to the cabin over an hour later he was hit by light, air and the tang of salt water and lye soap. The cabin was spotless, the inner door standing open on to what had been a fetid little cubby hole and was now clean and dimly lit with the light from the open porthole.

A water tub stood on the floor, his mirror and shaving tackle were on the shelf, a towel dangled from a nail and a cloth was draped decorously over the bucket.

Clem was sitting at the table with a large bodkin, some twine and a pile of newspapers. 'What are you doing now?' Nathan demanded.

In response, Clem lifted his hand. Neat squares of newspaper were threaded onto the twine. 'For the privy,' he said concisely. 'I found the newspaper by the galley range.'

'My God.' Nathan stared round a cabin that would have done a post captain proud. 'You'll make someone a wonderful wife, Clem.'

As soon as he said it he could have bitten his tongue out. The boy went scarlet, his expression horrified. 'Damn it, I was teasing, I don't mean…I don't mean what I was warning you about last night. The other men, if they see this, will just think you're a good servant.'

'Well, I did it for me, too,' Clem retorted. 'I've got to live here as well. I don't enjoy cleaning,' he added with a grimace.

'No. And you aren't used to it, either, are you?' Nathan spun a chair round and straddled it, arms along the back as he studied the flushed and indignant face opposite him. 'When you are angry, that lilting local accent vanishes completely. You've been educated, haven't you, Clem? You're from quite a respectable family.'

'I—' There was no point in lying about it. Clemence bent her head, letting her hair fall over her face, and mumbled, 'Yes. I went to school in Spanish Town. My father was a merchant, just in a small way.'

'So the loss of your ship was a blow? Financially, I mean?'

She nodded, her mind working frantically to sort out a story that was as close to the truth as she could make it. Fewer risks of slipping up later, that way. 'My uncle took everything that was left. He claims he's looking after it, as my guardian.' Indignation made her voice shake. 'I didn't feel safe any more, so I got a berth on the *Raven Princess*, in secret. Only she sailed early.'

'Couldn't you have gone to the Governor?' Stanier asked.

'The Governor? You have no idea, have you? No idea at all what it's like being a—' She stopped, appalled at what she had almost said.

'A what, Clem?' He was watching her like a hawk, she realised, risking a glance up through the fringe of ragged hair.

'A small merchant's son. Someone with no influence. Sir,' she added, somewhat belatedly.

'I think we can drop the *sir*, in here at least. My name is Nathan.' Clemence nodded, not trusting herself to speak yet, not after that near-disaster. 'So, we know about you now. What do you make of me, Clem?'

Make of him? What should she say? That he was probably the most disturbingly male creature she had ever come across? That she probably owed him her life, but that she could not trust him one inch? That she admired his style, but despised his morals?

'I think,' she said slowly, returning with care to her island lilt, 'that you are a gentleman and I know that you were once in the navy, if what McTiernan said yesterday evening in the tavern is true. And it would seem to fit with your character.'

The unthinking natural arrogance of command, for one thing. But she couldn't put it like that. 'You are used to giving orders, your kit is very good quality, even if it is quite worn. There's a broad arrow stamped on some of the instrument cases, so they were government issue once.'

Stanier—Nathan—nodded. 'You're right, Clem.' Something inside her warmed at the praise, despite the pride that was telling her she wanted nothing from him, least of all his good opinion. 'Yes, I'm the younger son of a gentleman and, yes, I was in the navy.'

'What happened?' Intrigued now, she shook back her hair and sat up straighter, watching his face. Something shadowed, dark, moved behind those blue eyes and the lines at the corners of his mouth tightened.

'I was given the opportunity to resign.'

'Oh.' There really wasn't any tactful way of asking. 'Why?'

'A little private enterprise here, a little bloody-minded insubordination there, a duel.'

'A duel?' Clemence stared. 'I thought naval officers weren't allowed to duel.'

'Correct.' Nathan's mouth twisted into a wry smile, but the bleakness behind his eyes spoke of complex emotion.

'Did you kill him?'

He shook his head and she felt unaccountably relieved. 'No, I did not.' It would be a horrible thing to have to live with—but why should she worry about the spiritual health of a King's officer turned pirate?

'Then what happened?'

'You can imagine how well that went down with my family. It was felt that my absence would be the best way of dealing with the situation. So I found employment here and there, legal and perhaps not quite so legal, and ended up in Kingston with no ship and no money.'

'Why are you telling me all this?' she asked. Instinct told her that Nathan Stanier was a proud, private man. He could not be enjoying sharing the details of his disgrace and penury with a scrubby youth rescued from the dockside.

'They say that a man has no secrets from his valet, and you are the nearest to one of those I'm likely to have for a while. You might as well know the worst about me from the outset.' He got up in a smooth movement that seemed to mask barely controlled emotion. Shame? she wondered. Or just anger at the situation he found himself in?

She could feel herself slipping closer and closer to letting her guard down with him and that, she knew, could be fatal. 'But I knew the worst about you already,' she pointed out, hauling herself back from the brink of blurting out who, and what, she was, casting herself onto that broad chest and giving up fighting. 'I knew you have taken McTiernan's money and that makes you a pirate. I really can't think of anything worse. Can you?'

Chapter Four

〜〜〜〜〜

Nathan spun round on his heel and stared at her. 'For a bright lad, you've a reckless tongue,' he remarked, his voice mild. His eyes, bleak, belied his tone utterly. 'Yes, I can think of worse things. Betrayal and treachery for two.' Then he laughed, sending a shiver down her spine. 'But you're right, they don't get much worse than this crew, I suspect, and now we're part of it.'

'Well, *I* didn't volunteer,' Clemence said bitterly.

'No, and I didn't save your ungrateful skin from that pack of jackals in order to get self-righteous lectures from you either, brat. So keep your lip buttoned, Clem, or I'll tan your breeches for you.'

She subsided, instantly. Let him think she was terrified of a beating; better that than have him lay hands on her. The vision of herself turned over Nathan Stanier's knee and that broad palm descending on her upturned buttocks made her go hot and cold all over. There was no way, surely, that he could fail to notice that she was a girl if that happened.

'I'll go and get our dinner, shall I?' she offered, by way of a flag of truce.

'I'm eating with the captain and Cutler.' Nathan was shrugging into his coat. Old naval respect for a captain must be engrained, Clemence thought dourly, if he felt he had to tidy himself up for that scum.

'Will they tell you where we are going?' she asked. If they docked at a harbour on one of the other islands, surely she could slip ashore?

'Hunting,' Nathan said. 'And not from a harbour, if that's what you are hoping for. McTiernan's got a hideaway, and I can show him a shortcut to get to it. Now, enough questions. Are you going to eat properly, if I'm not there to nag you?'

Disarmed by his concern, she smiled. Life was so complicated. It would be much easier if it was black and white, if he was an out-and-out villain, but he wasn't and liking, gratitude and the disconcerting tingle of desire kept undermining her certainty. 'Yes, I promise. I'm hungry after all that work.' Nathan was staring at her. 'What is it?'

'That bruise is getting worse,' he said abruptly. 'It looks…odd. You're all right otherwise? You're not seasick?'

'In this weather? No. I don't know what I would be like in a storm, though. My father used to take me on short sea journeys with him. The crews were very good, they'd let me go anywhere, even though I was a—a child,' she finished hastily.

The moment he was gone, she went to look at her reflection in his shaving mirror. Yes, her face was black, blue and purple on one side and still swollen. Her hair was lank and she plucked at it, wondering whether to wash it. It was horrible like this, but on the other hand it helped her disguise, and that was the most important thing. Clemence fished the bandana out of her back pocket and tied it round her forehead again, pulling it one way, then another for effect.

Then the irony of it struck her. Here she was, prinking and posing in front of a mirror, trying to make herself look as unfeminine and unattractive as possible, when all the time she should be on her way to England, to her aunt Amelia the Duchess of Allington, stepmother to the present duke, who was to give her some town bronze before her come-out next Season. They'd have the letter by now, telling them of her father's death, of her own *ill health*.

She should be in the luxury of her own cabin on a large merchantman, practising flirting with the officers and worrying that she did not have pretty enough gowns in her luggage.

A proper young lady in this situation should be in a state of collapse, not scrubbing out privies, swaggering about with a knife and sharing a cabin with an attractive, dangerous, good-for-nothing rogue. Depressingly, this proved she was not a proper young lady. On the other hand, if she was, she would still be in the Naismiths' power. Better to be a skinny tomboy and alive.

Clemence gave the bandana one last tweak and headed for the galley, her stomach rumbling with genuine hunger as it had not done for weeks.

Street was ladling an unpleasant-looking grey slop into four buckets. Clemence wrinkled her nose, hung back and hoped this was not dinner.

'There, that'll do for 'em.' The cook gestured to the two hands who were waiting. 'They got water?'

'Enough,' one of the men said, spitting on the deck close to Clemence's feet. 'Waste of space, the lot of them. Not worth nothing.'

'If the captain says keep 'em, we keep 'em,' Street said, his voice a warning growl. 'He's got his reasons. You check the water and let me know if they're sickening. I'm not taking a lashing for you if you let any of them die.'

'Yeah, yeah,' the man grumbled, hefting a couple of buckets and shuffling off, followed by his mate.

'Mr Street?' Clemence ventured. 'I've come for my dinner, sir.' The cook waved a bloodstained hand towards a rather more savoury-looking cauldron of stew. He seemed out of temper, but not with her, so she ventured, 'Are there prisoners on board?'

'None of your business, lad.' He swung round to glower at her. 'You keep your nose out of things that don't concern you if you want to keep a whole hide. And don't go down to the orlop deck, either. You hear?'

'Yes, Mr Street.' The orlop deck? Why mention that? It was the very lowest deck, below the waterline where the cables were stowed. There would be no cabins down there, just dark holds with bilge water, rats and darkness; it would never have occurred to her to visit it. The cook went back to wielding his meat cleaver on a leg of pork, so she took bread to sop up the stew, poured some of the thin ale into a tankard and retreated to her refuge on top of the barrels.

The stew was better than she had expected and her appetite sharper, but Clemence spooned the gravy into her mouth absently, her eyes unfocused on the expanse of blue stretching out to the horizon. If there were captives down on the orlop deck, then they would be common seamen, she assumed, otherwise, if they had any value, they would be up in a proper cabin being kept alive with some care.

And if they were seamen, then some of them might be men from *Raven Duchess*. She stared down at the planking, scrubbed white by constant holystoning, the tar bubbling between the joints in the heat. Somewhere down there below, in foul darkness, could be men in her employ, men who'd been kept prisoner for six months. Men she was responsible for.

'Then lay in the course you suggest through the channel, Mr Stanier. We'll take it at first light.' It was Captain McTiernan, Nathan at his side, Cutler behind them. All three men had their hands clasped behind their backs, just as she had seen her father pacing with his captains. It seemed impossible that pirates would behave in the same everyday way, but the more she saw, the more she realised they were not bogeymen out of a children's storybook, they were real men operating in the real world. Their work just happened to be evil.

Instinct made her wriggle down amongst the barrels as though she could hide in some crevice, then common sense stopped her. It was not safe to cringe and cower; if McTiernan saw her, he might assume she was spying on him. As they drew level she wiped her crust round the tin plate and drained her tankard with an appearance of nonchalance, despite the fact that her heart was thudding against her ribs.

McTiernan stopped, bracketed by the two men, and looked at her. Clemence stared back, trying, without much difficulty, to look suitably nervous and humble. His eyes were flat, without emotion, staring at her as though she was no more, nor less, than one of the casks. Her eyes shifted to the left. Cutler was more obviously assessing—now she knew what a lamb in the slaugh-terman's yard felt like. She shivered and glanced at Nathan, trying to read the message in the deep blue gaze. Warning or reassurance?

McTiernan blinked, slowly, and she half-expected to see an inner eyelid slide back into place like the lizards that scuttled up every wall in Raven's Hold. Then, without speaking, he turned. Clemence felt the breath *whoosh* out of her lungs just as there was a shout from above.

Everyone looked up. Something was falling. Wedged between the barrels, Clemence tried to wriggle away, then the tail of her shirt caught, jerking her back. She felt a sharp blow to her head and the world erupted into stars.

Minutes passed, or hours. Her head hurt. She was on her back on the deck and above her she could see the captain, staring upwards towards the mast-tops that seemed to circle dizzyingly with the ship's motion. Then someone bent over her. Nathan. The sick tension inside her relaxed; it was all right now. He was here.

'Lie still.' His hand pressed down on her shoulder and she lay back, closing her eyes. Her head hurt abo-minably, but the warm touch meant she was safe, she reasoned with what parts of her brain still seemed to be working. Something else, her common sense presum-ably, jabbed her. Nothing was all right, least of all the way she was feeling about this renegade officer.

'Is he dead?' Cutler. *If I'm dead, he'll eat me.* The words whispered in her mind; she was beginning to drift in and out of consciousness.

'No, just stunned. I'll take him below.'

'Flog the bastard.' It was McTiernan, his voice flat calm.

But I haven't done anything, she wanted to shout. *It wasn't my fault!* She shifted, trying to wriggle away, but Nathan's hand curled round and held her.

'Steady, Clem. He's angry with the hand who dropped the fid.' So that was what it was. Her memory produced the image of a heavy wooden spike. Point down it would have killed her.

'Because it hit me?' she murmured. McTiernan was this angry because a cabin boy had been hit on the head?

'No.' Her eyes opened as he knelt, slid one arm under her knees, the other under her back. 'Because it almost hit him.'

Nathan straightened with her in his arms. The world lurched, steadied, to reveal a man on the deck, cowering.

'Fifty. Now.' McTiernan turned on his heel and walked away, leaving the man screaming after him.

'All hands for punishment!' Cutler roared, making her start and try to burrow against the security of Nathan's hard chest.

'I'm taking the lad down,' he said. 'You don't need me for this and he's no use to me unconscious. I need to check his head.'

Fifty? Fifty lashes? 'That will kill him,' Clemence managed to say. Her view, mercifully, was confined to the open neck of Nathan's shirt, the hollow at the base of his throat, the underside of his jaw. She made herself focus on the satiny texture of the skin, the few freckles, the pucker of a small scar, the way his Adam's apple moved when he swallowed.

'Oh, yes, it most certainly will. Close your eyes, lie still, I've got you.'

Oh, God. He had got her, oh, yes, indeed. The realisation of her danger thudded through her throbbing headache seconds after Clemence let her head sink gratefully on to his shoulder.

She was closer than she had ever been to Nathan and his hands seemed to be in the places that were most dangerous—the curve of her hip, her tightly strapped ribcage. She couldn't see what had happened to the hem of her long shirt that she had been using to disguise the fact that there were no bulges in her trousers where a boy ought to bulge.

'I'm all right, you can put me down.' She was ignored. Of course, Nathan Stanier took no orders from scrubby boys. He would have to set her on her feet when they got to the companionway though, she reasoned, praying he was not intending to undress her to tuck her up in bed.

But it seemed that Nathan had thought out the logistics of descending steep stairs on a pitching ship with his arms full. He swung her round and hung her over his shoulder, one arm tight around the back of her thighs as he climbed down. 'Sorry if this jars your head, but we'll be down in a minute.' And they were and she was back in his arms almost shaking with the jumble of sensations, fears, emotions that were rattling round her poor aching head.

'There.' He put her down. Clemence opened her eyes and saw they were in their cabin. This was her bunk, thank goodness. She'd say she wanted to sleep…

But she wasn't safe, not yet. Nathan knelt in front of her, overwhelmingly big on the confined space, and tipped her forward against his chest so he could part her hair and look at her scalp.

'Skin isn't broken, but you'll have a nasty lump.' He didn't seem ready to release her, one hand flat on her back, holding her close, the other running gently through her hair, checking for lumps. Clemence let her forehead rest against his shoulder. Madness. Bliss. All her senses were full of him, his heat, the feel of him, the scent of him, the aura of strength that seemed to flow from him. She could stay like this all day. Safe. She began to drift.

'Clem?' Nathan's voice was puzzled. 'Why the devil are you trussed up like the Christmas goose?'

'Cracked ribs,' she said on a gulp, back in the real world with a vengeance. 'When my uncle hit me. I, er…fell against a table.'

'Rubbish. You'd have yelled the place down just now when I slung you over my shoulder if you'd got cracked ribs.' He slid his hands free and sat back on his heels beside the bunk. Clemence closed her eyes as though that could hide her. She wanted so much to believe he would protect her when he knew her secret, wanted so much, in the midst of this nightmare, to believe there was good in this flawed man. 'Clem, take your shirt off.'

'No.' She opened her eyes and met his, read the questions in them.

'Why not?'

There was nowhere to go, no lie she could think of, no escape. Eyes locked with his, braced for his reaction, Clemence said, 'Because I'm a girl.' And waited.

Silence, then, 'Well, thank God for that,' Nathan said.

'What?' She sat bolt upright, then clutched her head as the cabin swam around her. 'What do you mean, *thank God*?'

Nathan was looking at her with all the usual composure wiped off his face. He seemed a good five years' younger, grinning with what had to be relief. 'Because my body was telling me there was a woman around,' he confessed, running a hand through his hair. 'I kept finding myself staring at you, but I didn't know why. The relief of finding that my dissipated way of life hasn't left me lusting after cabin boys is considerable, believe me. What's your real name?'

'Clemence.' The release of tension on finding that he had not become a slavering monster bent on rapine turned into temper. It was that, or tears. 'And the relief might be considerable for you, but now I am sharing a cabin with a man who knows I am a woman and whose body is most certainly interested in that fact—a piece of information I could well do without, believe me! Forgive me, but *I* was much happier when you were simply confused and uncomfortable.'

'So, you think I am more likely to ravish Clemence than Clem, do you?' He rocked back on his heels and stood up, hands on hips, looking down at her.

She had made him angry again. Clemence lay down cautiously, too dizzy to stay sitting up. 'No, I don't think that. My cousin was going to force me every night until he got me with child and I had to agree to marry him. I may not know you, but I do understand that *you* don't treat people like that. But this…' she waved a hand around the confines of the cabin, the closeness of him, the privy cupboard '…this is not very *comfortable*. Not for a woman alone with a man she doesn't know.'

You wouldn't mistreat people you know as individuals, that is, she qualified to herself. Putting a pirate ship in the way of capturing and plundering merchant vessels and killing their crews, that was another matter. You couldn't tell that sort of thing about people just by looking at them, it seemed.

'My God.' He sat down on the nearest chair. 'No wonder you ran away. Which of them hit you?'

'My uncle. Why?'

'For future reference,' Nathan said grimly. 'This cousin of yours—he didn't—'

'No. I'm too scrawny to interest him at the moment. He was going to fatten me up.' Nathan's growl sent a shiver of pleasure down her spine at the thought of Lewis walking into the cabin and coming up against that formidable pair of fists. 'Are you going to tell anyone about me?'

'Hell, no! If you were in danger when they thought you a boy, you wouldn't be safe for one minute if they knew you are a woman.' He pulled out a chair and sat down out of reach of her, whether for his peace of mind or hers, she couldn't tell. 'How old are you?'

'Nineteen. Twenty in two months' time.'

Nathan's eyebrows went up and he raked one long-fingered hand back through his hair again, reducing it to a boyish tangle. Clemence resisted the urge to get up and comb it straight. 'This gets worse and worse.'

'Why?'

'*Why?* I thought you were fourteen, a child. Now I know you're not—' He stopped, frowning. 'We need to think about the practicalities of this.'

'There aren't any, not really.' Clemence sat up against the hard bulkhead with some caution. 'There's the closet, thank goodness, and now you know who I am I can just ask for privacy when I need it.'

'When are your courses due?' he asked, in such a matter-of-fact manner that she answered him before she had time to be embarrassed.

'Three weeks.' Goodness, she hadn't thought of that.

'Good.' Nathan was pretending to pay careful atten-

tion to a knot-hole in the table. 'You are doing very
well with the way you move. I guess you know some
young lads?'

'I used to run wild with them until I was fourteen,'
she confessed. 'What is that noise?' There were no live
pigs on board, surely?

'A man screaming,' Nathan said, getting up and
slamming both portholes shut. 'Try not to listen.'

'It's him, isn't it? The man who dropped the fid.'
Suddenly it was all too much. Somehow she had
managed to endure Uncle Joshua's threats, Cousin
Lewis's plans for her. She had acted with determination
and escaped, stolen a horse without a qualm, kept her
head when McTiernan and his men had seized her,
coped with two days on a pirate ship and now...

Clemence dragged her sleeve across her eyes and
sniffed, trying to hold back the tears.

'Stop it, crying isn't going to help him,' Nathan
said abruptly.

'They are killing him by inches, torturing him,' she
retorted. 'Can't you do anything?'

'No.'

She half-turned, hunching her shoulder towards him.
Of course he was right, there was nothing to be done. It
was just that she expected him to work miracles. Oh,
damn! Why had he discovered she was female? It
weakened her; she was turning to him for help he
couldn't give and which she shouldn't expect. The
moment she'd decided to escape from Raven's Hold she
had taken her own destiny into her hands, however
feeble they might prove to be, and now she was reacting
like Miss Clemence Ravenhurst, sheltered young lady.

'Clem. *Clemence.*' She shook her head, fighting to

try to regain her composure and her independence. 'Oh, come here.' Nathan sat down on the bunk and pulled her rigidly resisting body into his arms. He pressed her un-bruised cheek against his chest, muffling her ear into his shirt, and held his palm to the other side of her head so that all she could hear was his heartbeat, the sound of his breathing and the turmoil of her own thoughts.

'Clemence,' he repeated, his voice a rumble in her ear. 'That's an unusual name. But I've heard it before, not all that long ago, either. Can't think where, though.'

'You've had a few other things on your mind,' she suggested, trying to drag her imagination away from what was happening on deck.

Nathan gave a snort of laughter, stirring her hair. 'Yes, just a few.' His hold on her tightened, not unpleasantly. He felt very strong. It was a novelty, being held by a man other than Papa. He'd been one for rapid bear-hugs, her father, impetuous lifts so her feet left the floor as he twirled her round. 'How did you get this thin, Clem? I'd better keep calling you Clem, less risk of a slip.'

'Yes,' she agreed, her lips touching the soft linen of his coarse white shirt as she spoke. A fraction of an inch away was the heat of his skin; she could almost taste it. 'I was always slender. When my father died I didn't feel much like eating; then, when I realised what Uncle Joshua was doing, my appetite vanished all together.' She shivered and felt Nathan's hand caress gently down her swollen cheek.

'They made me eat the night I escaped. Apparently I was so skinny it would be unpleasant for Cousin Lewis to bed with me. He said I was like a boy.' Nathan stiff-ened and muttered something, but all she could hear was that low growl again. 'That's what gave me the idea. I still had the clothes from when I used to run wild as a child with the local planters' sons.'

'How did you get out?' He was talking to distract her, she thought, grateful for the attempt.

'The house is on a cliff and my room has a balcony overhanging the sea. I wrote a despairing note to make them think I had thrown myself over and I climbed up the creepers from the balcony, along the ledge just below the roof and then slid down some other roofs. I stole a horse from one of the penns about two miles away.' Nathan made an interrogative noise. 'You'd say farm, I suppose. Or agricultural estate. I threw my clothes and my plait of hair away far from the house. They'll think I'm dead, I hope.'

Clemence felt him lift his head. 'It's over.'

That poor man. He had probably done many awful things himself in the past, but he deserved a fair trial for his crimes, some dignity, not a brutal death for a tiny mistake.

Nathan didn't free her and she did not try to duck out of his embrace. It was an illusion, she knew, but even the illusion of safety, of someone who cared, was enough just now. She felt her body softening, relaxing into his. 'You've got guts. What did you hope to do?' he asked.

'Stow away, get to another island, find work.' The lie slid easily over her tongue without her having to think. However good he was being to her now, if he knew she was a Ravenhurst, guessed at the power and the wealth of her relatives, then she became not a stray he had rescued, but thousands of pounds' worth of hostage.

'And what do you want to do now?' he asked.

'Have a bath,' Clemence answered fervently.

Nathan chuckled, opened his arms and let her sit

back upright. 'We could both do with that,' he agreed. Free of his embrace, she could study him. His eyes were not just blue, she realised. There was a golden ring round the iris and tiny flecks of black. As he watched her they seemed to grow darker, more intense. 'I'll have to see what I can organise. It'll be cold water, though.'

She nodded, hardly hearing what he was saying, her eyes searching his face for something she could not define. It felt as though he was still holding her, as though the blow to her head had shifted her thoughts and her perceptions. He knew she was a woman now, and somehow that made her see him differently also.

'Nathan…' Clemence touched his arm, not certain what she was asking, and then he was pulling her into his arms and his mouth took her lips and she knew.

Chapter Five

How had he not realised immediately that Clem was a woman? Every instinct he possessed had been trying to tell him, and a life of near misses had taught him to listen to his instincts. He had been focused on getting into the crew of the *Sea Scorpion* and staying alive while he did so. Perhaps his brain had more sense than his instincts and put survival over sex.

Nathan held himself still, caressing her mouth with his as though she were made of eggshell porcelain. Oh, yes, not a girl but a woman. Young, yes, untouched certainly, but everything that was feminine in her had been in her eyes as she looked at him a moment ago, just as every male impulse was telling him to claim her now.

It was a long time since he had felt like this about a woman. Seven years, in fact. *But that was in another country, and besides, the wench is dead.* He shook himself; now was not the time to be thinking of those dark dramas and the poetry into which he had plunged in the aftermath of the scandal on Minorca.

She was transforming under his hands, that thin body

curving into him, her boyish gestures becoming languid and feminine. The strong part of him, the code of honour he had been brought up in, the naval discipline that had formed him and had all but broken him, were enough to stop the animal within from pressing her back on to the hard bunk and taking her, but they were not enough to stop him kissing, holding, inhaling the female scent of her skin. In the brutal masculine world in which he was trapped, that scent was like everything civilised and beautiful.

If he tried to take her now, he probably could. Not because she was wanton, but because she was frightened and he represented all she had of safety. He sensed that in her near collapse into tears and could only admire the way she had summoned up her courage to keep fighting. That alone was enough to restrain him, he realised, sliding his tongue between her lips, sweeping it around to taste her, tease the sensitive tissue. Clem gave a little gasp, her breath hitching, and he lifted his mouth away.

Too much, too soon. *She is so fragile*, Nathan thought, as he ran his thumb gently under the downswept lashes that shielded those big green eyes and feathered her un-damaged cheek. Despite her height, her bones felt slender; despite her deceptively boyish appearance, the high cheek-bones and pointed chin had a charm that spoke of delicacy.

He couldn't imagine the courage it had taken for her to escape the way she had, the guts she needed to cope and adapt to finding herself here on what must seem a ship from hell.

'I think that cold bath is probably a good thing for any number of reasons,' he said, finding his voice oddly husky.

'I—' She opened her eyes and looked at him. 'What happened?'

'I kissed you.'

'I know that.' She gave him a look part-exasperation, part-amusement, wholly female. 'Why? I mean, why did you stop?'

'Because I shouldn't have started and, having started, I knew damn well I shouldn't continue. I don't seduce virgins, Clem.' *Although one once seduced me.* And now he really had opened a Pandora's box of troubles for himself. He didn't need his imagination any longer to guess how she would be in his arms, he knew. He needed no fantasy to conjure up the sweet softness of her mouth or the taste of her.

Nathan stood up and went to sit on the far side of the table. No reason to let her see just how aroused that insane kiss had made him.

'Thank you,' she said politely, making him smile despite himself. 'But you shouldn't take all the blame. I enjoyed it and I feel better for you holding me. I've missed being hugged,' she added, rather forlornly.

Oh, God! There was nothing he would like more than to hug her. And kiss her. And take off those boy's clothes and unwrap the binding around her small breasts and kiss the soft, compressed curves beneath. And lay her back on that hard bunk and—

'I must go up on deck. I'll tell them I want a tub sent down and some water and they are to be quiet about it because you are very sick from that blow to your head.'

He stood looking down at Clem, fighting the urge to grab her, bundle her into a boat and get away. Which was impossible. There were things he had to do and no one girl was going to prevent him doing them.

Clemence. He said the name in his mind, savouring the sound of it, a sort of fruity sweet tang of a name. Tart and challenging, yet mellow, too. She nodded, watching him. She was thinking hard, he could tell, but those thoughts were hidden. She had learned well in those nightmare weeks at the mercy of her relatives.

'I'll get into bed, pull up the blanket and pretend to be dozing. When they've gone I'll wedge the latch before I take my bath.'

That did it. The image of Clem standing up, slowly pulling off that shirt, unbinding her breasts, stepping shivering into cold water, her nipples puckering, was so vivid Nathan drew in a deep, racking breath. Her eyes slid down his body, stopped, widened. 'Good idea. I'll knock when I come back.'

Clemence sat staring at the back of the cabin door for some minutes after it had shut abruptly behind Nathan. So, not only was she sharing a cabin with a man she desired and who had discovered she was a woman, but a man who was showing unmistakable evidence of the fact that he desired her, too.

She understood the theory of lovemaking, naturally. But she had never observed the—her mind scrabbled rather wildly for a word—the *mechanism* before. And she had produced that effect on him. The feeling of gratification was something to be ashamed of, she told herself severely.

What would she have done if Nathan had done more than kiss her? Protest or yield? She had a sinking feeling that she would have yielded. No, worse, she would have positively incited him. She had seen those sculpted muscles; now she wanted to caress them.

Shame, confusion, arousal were all uncomfortable

internal sensations when you had just had a nasty thump on the head. Clemence slid down under the blanket, pulled it high over her ears and closed her eyes, thankful to be still for a while. If she could slip into sleep, she could pretend *this* was the dream.

The sound of voices, the rattle of the door opening, jerked her out of her doze, rigid under the blanket. It seemed a very slight barricade. There was a thump on the floor, some more banging about, then the door closed again. Cautiously Clemence sat up. There was a small half-barrel on the floor, just big enough for a person to sit in with their knees drawn up, and two big buckets of water and a jug.

She slipped out of bed and wedged the latch on the door with her knife, then went to dip a finger in the water containers. The buckets were salt, but the jug was fresh for her face and hair. A rummage through Nathan's kit bag produced a new block of green soap. She sniffed. Olive oil. On the side were imprinted the words *Savon de Marseilles*. And there was a luxuriously large sponge as well. French olive-oil soap and sponges? Had he been in the Mediterranean recently? She sensed there was a lot he had not told her.

Clemence stripped, sighing with relief as the linen strips uncoiled from around her ribs. She ran her hands over her torso, massaging the ridges where the bandages had cut into her skin. Nathan's hands had rested there, and there—and just there.

She stepped into the tub, shivered and hunkered down, gasping as the cold water covered her belly. Her head throbbed; the strange new pulse between her thighs throbbed, too, despite the chill of the water, and she realised the fear that had been ever present in the pit of her stomach for days had gone at last.

There was no logical explanation—it was dangerous folly not to be frightened. Clemence reached for the block of soap and began to work up a lather.

Nathan tapped on the door, wondering at the apprehension that gripped him. What was he going to find inside? His imagination reacted luridly to months of enforced celibacy at sea; it suddenly seemed a long time since he had left England and paid off his mistress. The remembered sweetness of Clemence in his arms conjured up the vision of a slender, naked woman, dripping with water, a nymph uncoiling herself from her tiny pool. The reality, when the door opened, was Clem, wet hair tousled, cheeks glowing and exuding a healthy, and less than erotic, smell of olive-oil soap.

In her clean second-hand clothes she looked the perfect well-scrubbed youth until she met his eye and blushed, rosily. Heat washed through his body and he gritted his teeth. 'Better?'

'Yes, much, much better, thank you. I found some birch-bark powder in your medical kit and that helped my headache, and the bliss of being clean, I cannot describe.' She gave a complicated little wriggle of sensual satisfaction, causing his loins to tighten painfully, and smiled. 'It is horrible being dirty; I don't know why it is so difficult to get boys to wash. Surely no one is willingly dirty?'

Nathan found he was not up to discussing any subject touching Clemence and the removal of clothes. She followed his eyes to the tub of dirty water, perhaps assuming his silence was irritation. 'Sorry, I was just trying to work out how to empty it.'

'I'll use the empty bucket and bail it out through the porthole.' He tossed his waistcoat on to the bunk and rolled up his sleeves. 'You've been very thrifty with the water.'

She was looking at his bare forearms. Nathan watched his own muscles bunch as he hefted the bucket and found, to his inner amusement, that he was endeavouring to make as light work of the task as possible. *Poseur*, he mocked himself. *Showing off like a cock with a new hen.* He remembered the *frisson* of pleasure when he had sensed Julietta's eyes on him in his uniform, the temptation to swagger to impress her.

'There isn't much space in the tub,' Clemence pointed out, jerking him back to the present. 'And there'll be even less room for you.'

Nathan chucked a pail full of water out of the porthole, his mind distractingly full of the image of Clemence curled up in the tub. 'You'll have to scrub my back, then, if I can't reach,' he said, half-joking.

'I suppose I could,' she said doubtfully. 'With my eyes closed, of course. Have you a back brush?'

'No. I was teasing you.' She smiled at him, unexpectedly, and he found himself grinning back. 'Are you usually this calm about things, Clem? I would have thought you fully justified if you were throwing hysterics by now.'

'It wouldn't do any good, would it?' she pointed out, folding discarded clothes with a housewifely air that contrasted ludicrously with her appearance.

'I wish my father was alive and I was at home with him, or, if that cannot happen, I wish my uncle and cousin were the men Papa believed them to be. Or, worst come to worst, I wish I had stowed away on a nice merchantman and was now having tea in the captain's wife's cabin. But if wishes were horses, beggars would ride and having hysterics would not be pleasant for you.'

'That's considerate of you.' Nathan poured clean water into the tub and began to unbutton his shirt.

'It is in my interests not to alienate you,' Clemence pointed out, all of a sudden as cool and sharp as fresh lemonade. She sat down on her bunk, curled her legs under her and faced the wall.

'What's the matter?' Nathan asked, his fingers stilling on the horn buttons.

'I do not want to have to go into the privy cupboard while you have your bath.'

'Oh. Yes, of course.' He would have stripped off without a second thought, Nathan realised; he was so focused on not pulling her into his arms that he was forgetting all the other ways he could shock or alarm her.

The shock of the cold water as he crouched down was a blessed relief for a moment, then the absence of the nagging tension in his groin was replaced by the sobering reality of protecting a young woman on the *Sea Scorpion*. Clemence would be safer in a dockside brothel—at least she could climb out of a window.

Nathan shook his head in admiration as he scrubbed soap into his torso. Out of a window overhanging the sea, up creepers, along a roof, stealing a horse… Now that was a woman with courage and brains. He had been brought up to regard the ideal woman as frail, clinging and charmingly reliant upon a man's every word. And he had found himself one who apparently embodied all of those attributes combined with the exotic looks of half-Greek parentage. The only fault his mother would have found with her—at first—was her lack of money.

They had all been well-dowered young ladies, the candidates for his hand that his mother had paraded before him. She always managed to completely ignore the fact that, however worthy her late husband's breeding might be, he had gambled all the money away and that their elder son had to manage a household with the parsimony of a miser. The need for Nathan to marry money was not spelled out, but he was always aware that if he did not, then he could expect to exist upon what the navy provided.

So, the daughters of well-off squires, the grand-daughters of merchants, the youngest child of younger sons of the minor aristocracy were all considered—provided they brought money with them. And, while most of them seemed pleased at the thought of a tall naval officer with a baron for a brother, Nathan had found the entire process distasteful. His mother, he was well aware, had made a *suitable* match to a man she despised. His brother Daniel had wed the sour-faced youngest daughter of an earl because of her breeding and her dowry—substantial, Nathan had always assumed, because of the need to get her off her family's hands. Neither gave him any desire to marry for money.

So he had married for love. More fool he.

Now, of course, any of those well-dowered damsels would flee screaming if they found themselves alone with him. Nathan grimaced and stood up, slopping water everywhere, and began to wash his hair. Too much to hope that Clemence had left him any fresh water, he reached for the jug and found it half-full.

'Admirable woman,' he said, pouring it in a luxurious stream over his head. 'All this fresh water left.'

'I don't need much now my hair is short,' she said, her shoulders still firmly turned away from him.

'Was it very long?' Nathan stepped out, splashed through the puddles and found a linen towel.

'To my waist,' she said with a sigh. 'My only beauty.'

'Your what?' Nathan balanced, one foot wrapped in the towel as he dried his toes, and stared at the back of her head and the damp mop of hair that, when dry, was all the colours of pulled taffy. 'That I cannot believe.'

'I am not fishing for compliments,' Clemence said, apparently resigned to her looks. 'I know I am too tall, too slim and my face has too many angles. My papa used to say that I was as flat as a kipper in front, but I've never seen a kipper, so I don't know.'

Nathan swallowed. This was more information than he felt able to cope with, even after a cold bath. The memory of her body moulding into his came back. Even with her bosom bound, he knew perfectly well that kippers were not that shape.

'You've lived on Jamaica all your life, then?' he asked, pulling on his loosest trousers and snatching at an innocuous topic of conversation.

'Yes. Papa and Mama came out here just after they were married. Papa was a younger son, like you.' She sighed. 'Mama died ten years ago of the yellow fever.'

'It isn't a very healthy climate,' Nathan said sympathetically, finding a clean shirt.

'I know. But I don't seem to catch things, perhaps because I was born out here. Have you finished?'

Clemence was getting a crick in her back from sitting hunched up and her imagination was uncomfortably exercised by the knowledge of what was going on behind her, her ears following every splash, the sound

of Nathan working up a lather on bare skin, his sigh of
pleasure when he tipped the fresh water over his head,
the flap of his shirt as he shook it out.

'Yes, I'm finished.'

She swung her bare feet off the bunk and grimaced
as they hit a puddle. The floor of the neat cabin was
awash with more water than she believed had been
brought in, there were wet towels on the chairs, dirty
clothing discarded into the wet.

'Tsk!' She stood regarding it, hands on hips.

'You sound like my mother,' Nathan said, standing
unrepentant in the middle of the damp disorder.

'Why are men so messy?' Clemence demanded.
'Women aren't messy; at least, I'm not.' She bent to pick
up a towel and started to mop at a puddle. 'Mind you,
that's easy to say when one has servants, I suppose.'

'Do you keep slaves?'

'No! Papa never did, we don't agree with it. And
since the trade was abolished ten years ago, he was cam-
paigning to abolish keeping slaves, too. But, of course,
the planters say it is uneconomic to grow sugar using
waged labourers and the Americans rely on slave labour
as well, so our planters say it is uneconomic to change
because of the competition. It was easier for us, being
merchants, to stick to our principles. Uncle Joshua and
Cousin Lewis,' she added with a grimace, 'are planters.'

'I'd like to meet those two,' Nathan remarked. She
saw his fist clench against his thigh and once again entertained the fantasy of it lifting Lewis off the floor with
a solid punch to his insipient double chin.

'I hope I never see them again. Are all those clothes
dirty? Only I'll use them to mop up with if I'm going
to have to wash them anyway.'

Nathan started to scoop dirty water out of the tub. 'You shouldn't have to clean and wash for me.'

'I'm your cabin boy, remember? And I don't expect there's a fat, cheerful washerwoman on board, now is there?'

'No. How's your head?'

'All right, unless I touch it.' In fact, strangely, she felt better than she had for days. Food and fresh air must be helping, but perhaps it was also the stimulus of taking events into her own hands. From somewhere her courage had returned; however awful this was, at least she was no longer a passive victim. And Nathan knowing she was a woman was not awful at all, although it should be.

It was not going to end happily, this odd relationship with a gentleman gone to the bad. Of course, if this was a sensation novel, she would redeem him by the end of the last chapter and they would sail off into the sunset together to a life of idyllic, romantic love on some enchanted island. Kept alive, presumably, by tropical fruits, fish and the odd shipwreck. But how did you redeem a pirate?

Clemence rolled her eyes at her own folly. She could just imagine Nathan's reaction to her sitting him down and questioning his motives, suggesting he ought to reform because, basically, he was a good man. He had told her about his fall from grace with the navy, the downhill path that had brought him here. His heart wasn't in it, she was sure, but he was not going to admit that to her.

And did she want to sail off with him' Of course she didn't, she was destined for London, a Season and a gentleman of impeccable breeding, wealth, manners and prospects. Miss Ravenhurst could set her sights just as high as she pleased, she thought, finding them resting speculatively on one well-muscled back just in front of her. And she was independent enough to do just as she wanted.

But now she was a laundry maid, not a lady, and likely to be for the foreseeable future. She began to scoop up sodden washing. That olive-oil soap seemed to lather fairly well in salt water and Mr Street would tell her where to hang the laundry to dry.

The door banged back, making her start and drop the clothes. Peering up through the table legs as she crouched to pick them up, Clemence saw the figure in the door. McTiernan.

'The wind's picked up,' he said abruptly to Nathan, ignoring her. 'You'll take us through the passage tonight, Stanier.'

She saw Nathan's bare feet flex on the deck, as though adjusting his stance for action, but all he said was, 'That's a tricky passage in daylight, let alone in the dark.'

'There's a moon. You're supposed to be the best, Stanier. We touch anything, I'll have you keelhauled.'

'When was the last time *Sea Scorpion* had her bottom scraped?' Nathan asked, as though the question of being dragged under the barnacle-encrusted belly of the ship was an interesting academic point.

'It's overdue,' the captain said as he turned on his heel, leaving them in silence.

'How many times have you done that passage?' Clemence asked as casually as she could.

'Never.' He began to gather up instruments, polishing the lenses of his sextant. 'I've heard about it, I've studied the charts, that's all.'

'Oh. Mr Cutler will help, won't he?' she worried,

throwing the wet bundle into a corner and fetching his notebook and the roll of charts, her stomach swooping with apprehension.

'I don't think our first mate likes me much.' Nathan squinted at a pencil point and reached for his knife to whittle it. 'I think Mr Cutler would be quite happy if we nudged a head of coral or a nice sharp rock. Not enough to do any damage, you understand, just enough to upset the captain.'

'Can I help?' She had no idea how, and anyway, he'd just dismiss the offer. She was a girl, after all, men didn't accept help from women, not when it really mattered.

Nathan looked up, his blue eyes hard and steady, studying her as he had that night in the tavern. 'Yes, you can.' He nodded towards the bunk. 'Get some rest now, it's going to be a long night. I'll come for you.'

Clemence finished tidying up, a tight knot of anticipation and apprehension in her stomach. Nathan wanted her help, he didn't just dismiss her or belittle her. His eyes searched hers so intently and he seemed to find something there; she had no idea what.

Obedient, she lay down on her bunk and closed her eyes, but it was a long time before she slept.

Chapter Six

Clemence stood a pace behind Nathan, clutched the sextant and shivered. The evening air was not cold, far from it, but the sense of menace hung like a chill fog around the poop deck.

'Well?' She forced herself not to cringe closer to Nathan as McTiernan swung round. 'What are we waiting for? Enter the channel.'

'When the moon is up,' Nathan said, a statement, not a request. 'We'll beat up and down here until it is.'

McTiernan's eyes narrowed, but he nodded abruptly to the steersman. 'As Mr Stanier orders.'

The atmosphere had changed from merely frightening to something else entirely. The pirates were hunting, she realised, the scent of blood was in their nostrils and the channel was the equivalent of a track through the forest that would lead them to their prey.

She watched Nathan's supple back as he bent over the chart spread out on the hatch, wondering how he managed to look so relaxed and confident under such pressure. It was, she thought, remembering that first

startling glimpse of him naked, a beautiful back, un-
blemished golden skin over long, strong muscles.

'You, boy. Fetch coffee.' Cutler's voice, as precise as
his clothing, made her jump. Setting the sextant down
carefully by Nathan's right hand, she turned to obey.

'And a lantern, Clem,' Nathan added.

It filled the time, getting the coffee for the men on
the poop deck, finding a lantern, but not enough. What
if they did hit a rock or a reef? What if the *Sea Scorpion*
was holed and there were men, as she suspected, captive
down in the dark hell of the orlop deck?

She wished she'd mentioned them to Nathan, but
now was not the time. Slowly the moon rose, then, at
last, the sea was washed with silver. The land, the forest
tumbling down to the sands, was stark black and white
and, between two headlands, a ribbon of water marked
the treacherous shortcut to Lizard Island.

'Two points round,' Nathan said to the man at the
wheel, and it seemed that at least half a dozen people
let out pent-up breath. 'I suggest you reef more sail, Mr
Cutler. I need control, not speed now.

'Clem, get up to the bows with the leadsman. He'll call
depth and what's coming up on the lead, but I want you
to scrape some off and bring it to me, every cast. Run.'

The mate on the *Raven Duchess* had shown her how
to cast the lead when she was young, although she had
never had the strength to make the throw that sent the
weight on its knotted cord out ahead, and she knew how
the hollow in the end was filled with tallow to pick up
whatever was on the sea bed.

The hand was swinging and casting now, counting out
as the knots flew past his fingers, then shouting the result
as the line went slack. He hauled the lead up, dripping.

'I've got to take some of the bottom for Mr Stanier,' Clemence said, pulling out her knife and scraping off the coarse sand that clung to the tallow. She ran back as the man cast again, her hand spread palm-up in the lantern-light for Nathan to study.

She was shaking. He took her wrist in one warm hand to raise it closer and his thumb caressed briefly over the delicate skin of her inner wrist. 'Black sand and no shell.' He picked up the notebook and made a note. 'Again. Run.'

Back and forth, back and forth, for what seemed like hours. The leadsman's monotonous chant was the loudest noise on deck and her palm grew sore from rubbing off sand and shell. There was hardly time to watch Nathan as she wanted to, his face rapt and remote as he studied chart and notes, the outline of the dark land and the set of the sails. He sent a hand forward to climb out along the bowsprit to watch ahead for the tell-tale foam of waves breaking over almost submerged rocks, but the real danger, she knew, were the heads of coral that lurked unseen just under the surface, ready to rip the bottom out of a ship.

The islands on either side grew closer and closer as they crept along on reefed sails. Cutler put two men on the wheel. No one was speaking now, except the leadsman and the watchers.

Then Nathan picked up a telescope, strode to the side, caught hold of the rigging and began to climb until he reached just below the yards, hooked one arm into the ropes and leaned out, his eyes fixed on the sea ahead.

'He'd better know what he's doing,' a soft voice said in Clemence's ear. McTiernan. The hair on her neck stood up as he laid a hand on her shoulder.

'He does, Cap'n,' she said stoutly, staring up at the dark figure silhouetted against the sky, and found she believed it. There was a call from the bows. 'I've got to go, sir. The leadsman.'

She wriggled out from under his hand and scurried off as Nathan began to call down course corrections to the wheel. What sort of captain put his whole ship at risk, just to test out one man? *An insane one*, the voice in her head said. It was almost as though McTiernan saw Nathan as a threat.

'No bottom!' the leadsman sang out, pulling up a clean weight, and she relaxed a little, leaning against the rail while he prepared to cast again. Nathan was coming down the rigging now, moving like a shadow to jump on to the deck and go back to stand beside the captain.

Yes, no wonder McTiernan was wary of him—they both had an intangible natural authority, a charisma. Cutler could dominate, but she couldn't imagine him leading, whereas McTiernan had the mesmeric quality of a snake and Nathan simply exuded the confidence that what he said, went.

He had found the deep channel, it seemed, the lead kept coming up clean, or with white sand at depth, and on the last call he brought her back to stand by his side.

'All right, Clem?' She nodded. 'Enjoying yourself?'

Enjoying myself? Is he mad? We're on a pirate ship captained by a homicidal maniac, sailing through a dangerous channel he's never sailed before in the dead of night and he asks me if I'm enjoying myself? 'Yes,' Clemence said, realising it was true. For the moment she was one of this crew, with a role to play—that was part of it. And she was close to Nathan, watching him work, and that, overwhelmingly, was the whole of it.

'Good. Pass me the sextant, will you, and find something to take notes.' He began to take star sights, calling out figures for her to write in columns.

'Where did you get your education, boy?' Cutler, bent over to look, far too close at her shoulder.

'School, sir. Spanish Town, before we lost our money, sir.'

'Clem, those figures.' Nathan put down the instrument and jerked his head. She came to stand at his side, holding the notebook flat while he ran his finger down the column. 'Good, you've a clear script, boy.'

'How much longer?' she ventured, wanting to slip her hand into his, whether in gratitude at the praise or for giving her an excuse to move away from Cutler, or simply to touch him, she was not sure. But it was not hard, in this company, to resist the urge.

'Soon.' As he said it, the hand in the crow's nest shouted down.

'Open water dead ahead!'

'I suggest we drop anchor, Captain.' Nathan made a mark on the chart and turned it towards the man. 'It will be dark soon, with moonset. I imagine you do not want to be in open water when the sun comes up, not without a chance to reconnoitre first. We won't be the only craft seeking shelter in this group of islands.'

'Aye.' McTiernan looked down at the map, then up at Nathan. 'It seems you're as good as you say.' He nodded sharply. 'Make it so, Mr Cutler.' Nathan snapped his fingers at Clemence and began to roll up his charts. She hurried to pick up the sextant and telescope, stuffing the notebook into the pocket in her waistcoat tails. 'Where the hell do you think you're going, Mr Stanier?'

'To correct this chart and then to sleep, Captain.' His

voice was level, but Clemence caught the challenge under it and her heart began to pound. He waited, a long few seconds until McTiernan nodded again, before he deigned to explain. 'If we need to bolt back up this channel in a hurry, I want this chart accurate, because it most certainly isn't now.'

They were almost at the hatch before the captain spoke. 'Five bells, Mr Stanier.'

'Aye, aye, sir.'

Clemence padded after Nathan, her arms full, yawning hugely, excitement and relived tension bubbling inside her. Inside the cabin she put her load on the table and turned, unable to suppress the broad smile that seemed to crack her face.

'You were wonderful! So cool with that vulture watching every move, I couldn't believe it. And there was so much wrong with the chart, I saw all those marks you were making, all the errors you found.' She stared at him, admiration and something else she could not quite identify animating her. 'It was *marvellous*.'

'It was a bloody miracle.' Nathan leaned back against the door and let his head rest against the panels, eyes closed. 'I never, ever, want to have to do something like that again, so long as I live.'

'But you made it look so easy,' Clemence protested. He was tired, that was all, she told herself. All her security rested on this man being invincible. Nathan opened his eyes, met hers and then held out his right hand; it was shaking very slightly. He dropped his gaze to it, staring until the tremor stopped.

'That, Clemence, is the trick. Never, ever, let them see you feel fear, never, in action, let yourself believe you are afraid.'

'*You* get scared?' she asked, disbelieving.

'Only a fool does not feel fear. Listen to it, hear what the warning is, do what you can to prepare for the dangers and then, when it is time to act, put the fear aside.'

'I thought I was weak, being frightened,' she admitted.

'No, sensible. And human.' He had closed his eyes again, leaning back against the door as though too weary to move to the chair.

Clemence went and wrapped her arms around his waist, laid her cheek on his chest and hugged, hard.

'Ough!' Nathan huffed, half-laughing. 'What are you doing?' He made no move to escape her embrace, rather seemed to relax into it.

'Hugging you. You need a hug. You deserve a hug— I don't expect you get many.' His chest moved, he was laughing, silently. Clemence felt her cheeks getting hot. 'I don't mean *that*; the sort of hugs you pay for. I mean friendly hugs.' She unwrapped her arms and pulled out a chair, tugging at his sleeve. 'Sit down, you are far too big to haul about. I suppose you'll insist on doing that chart before you'll sleep. I'll go and get some coffee.'

When she got back with a beaker of the thick black liquid he was dead to the world, his head on his folded arms, the pencil fallen from his hand, his hair in his eyes.

Clemence set down the beaker and moved the pencil, resisting the impulse to smooth back the thick hair, play with the sun-bleached tips. Best to let him sleep. She climbed on to her bunk and sat watching him, feeling again the strapping of muscle over his ribs, the long back muscles where her palms had pressed, the heat of his tired body.

Flawed, complex, beautiful, dangerously enigmatic. She was very much afraid that she was… Her lids drooped.

* * *

'Clem!' Nathan's hand fell from her shoulder as she woke with a start. 'Time to wake up, nearly five bells.'

Her neck had a crick in it and she felt hot and sweaty. 'Oh.' She stretched. 'Have you been to bed?'

'No, I slept for half an hour, drank my nice cold coffee and altered the chart.' He jerked his head towards the privy door. 'I've finished with the cupboard.'

Last night's moment of vulnerability had gone. This morning Nathan was all business, making notes, sorting through the rolls of charts, his hands rock-steady. Clemence took herself off to the cupboard and emerged, ten minutes later, considerably more awake.

'Nathan?'

'Mmm?'

'Did you know there are prisoners on board?'

'No.' He put down a pair of dividers and stared at her. 'Where?'

'Down on the orlop deck.' She explained what she had heard and seen.

'But McTiernan doesn't take ordinary seamen, he slaughters the lot.'

'I know. So why does he want these? And some of them may be from my father's ship. I can't leave them down there.'

'Oh, yes, you can. Unless you want to join them, that is.'

'Nathan, please.' She dragged a chair up and sat down, knee to knee, her voice wheedling. 'You can do something, surely?'

'Don't you dare try that wide-eyed stuff on me, Clem,' he warned. 'It irritates the hell out of me at the best of times and, just now, it's damned dangerous.'

'Sorry.' She didn't know what had come over her. Normally that sort of eyelash fluttering, *Oh, Mr Stanier, you are wonderful, won't you do it for me?* irritated her, too, when she'd seen other young women trying it on men.

Clemence knew she was hopeless at flirting; she always had been, feeling a complete idiot making eyes at boys she'd known all her life and pretending to be five foot one and a fragile little bloom when she was nothing of the kind. Attempting to deploy her inept feminine wiles on Nathan Stanier was madness. Feeling as she did about him was even madder.

'I'll see what I can find out,' he conceded. 'Come on, breakfast time.'

Street was frying yams when they made their way to the galley, the savoury smell making Clemence's mouth water with longing. Nathan raided the skillet of bacon, peering into the pots that bubbled, their contents sloshing back and forth with the motion of the ship as they slid between the restraining bars on the range.

'That's surely not our dinner, is it?' He dipped a cautious finger into one pot.

'Nah, that swill's for the cargo.' Street grinned.

'You are not much concerned with keeping them alive, then?' Nathan sucked his finger clean, grimacing.

'Not what you'd call a high-value cargo, field hands,' Street remarked. 'But I keep them alive, as much as food and water will do.'

'It's slaves down there, then?' Nathan queried, pouring himself thin ale and draining the tankard.

'They will be, by the time we get them to St Martin. The French'll buy anything, they're that short since the Peace, what with the trade being outlawed.'

'So captive merchant crews are sold to the French islands and just conveniently vanish into the upland plantations out of reach of any English help? Good business idea.'

Clemence was positively hissing with indignation by the time she and Nathan found a deserted piece of deck to lean against the rail and eat.

'The bastard! I'd like to—'

'Quiet! At least we know he wants them kept alive. If they're worth money, they've a good chance of getting off this ship. I was worried he was keeping them for sport—shark bait or something.' Nathan tossed a piece of bacon rind over the side as though to make his point.

'What? He wouldn't? Alive, you mean?'

'He would and he does. He's got a very strange idea of entertainment, has our captain. He isn't called *Red* because of his taste in spotted kerchiefs, it's because blood's red and he likes it. Lots of it.'

'You…you're frightening me,' Clemence managed to say around the constriction in her throat. She didn't want him to treat her like a sheltered little girl, but like a grown woman. On the other hand, there were some details she could very well do without.

'Good. Be very frightened—you are less likely to do anything foolish.'

'I'd heard he had a dreadful reputation, but I didn't know he was like that.' She shuddered. But she couldn't just let men she knew be sold off as slaves. She would have to think of something.

'Mr Stanier!' The light was breaking through, chasing the night back into deep pools of shadow either side of the channel. Ahead, in the open sea, a brisk breeze was making white horses on the wavelets.

'Coming, sir.' Nathan pushed his ale into Clemence's hands. 'Now, things get lively.'

Nathan studied the open waters of the Windward Passage as *Sea Scorpion* slipped out of the channel and turned starboard to the sheltered deep anchorage between Lizard Island and, at their back, the scatter of islands they had picked their way through the night before. Ahead was the major route for shipping between Hispaniola and Cuba and topsails were distantly visible. Closer to the island the white lateen sails of fishing boats dotted the sea—small fry, safe from the big shark.

He turned on his heel, seeming to glance casually over the forested slopes and rock-strewn beaches behind them. Somewhere, if things had gone to plan, spy glasses were watching them and messages were being sent to a middling-sized merchant vessel with a conveniently damaged mast. It would come limping out of shelter, like a bird with a broken wing, right under the nose of the *Sea Scorpion*—and McTiernan would not be able to resist.

'You seem pleased with life, Mr Stanier.'

'Who wouldn't smile at a morning like this, Mr Cutler?' On his other side he sensed Clem stiffening, but she neither pressed closer to him nor moved away. She was scared of Cutler, but she had guts.

'Drop anchor!' There was a roar as the pinions were knocked out and the chain rushed free, the anchor dropping through clear water to the sand beneath, then a few moments of peace again until the bo'sun began ordering the hands to their morning chores.

'You're not expecting any business along yet?'

'No.' Cutler was looking up into the rigging, his eyes checking, evaluating every knot and sheet. 'Those fat lazy merchantmen won't stir themselves for a while yet.'

Beside him Clem gave a muffled snort and Nathan kicked her lightly on the ankle in warning; the last thing they needed was her giving Cutler a lecture on the superiority of merchantmen over pirate vessels.

A jolly boat was swung out with water casks to fill at the stream that burst out of the forest on to the beach in a miniature waterfall. Even without the telescope he could make out the spreading pool beneath the fall. 'Imagine swimming in that,' Clem said wistfully.

Nathan looked at her. Leaning with elbows on the rail, chin in hand, rear end stuck out, she was lost in a daydream. With no difficulty at all he joined her in it. Somehow he had no trouble at all imagining Clemence naked, slipping like a fish through the water, coming up to the surface laughing, her hands full of shells, walking towards him, small high breasts covered in sun-reflecting droplets…

He looked again and hissed, 'Stand up straight and pull your shirt down.'

She jumped to obey, startled question in her eyes.

'You might be too thin,' he muttered in her ear, 'but no lad has got a backside like that!' *Oh, God, and now that was in his head, too, pert and rounded, just asking to be cupped in his palms like a ripe peach.*

She went pink, but looked pleased. 'Really? That's good. I must be putting weight on.'

Women! 'It is no such—'

'Sail ho!' The cry from the masthead had everyone turning towards the rail. There, emerging slowly from behind the headland, was a small merchantman, sail drooping, mast oddly angled, crew swarming over the rigging in frantic activity.

'Raise the anchor!' Cutler roared and the bo'sun came at the run, starter in hand, shoving and bullying the hands into place around the capstan. Men were climbing the rigging, making for their designated places on the yards ready to lower the sail, and the lids of sea chests crashed open as the crew left on deck armed themselves.

'Get below.' Nathan pushed Clem towards the companionway.

'No!' She dug in her heels, then saw the look on his face. 'I'll go down before we close with them,' she promised.

'Do that. This is going to be a hot fight.'

'How do you know?' Clem demanded, half-running to keep up with him as he made for the nearest arms' chest to find a cutlass. 'It's a small ship.'

'Instinct,' he lied, mentally kicking himself for the slip.

'But they aren't heavily armed,' she continued to speculate.

'Spare me your views on marine strategy,' Nathan said coldly, desperate to stop her talking.

'Sorry.' She subsided, shooting him a side-long look from under her lashes that was pure feminine speculation.

The anchor was up, the sails crashing down, beginning to fill as the hands scrambled back to the deck. Nathan tried the edge on the cutlass with his thumb and studied the men on the poop deck. Just behind the steersman, that was the place.

Sea Scorpion began to move, nosing out towards the sea and its victim. 'Hoist the bones,' Cutler yelled and a man ran to the main mast and began to lash an odd bundle to it.

'What's that?' Beside him Clem craned to see.

'The skull and cross-bones,' Nathan said grimly, watching it jerk up to the foremast.

'But…that's not a flag. Those are real…' Clem turned away, her face white as she saw the gulls swoop to feast on the remains that still clung to the pathetic relics.

'I told you, our captain has a novel sense of humour.' To say nothing of a unique personal style. The merchantman had seen them now. Its few gun ports dropped open; across the water there was the sound of shouted orders, the rumble of gun carriages. The armament looked pitifully small, but that was all to the good, Nathan thought. They didn't want a long-distance gun battle, they needed hand-to-hand fighting if the trap was to be sprung on the *Sea Scorpion*.

Beside him Clemence gasped. 'They are running out their guns—what if we're hit? The men down below won't have a chance.'

'Nothing we can do. Clem, be quiet—'

There was a shout from the crow's nest. 'Cap'n! Big merchantman, just coming into sight off the starboard bow!'

There was a rush for the rail, telescopes trained beyond the stricken ship. Minutes passed, then, 'It's the *Raven Princess*, Cap'n!'

Chapter Seven

'**Y**es!' For the first time Nathan saw McTiernan animated. The captain slammed his clenched fist into the other palm. 'Leave this one, it isn't going far.' He turned to the wheelman, firing rapid orders as Cutler shouted up to the sail handlers.

Sea Scorpion swung round, away from her crippled victim towards the richly tempting prize of a great ocean-going craft bound for London. 'Hell!' Nathan let the one word escape, then shut his lips tight. The rat had so nearly walked into the trap and now, whiskers twitching, it was off after a bigger, tastier piece of cheese and there was absolutely nothing he could do about it.

'No, oh, no.' Clem's whisper cut through his own furious thoughts. 'Not the *Raven Princess*.'

'Why not?'

'I…I know the captain, some of the crew. That was the ship I was making for when McTiernan stopped me.'

It must be the thought of what would have happened to her as a member of a captured crew that was making her so distressed. She was going to cry in a minute, he could see her full lower lip begin to tremble.

'Clem,' he hissed, 'if you can't control yourself, you'll have to go below. There is nothing either of us can do about this.'

'Why should you want to?' she spat at him, her face contorted with anger. 'You're one of them, you'll share the killing and the booty and the plunder and I expect you'll want me to wash the blood off your clothes when you come back from getting it.'

'Clem, shut up.' He took her arm and shook her. 'You are attracting attention.'

'I will not stand by and—' His hand over her mouth cut off the threat. Nathan wrapped his other arm around her waist and hoisted her off her feet, kicking and struggling. Her buttocks squirmed against his groin, sending desire lancing through him, deepening his anger. His entire strategy was going to hell in a handcart and this damned woman, who hadn't the sense to be terrified, was going to give it a final shove off the cliff if he couldn't shut her up.

'What the devil are you about, Mr Stanier?' Cutler shouted down from the rail of the poop deck.

'He's frightened, Mr Cutler, but he won't go down. He'll be a damn nuisance under our feet, I'll dump him in the cabin and be right back.'

Ruthless, Nathan slung Clem over his shoulder with considerably less care than he had shown the day before and got her, struggling and cursing at him, down the companionway.

'Will you shut up, Clem?'

'Put me down!' She fetched him a painful thump in the kidneys with a clenched fist. Nathan dropped her on to her feet and pushed her back against a bulkhead, keeping one hand pressed to her shoulder to hold her still. The deck around them was deserted, everyone was either above decks or at the guns.

'There, you are down.' She glared at him, hands fisted on her hips. 'Now, show some sense and *shut up*.'

'There was no need to manhandle me.' She pushed the hair out of her eyes and tugged at her shirt tails.

'There was every need.' She wriggled and he brought up his other hand and pinned her against the wood. Even under the strapping he could see the rise and fall of her bosom, catch her feminine scent, hot, furious, heady.

'You *pirate*, you bully, you—' The injustice, even though she had no way of knowing the truth, was the final straw. Wrestling with her had stimulated an erection that ached, his hands could feel her heat, he could hear her panting breaths, his nostrils were full of her.

Nathan took a step forward and kissed her hard on the mouth with none of the delicacy and restraint he had used before and with the full force of his angry frustration behind it.

Clemence's gasp of shock was swallowed up by the fierce open-mouthed kiss. She grabbed his wrists, but she might as well have been wrestling with the capstan bars. Something slid through her, a strange mixture of anger and triumph that she had provoked him into this violent acceptance of her femininity.

But the anger was winning—the logical emotion, the wise one. She jerked up one knee and he moved in like a swordsman, almost as though he had expected it, turning her aggressive gesture into weakness as she found him between her thighs, his whole body pressed against her, the heat of his erection searing against her belly.

His tongue was in her mouth, thrusting. Clemence closed her teeth and he jerked back and looked down at her, his face stark. 'Clemence—*hell.*'

Panting, she stared at him from a distance of perhaps six inches. He looked shaken, yet still angry. *He should be grovelling at my feet.* Nathan met her stormy gaze and something deep in those blue eyes stirred, despite the expression on his face. He desired her, it was not just anger at her outburst.

Before she could think, Clemence let go of his wrists and seized his head, dragged it down to her lips again, clung for a few dizzying moments and then pulled free.

'Are you sorry? I should hope so,' she said shakily. 'So…so am I. Sorry.' Slowly he lifted his hands away from her shoulders and she stared back at him, each of them cautious, as if they were two wrestlers not knowing if the other truly had called *quits.* 'May I come back on deck? I won't say anything, I promise.' There was nothing she could do, except watch and pray that *Raven Princess* could outrun them. And if the worst happened, then it was her duty to stand and watch it, not cower in her cabin with her head under the pillow.

'Clemence, what just happened was madness.' Nathan touched her swollen lower lip with the back of his fingers.

'Well, it wasn't very sensible,' she agreed shakily, 'but I think we can forgive ourselves, because otherwise we are going to have to spend some very long, silent hours in that cabin.' He was still looking grim, but that produced a reluctant grin.

'Come on, then. Hell, your mouth is swollen. You look as though you've been kissed hard.' Clemence narrowed her eyes at him. Nathan shrugged, his smile twisting wryly, raised his wrist to his mouth and bit with a grimace. Blood welled from the puncture and he smeared it onto her lip and down her chin. 'There. Look cowed, I've cuffed you, cut the inside of your lip.'

'All right.' Feeling quite adequately cowed, and more than a little confused, Clemence dug a bandana out of her pocket and held it to the side of her mouth, bracing herself for their reappearance on deck and Cutler's hard stare.

But there was no need to fear they were of the slightest interest to anyone; as they reached the rail there was a shout from above. 'Frigate!'

McTiernan froze, then a stream of low-voiced invective hissed from between his clenched teeth. Most of the words meant nothing to Clemence, but the sheer malevolence of it chilled her to the bone.

Beautiful, sunlit, the white sails of the distant naval ship strained in the wind, bringing her into a direct line between hunter and hunted. Clemence thought she had never seen anything more wonderful in her life.

'There's time to take the smaller ship.' Her jaw dropped as Nathan called up to McTiernan. He began to climb to the poop deck. 'We could board her, grab any portable valuables. Cut and run.'

Nathan? Clemence stared, disbelieving, as the men talked. Yes, she could accept, just, that he was the navigator, that when they went into action he would take part, but that he would deliberately incite McTiernan to take a helpless ship shocked her to the core.

'No, that bastard will see us, the visibility is too good. Mr Cutler, take us back behind Lizard Island and into the pool, we'll skulk like curs until that damn King's ship's gone and then...' he showed his stained teeth in a humourless grin '…then we'll take the next thing that shows a bowsprit, and God have mercy on them, because I won't.'

Clemence did not need any instructions to stay out of the way. She retreated to her perch amongst the casks and watched, blank-eyed, as the ship turned tail back into the shelter of Lizard Island. The watering crew were waiting on the beach, but the *Sea Scorpion* kept going. Surely McTiernan was not going to abandon his own men and a valuable jolly boat?

Puzzlement broke through her misery as she saw the topsails were being reefed in, then the mainsail. Boats were lowered, lines thrown out to them. As *Sea Scorpion*'s speed dropped to a glide, the boats took up the slack and began to steer her towards what seemed to be sheer cliff. Men in two of the boats that were not towing rowed right up to the tumbling vegetation and she realised that they were pulling back a screen of greenery to reveal the tight mouth of an entrance.

Slowed to walking pace now, the ship slid forward, her shadow black on the white sand, fish shoals darting away as though at the approach of a giant predator. They were through the screen, into an almost circular sea pool. Clemence had seen inlets like this before, caused when the roofs of caves collapsed; she'd even swum in one in the days before she had become a virtual prisoner, a million years ago.

So, this was McTiernan's secret hideaway and, thanks to Nathan showing him the shortcut through the sea passage, he was now even closer to Kingston harbour and had an ideal route to surprise the rich merchantmen leaving it.

The jolly boat with the water casks came through the

gap in the wake of the flotilla of rowing boats, and the screen of creepers was hauled back into place. It was perfect, Clemence realised, standing up on the casks to look around. There was even a beach at the far end big enough for some shacks. Used, no doubt, for storing plunder. The only thing it was lacking was a source of fresh water, hence the laborious business of filling the casks from the waterfall further along the beach.

The anchor chain roared out through the hawsehole and *Sea Scorpion* came to rest, bobbing grotesquely in its idyllic setting like its namesake in the middle of an exquisite Meissen bowl.

'There you are.' It was Nathan, hands on hips, eyes screwed up against the sun dazzle.

'How could you?' she hissed.

He leaned in close with a jerk of his head to bring her hunkering down so he could murmur in her ear. 'Would you believe to try to delay us for the frigate to arrive?' he enquired.

'And risk capture yourself? How naïve do you think I am?' Nathan opened his mouth to speak. 'No, don't answer that.'

'Which?' He raised one eyebrow, infuriating her further. 'The answers are—possibly, but it might be a profitable risk to take for the reward and, no, not naïve, just somewhat sheltered from this sort of thing.'

'What sort of thing? Double-dealing, back-stabbing, money-grubbing treachery? I thought you disapproved of betrayal and disloyalty.'

'I do, when I'm dealing with human beings with some basic moral sense. This lot are fair game.' There was the sound of footsteps on the boards. Nathan drew back and added, at a normal volume, 'And next time, do what you're told, when you're told, or you'll get more than a cuff in the mouth. Understand?'

Over his shoulder Cutler loomed. 'Yessir, Mr Stanier,' Clemence said, nodding frantically and holding the kerchief to her mouth. 'Sorry, sir.'

'Let me know when you get tired of the brat, Stanier,' Cutler said, his gaze sliding over Clemence. 'I'm sure we'll find a use for him.'

'Not while I've a pile of washing needing doing,' Nathan said easily. 'Shift yourself, Clem, I want that cabin shipshape when I come down.'

Escaping below decks was a relief, even with a pile of dirty clothes to wash in the hot seawater she dipped from the cook's big cauldron. He made no fuss about her taking fresh for rinsing either, with the supply now easily replenished.

Clemence scrubbed and wrung and dipped, regarding her wrinkled fingers with something like dismay. Her skin was becoming tanned, her fingernails chipped, the soft palms a thing of the past. How pampered she had been, she realised, pushing sweaty hair back from her forehead and attacking her stained trousers.

She had supervised the household, studied her Spanish and French and her music, written to friends and relatives, shopped—and thought herself busy. The promised London Season would have been nothing but shopping and pleasure with only one task before her, the finding of a suitable husband.

Well, she wasn't going to find one now, even if she emerged alive and unscathed from this adventure. Clemence sat back on her heels, jolted by the thought. She had been so set on escaping from the Naismiths that the consequences had simply not occurred to her.

She had never found a gentleman on Jamaica who stirred more than a flutter in her heart and she had cherished no particular daydream of the one she would find in London, but it was a shock to realise that no gentleman was going to want her now, virgin or not.

And the fact that the only man who did stir her was Nathan Stanier was not much consolation, either. She had a lowering thought that the effect he had on her was purely physical, which probably showed she was wanton, and the notion that she was falling in love with him was simply the product of enforced intimacy, gratitude that he had saved her and the disturbing effect of whatever it was that seemed to spark between them.

Just sex, Clemence thought gloomily, sucking the finger she had rubbed raw in an attempt to get the coffee stains out of her shirt. It certainly was for him. All she was to Nathan Stanier was an inconvenient stray who brought the added complication—to one who had at least been brought up as a gentleman—that if he made love to her he would probably feel guilty about it afterwards.

She ought to feel guilty just thinking about sex, she knew that. Well-bred young women had to pretend they knew nothing about it and did not want to know either. The first was nonsense, of course. You couldn't live on a tropical island, surrounded by burgeoning fertility, hot nights and the amazingly lax morals of a good part of the European population without grasping rather more than the essentials.

As for the second unspoken rule, well, she had never wanted a man before, so the subject had been of academic interest up to now. There had been Mr Benson, of course, whose classically handsome profile had troubled her dreams a little for a week or two, and the oddly flustered feeling that the attempts at flirtation of some of the bolder naval officers provoked, but that was all.

So this almost constant awareness of her own body, the slightly breathless feeling of anticipation the entire time, the embarrassingly persistent pulse that made her want to squeeze her legs together in a vain attempt to calm it, those were all Nathan Stanier's doing. Those two kisses, one so gentle, one so angry, had completely undone her, plunged her into a state where all she wanted was to have him make love to her. Completely. After all, if she survived this she was going to be ruined. She might as well get some benefit out of it…

'Penny for them?'

The bar of soap shot out of her clutching fingers and skidded across the cabin. Clemence twisted round with a muffled shriek, lost her balance and sat down in a puddle. Nathan, just inside the door, regarded her with that infuriating eyebrow raised and an expression on his face that convinced her that she must look a complete idiot. A completely undesirable idiot.

Her face, of course, would be scarlet, what with lust and embarrassment and the heat and the steam from the hot water. Her hair, she could feel, was hanging in lank rats' tails, she had washerwoman's fingers—and it was all his fault.

Clemence counted to ten, in Spanish, backwards, thought, *Imagine you're at dinner at the King's House with the Governor*, and managed not to shriek at him. 'I am hot, I am tired, I am upset and I have about a hundredweight of wet washing to wring out,' she articulated with dangerous calm and produced a small tight smile that had the desired effect of lowering that eyebrow.

'Right.' He came fully into the cabin, shut the door

and retrieved the soap from under her bunk. 'Let's tackle the easy things first. I'll wring. Do you know where you can hang these out?'

'Mr Street showed me, between decks, forr'ard of the sail-maker's station.' This was the man she was having utterly improper fantasies about and here they were, discussing the laundry. Something of the trouble in her thoughts must have been reflected on her face because, as Nathan heaved the tub of wet clothes on to the table, he regarded her quizzically.

'I was thinking about what is going to happen to me if I ever manage to get out of this,' she admitted.

'We'll think of something.' He began to twist the sopping garments, the tendons on his wrists standing out sharply. Clemence watched the play of muscles under the thin linen sleeves. Those were the hands that had pinned her to the bulkhead a short while ago, had made her feel helpless and powerful, both at the same time. She wanted to feel them on her again, wanted to try his strength, stroke his naked skin, lick the paler skin just below the lobe of his ear…

'Put them in here.' She snatched up the empty water pail and put it on the table, almost hopping from foot to foot in her anxiety to be out of the cabin. It was suddenly too small. Or perhaps he was too big.

Nathan was still there when she returned, only now he was stuffing things into the big leather satchel. 'Where are you going?' He wasn't leaving, surely?

'I told McTiernan I want to go along to the headland, get height and take bearings. I thought we could deal with some of your other woes while we were at it.' He was going to make love to her? There was silence while she stared at him, feeling the blood ebb and flow under her skin. 'Clem? You don't mind a walk, do you? You said you were feeling hot and tired—the exercise will do you good.'

'Right, yes, exercise, of course,' she gabbled. He wasn't a mind reader, the words *Take Me* were not emblazoned on her forehead, he was talking about her complaints, not her fantasies. Clemence struggled for some poise. 'Can I help with anything?'

'Go to the galley, get something to take with us to eat.' He tossed her another satchel. 'I'll see you on deck in a minute.'

One of the hands rowed them across to the huts on the beach and pointed out the path through the trees that led to the stream. 'Looks as though it will be a gentle slope until then,' Nathan said, swinging the bulky satchel over his shoulder. 'Then it will be a stiffer climb to the headland. Can you manage?'

Clemence nodded, following at his heels. Already, just being clear of the ship, she was feeling better. She looked back, catching a glimpse of it through the trees as it rode at anchor: black, waiting, sinister. Down in the deepest, darkest part men were huddled in abject misery, dying perhaps. She felt so helpless.

'Forget the ship for a while.' Nathan was looking back over his shoulder.

Clemence nodded and ran to catch up; until she could think of something positive to do, it was futile to keep worrying at the problem. They walked in single file, silent, for perhaps half an hour until the sound of falling water drew them to the stream. It fell over a waterfall into a deep pool that, in turn, drained through the trees, over the cliff and into the pool they had seen on the beach.

It was a magic place, sunlight filtering through the leaves, the cool water cupped in a ring of rocks, the foaming lace of the waterfall. They stood looking at it, side by side, then Nathan said, 'You could swim when we come back down. It is safe up here, not like the beach pool.'

It made Clemence feel better just thinking about it. 'I could?'

'I'd stand guard.' Nathan turned away and began to strike off up a steeper path.

Goodness, he's fit, Clemence thought, aware that she was puffing as she climbed in the wake of his long stride. Weeks of enforced inaction inside, hardly any food, the immobility of grief, had taken their toll on someone used to walking and riding every day.

Nathan stopped and waited for her as the forest gave way to the bare slopes above. 'Here.' He held out his hand and Clemence put hers into it. 'I used to be able to walk for miles,' she lamented, allowing herself to be towed up a steep bit. 'And I rode every day. And only a few years ago I was climbing trees and playing in the cane fields and now I'm panting over one little hill.'

'Not so little. Look.' Nathan released her hand as he gestured and she realised they had climbed to the top of Lizard Island. The sea spread out in front of them, islets dotted like spilled beads on crushed blue velvet. The frigate had come up with the damaged merchantman and even without the telescope Clemence could see the activity as sailors from the warship helped the crew with the rigging.

'They'll be safely on their way soon,' she commented, pointing. 'And they'll tell the frigate which way we went as well.'

'They won't find us, not unless we signal,' Nathan broke off, looking thoughtful. 'Fire would do it, but there's no point up here, that wouldn't pinpoint anything and I presume you'd have a fixed objection to setting the *Sea Scorpion* on fire.'

'With the holds full of trapped men? Yes, I would!' She sat down on a smooth boulder and regarded him. 'Would you really betray McTiernan and the crew?'

'For the bounty on their heads? Yes. I could do with the money.' Nathan had the glass to his eye, scanning not just the sea, but sweeping round to the larger island behind them and the wooded slopes falling away from their viewpoint.

'That seems…'

'Risky?' He lowered the glass and studied her face. Clemence knew she was frowning.

'Well, yes, that of course, McTiernan would have your liver. But you signed up with them.'

'Honour amongst thieves? You think I should be loyal to that crew of murderous vagabonds?'

'I know it sounds wrong.' She struggled with it some more. 'It is just that two wrongs don't make a right.'

'So loyalty is an absolute virtue and, having joined the pirates, I must remain one? My shipmates, right or wrong?' Nathan rested one hip on a rock in front of her. 'You are a severe moralist, Clem.'

'Oh, no, never that!' Clemence protested. 'I don't want to judge.'

'But you are judging me?'

'Yes,' she conceded miserably confused. 'I know I am.' She hated the moral ambiguity, *his* moral ambiguity. Why couldn't he be a hero, purer than pure? How could she be trembling on the brink of falling in love with a man like him?

Chapter Eight

'So, you can't trust a pirate turncoat?' Nathan enquired.

'I shouldn't. But I do about some things.' She scuffed the gritty soil under her toe. 'I trust you not to betray me, even when I do foolish things.'

'Yes, you can rely on me for that. But you couldn't trust me not to kiss you,' he pointed out.

'I wanted you to,' she said baldly, still staring at her toes. 'Both times. And you stopped at a kiss. Thank goodness,' she added hastily.

'You are a virgin, Clemence,' he said, his voice harsh. 'I am—I *was*—a gentleman. I told you, I do not seduce virgins.'

'No. Of course not.' When she dared to look up again, Nathan was on his feet, using the rock as a rest while he made notes. 'Can I help?'

'No, thank you,' he said absently, squinting at the horizon and then looking back at his notes. 'Why not lay out the food and we'll eat? Have a look over there—' He waved towards an outcrop of tumbled rocks. 'There might be a good view on the other side of those. I'll be along in a minute.'

Clemence gathered up her satchel and made for the rocks. She had been wondering how to discreetly slip away and find a rock to shelter behind to make herself comfortable; Nathan was being very tactful.

As Clemence disappeared around the heap of rocks Nathan pulled a mirror, the size of his palm, from his pocket and angled it to the sun, moving it in a jerky rhythm. 'Look this way, damn you,' he muttered. The frigate still rode beside the merchantman, its flag hoists inactive. Somewhere out on that blue expanse was the fishing boat that had been dogging their steps and had signalled ahead when they entered the channel last night. It was gratifying that they had second-guessed McTiernan's movements, set the first decoy up at the right place.

Appear to leave, stay close, use second decoy, he signalled, over and over. Finally a dark dot appeared against the white canvas, struggling up towards the to'gallants. He put the mirror back in his pocket and raised the telescope.

Acknowledged. Stand by. Two days. Two more days eyeball to eyeball with McTiernan and Cutler. This had better be worth it, although just at the moment he was coming to the conclusion that simply getting out with a whole skin was the most he could hope for. A whole skin and Clemence.

Nathan scrubbed a hand through his hair. It was bad enough having those clear eyes judging him for being a pirate, let alone a turncoat pirate. The temptation to justify himself to her was strong, but if she knew the truth it would only put her in more danger than she was already. He would just have to add her disapproval to the other burdens of the situation.

With the telescope tucked under his arm, Nathan

went to see what she had managed to find for their picnic. 'A whole chicken? How in Hades did you manage that?' It was small and scrawny, but even so, a chicken was a chicken.

'I snivelled a bit. Said you'd hit me and I wanted something to put you in a good mood,' she confessed with a grin. 'Mr Street had just fished three birds out of the pot. He said I had probably deserved a good thrashing because all boys were the spawn of the devil, but he was smiling, so I grabbed a chicken and a loaf and some of the butter and things.' She gestured at the spread.

'You'd make a very promising conman, young Clem.' Nathan hunkered down and began to tear the fowl apart. 'What would Miss Clemence be doing now, assuming your uncle hadn't turned out to be such a villain?'

'Oh, managing the household, sewing, meeting friends. I've got a nice garden.' Something about the way she was so focused on the food and so off-hand with her brief description made him suspicious.

'Courting a handsome local lad?'

'No!' That was very vehement. 'I know them all too well—it would be like courting my own brother.'

'Dashing naval officers, then?' Nathan settled down, propped himself on one elbow, and began to gnaw at a chicken leg. 'I hear the uniform attracts the ladies.' *I know damn well it does—that and a fat purse of prize money.*

'Don't you know from your own experience?' she asked, looking up, her eyes very green in the sunlight. The scruffy urchin had vanished and in his place was a young lady regarding him from beneath haughtily lifted eyebrows.

'I was at sea a lot of the time,' he said, treading cautiously, unsure whether she was testing his story or simply showing feminine curiosity about the women in his life.

'Oh, yes, I recall you telling me about your career. You obviously had far more exciting things to be doing than courting gentlewomen.' Clemence lobbed a chicken bone over one shoulder into the undergrowth, the young lady vanishing again. 'No, I never found the naval officers very tempting, either. They were so determined to see how far their flirtations would get them before they could escape again to their ships, leaving a trail of broken hearts in their wake.'

'Did you go to receptions at the King's House?'

'Oh, yes.' Clemence spread butter on a crust with a lavish hand. 'Goodness, I'm so hungry—it must be the sea air.' She tucked a lock of hair back behind her ear and waved the crust for emphasis. 'I don't know about England, but here virtually the entire white population is on visiting terms and is invited to receptions by the Governor.

'Society is so small that the social divisions almost disappear. Visiting ladies always say that balls and routs are complete romps and turn up their noses at us when they find themselves sitting next to an attorney or a shopkeeper at a dinner party, but it would be ridiculous if society were confined to a handful of leading planters and the richest merchants.'

'So, no young man to deliver you back to,' Nathan mused, realising he was not finding that thought displeasing.

'It is a trifle premature to think about getting back safe to Kingston, is it not?' Clemence asked.

'Perhaps. I like to plan ahead. What's your surname,

Clemence?' he asked, realising that she had never told him. Now why not?

'Browne.' The response was so quick, he should not have been suspicious, but there was something about the way she held his eyes, as though daring him to challenge her, that told him she was lying. No, she did not trust him, not wholly. Sensible woman.

He nodded and she leaned against a rock, apparently sated, and tipped her face up to the sun. The shaggy hair fell back, giving Nathan a clear sight of her face. The swelling had gone down, the bruises were turning yellow. Soon the disfigurement would be gone, any lingering traces disguised by a healthy tan. How easy would it be to hide the fact that she was a girl when that happened?

Two days to survive before this all came to a head. Nathan shifted uncomfortably. Lying around felt wrong, even though there was nothing he could do now. He had gone into this deception knowing there was a good chance he would not come out of it. At the time, the gains had seemed worth the risk and he had always been ready to play the odds, especially when he did not much care about his own skin. Now he was responsible for Clemence and there was no one he could rely on to protect her if the worst happened. He had to stay alive— which might not be something he had much control over.

Although there were the men in the hold. Would they be in any condition to fight if he could free them? It would shorten the odds, although the timing would be critical.

'You look grim,' Clemence observed, head on one side. 'And tired. Are you sleeping at night?'

'Yes, I'm sleeping.' And dreaming. His dreams seemed to be full of smoke and blood and the rattle of that disgusting bundle of rotting bones at the masthead.

He woke every time feeling as though he'd just fought a ship action. It was curiously pleasant to have someone to worry about him.

'Good.' Clemence closed her eyes again and he sat and watched while she dropped off. Her mouth opened a little, her breath came in foolish whiffles and her long limbs relaxed into an endearing, graceful sprawl. Nathan wanted to crawl over, put his head in her lap and sleep, too, perhaps to wake and find she was stroking his hair. Instead, he sat up and thought, long and hard.

Clemence woke, feeling warm and relaxed and safe. Her eyes were closed, but she could feel Nathan watching her, those deep blue eyes resting on her face. Why did she have to meet him when she was looking absolutely at her worst? Hair hacked off, face black and blue, what small curves she had ruthlessly suppressed, nothing but a scruffy urchin.

He had kissed her twice, and had managed to restrain his passionate impulses very effectively. What would he think of her if he could see her all dressed up, her hair grown again, her bruises gone? Nothing, probably, just that here was another young lady. And if Miss Clemence Ravenhurst met Mr Nathan Stanier on Jamaica, she assumed he'd be in shackles and on his way to the gallows and in no state to flirt.

On that disturbing thought she opened her eyes wide. Nathan smiled at her sleepily. Whatever happened, she had to make sure he did not get caught if, by some miracle, they got safe back to Kingston. He probably had some gallant notion of delivering her to the Governor; she would have to stop that. He might think he was looking after her, but she suspected it might work both ways.

'I think I can swim now without sinking,' she announced, gathering up the remains of the food.

'How long has it been since you have swum?' he asked, stopping to help her down the steep part again.

'Just before my father died,' she confessed, amused to see that he looked faintly shocked and, perhaps, intrigued. 'There are lots of bathing pools on the island and many ladies swim. You have to be careful around the swamps, of course, because of the unhealthy airs, but the fast-flowing streams are safe.'

A little *frisson* ran through her. Nathan was studiously not commenting, which meant, perhaps, that his imagination was running riot, a fact that ought to embarrass her, but did not. It seemed that being kidnapped by pirates resulted in a deplorable lowering of one's sensibilities.

'Ladies swim in England, don't they?' she asked. 'In the sea, at any rate. I've heard about bathing machines.'

Nathan gave a snort of laughter. 'Yes, they swim—or at least, immerse themselves in the sea. They wear strange flannel bathing dresses and are guarded by fierce women with arms like blacksmiths whose job is to dunk them right under.'

'What on earth for? It sounds horrible.' And wet flannel. Ugh. The joy of swimming was to be naked, to feel the water slide like silk over your limbs, to hang, suspended like a bird, weightless.

'Because one does not swim for pleasure in England, one does it for one's health.'

'I'm sure the men don't put on strange flannel garments and submit to being dunked,' Clemence retorted. 'I'm sure you swim naked where you want to and it is up to the ladies to keep out of the way.'

Was it her imagination or was the back of Nathan's neck becoming flushed? It was probably just the heat—surely she wasn't embarrassing him? As they reached the pool, he turned aside. 'I'll sit here on this log and keep an eye on the path up from the cove,' he said, to her ears sounding somehow constrained as he stood with his back to her and the water. 'There are towels in my pack.'

'Thank you.' Touched by his thoughtfulness Clemence reached out, then pulled her hand back. He might misinterpret her action and imagine she wanted… something. She caught herself up, turned her hand towards the satchel and pulled out a thin linen towel. He would be correct—she *did* want him and he was being gentlemanly about his needs, so provocation was not the action of a lady.

She looked down at her filthy feet as she heeled off her shoes and chuckled. Those weren't the feet of a lady, either, or the hands. The sight of her masculine attire draped on the bushes would doubtless give her unknown Aunt Amelia in London hysterics, and as for the tale of what had happened in the last few months— well, she couldn't imagine beginning to try to explain that to a well-bred society lady.

The water was cool to a cautious toe. Clemence sat on a rock and slipped in before she could think about it, vanishing straight down into the depths. She surfaced with a strangled shriek.

'Clemence! Are you all right?' She pushed the dripping hair back from her face with both hands and hung there, treading water and looking up. Nathan, knife in hand, was poised on the brink of the pool above her.

'Yes, sorry I startled you. I'm fine, but it is deep and cold and I jumped right in.' After that first searching look, he was now staring firmly ahead into the bushes on the far side. Clemence glanced down at herself. Here in the shade all she could see though the greenish water was the pale shimmer of her body. Possibly, from above, she was rather more revealed, but that was all the more reason for them both to be on the same level.

'Why don't you swim, too? It is so refreshing once you are in.'

'Is it deep right across?' he asked, still not looking down.

'Yes, very. We could stay back to back, that would be perfectly proper,' she coaxed. And cold water was very dampening to male passion, she had heard, so he would not have to exert any will-power. Making that as an additional argument might not be a good idea, so she contented herself with paddling off under an overhanging fern to allow him to undress in privacy.

'Close your eyes.' Clemence squeezed them shut, then opened them just a crack in time to see Nathan's naked body slice through the surface in a shallow dive.

He surfaced, hair otter-sleek to his head. 'It's freezing, woman!' But he was grinning as he sent a great splash of water towards her with a sweep of his arm. So much for modestly swimming back to back.

Clemence ducked and swam underwater across the pool, glimpsing the pale length of his body through the green haze, then popped up behind him. 'Not if you move about,' she called, turning on to her back and kicking up a shower of spray to cascade on to his head. Nathan dived like a dolphin, arching up, leaving her with a startling image of fluid body, taut buttocks and long legs, then the surface of the pool was empty except for her and the spreading rings of ripples.

'Nathan?' she queried foolishly into the sudden silence, as something seized her ankles and she was pulled down by ruthless hands. Clemence shut her mouth just in time, kicked and they released her, only to fasten on her waist and propel her up, breaking the surface and tossing her into the air.

She landed with a huge splash, flailing and laughing and spouting water. 'Wretch!'

'That's for luring me into your freezing pool.' He swam lazily towards the little waterfall and levered himself up on braced forearms, twisting to sit on a concealed ledge just under the surface, the cascade breaking over his head and shoulders so he was almost lost in foam. He looked, Clemence thought, like a water god waiting to surprise travellers or perhaps to pounce lustfully on a passing nymph.

She was the nearest thing to a nymph available, she speculated, paddling gently on the spot, watching Nathan who, with closed eyes, was luxuriating in the pounding massage of the water on his shoulders. There was a clump of lily-like blooms growing beside her sheltering fern, the flower trumpets a rich amber yellow with nodding dark-brown stamens. Clemence reached up and broke one off, then tucked it behind her ear.

With her bruised face she would look ridiculous, she was quite certain, but it might make Nathan smile; somehow, his pleasure had become important to her. She swam slowly out into the middle of the pool and waited for him to open his eyes. When he did, he just stared. Her heart sank; he was not amused, merely baffled by her behaviour.

'Clemence,' he managed after a long minute, probably at a loss for anything nice to say.

'I know, I look an idiot, I was just thinking you look like a water god and you ought to have a nymph and I was trying to appear more nymph-like because I thought that would amuse you, but obviously I don't and you aren't...' She was babbling. Slowly her voice trailed away, the heat of her blushes burning her cheeks.

Nathan simply slid into the water and took two long over-arm strokes to reach her. He put one hand either side of her waist, Clemence lifted her hands to his shoulders and they hung together in the green water, a foot apart, staring into each other's eyes.

'Yes,' he said slowly. 'That's what you are, a water spirit with your big green eyes and those fey looks and your long, graceful limbs made for slipping through clear water.'

'Me?' The word came out on a gasp. He was so close she could feel his body heat through the water. She could see down below the surface, down to the dark hair on his chest, narrowing to where she dared not let her gaze follow. Under her palms she could feel the bunch and flex of muscles as he trod water, supporting her, and the ripples their floating bodies made washed against her skin like the touch of a thousand caressing fingers.

'Yes, you,' Nathan said. He did not seem to have the same inhibitions about looking down through the water as she had. 'And I can't recall who you said likened your figure to a kipper, but all I can say is, they have been eating some very odd fish.'

'I'm flat...'

'You shouldn't listen to other people.'

'Just to you?'

'Yes, I know what I'm talking about. You have curves

in all the right places, Clemence.' His hands slid down to her hips and then back to her waist.

'But—' She stared down at her chest, biting her lip. Their bodies glimmered pale as ivory through the greenish water as though seen through thick old glass. Oddly, there did seem to be rather more bosom than she had possessed when she'd fled Raven's Hold.

'And you have the loveliest breasts. Perfect.' Before she could flutter her feet and propel herself away, his right hand came up, cupped, just below her left breast. He did not touch her, yet the upward pressure on the water seemed to support the flesh, caress it. The nipple stiffened betrayingly. 'Perfect,' Nathan repeated. Then he was swimming away from her to the bank.

Confused, delighted, aroused and painfully shy, Clemence turned, thankful for the cool water against her hot cheeks as she heard Nathan splashing as he got out of the pool behind her.

There were the sounds of him moving away, then she sensed she was alone. *Perfect?* He thought her body was perfect? It must be a long time indeed since he had lain with a woman if that was what he thought, Clemence told herself. On the other hand, men did seem to be able to get physically excited by *anything* female, which was very odd of them.

Take Cousin Lewis, for example, she mused, as she climbed out of the water and reached for the towel. He had made it very clear he thought her unattractive and yet he was also supremely confident that he could have sex with her and leave her with child, even though he had a beautiful and passionate mistress under the same roof.

She towelled herself, then wrapped the linen strips tight around her breasts again. She was beginning to hate the hot restrictive feeling, so much worse than the carefully structured support of light stays. But Nathan was right; for some reason, perhaps the food and fresh air and exercise, her small curves were coming back and she could not risk discovery for the sake of comfort.

'Are you decent?' He sounded as detached as if they had just been for a country walk with a chaperon, not swimming naked in a tropical pool.

'Perfectly,' Clemence assured him, managing to sound equally genteel. 'I wish I'd brought a comb, though.'

'Here.' Nathan produced a battered bone comb from the depths of a waistcoat pocket, eyeing her critically as she raked it through her hair.

Clemence shook her head to produce a tousled look and squinted at him through her damp fringe. 'My hair was my only beauty; I used to be able to comb it out almost down to my waist. Cutting it off hurt, but at the time I'd have shaved my head if it got me out of there.'

'Is that what they told you? That your hair was your only beauty?' Nathan shook his head. 'Obviously big green eyes like forest pools are two a penny on Jamaica. Come on, nymph, or the captain will have us holystoning the decks as punishment for being late back.'

Clemence found she was grinning foolishly as she followed Nathan's wide shoulders down the path. He thought her eyes were beautiful, he thought her figure was beautiful, he thought… She let herself slip into a daydream where her hair had miraculously grown again and Nathan was no navy renegade turned pirate, but instead appeared in elegant full-dress naval uniform to claim her hand, rescued her from the Naismiths, swept her off to his bedchamber…

'What's the matter?'

'Um?'

He was looking back over his shoulder at her. 'You sighed.'

'Oh. I suppose I'm tired, a little. Don't take any notice.'

Because I certainly cannot! Miracles do not happen, dreams do not come true and reality is just that. Real.

As she thought it, they came out of the trees and there, before them, was the hidden harbour, the *Sea Scorpion* in its lair at the centre. Quiet, malevolent and deadly. Clemence stared, all her sensual daydreams shrivelling like a love letter thrown on to hot coals. Here was her reality.

Chapter Nine

'Well?' McTiernan was there as they climbed the ladder up to the main deck. Clemence clenched her hands on the wooden rungs, her head just below the soles of Nathan's shoes as the cold voice sliced away what remained of the warm glow inside her. 'What did you see?'

Nathan finished his climb, swung his leg over the side and dropped to the deck before he answered, turning away with McTiernan and leaving her to scramble up unaided and mercifully unregarded.

'The frigate's still there, helping the merchantman with its rigging. It's got no boats out, they haven't swung their cutter over to go exploring. My guess is that they think we're long gone.' Nathan produced his notebook, opening it up to show something to the captain.

'Those two islets? Yes, what about them?'

'From up high you can see there's a shallow sand-bar between them, but you can't detect it on the surface and the Admiralty charts don't show it, either. No rocks or coral heads and there's deep water either side. If we can get our angle of attack right, we ought to be able to drive a ship on to that and board it at our leisure. No need to pound it to bits and you can kedge it off again undamaged when you are ready.'

'Show me on the chart.' Clemence went and leaned on the mast on the far side, pretending to pick her teeth with a wood splinter. 'Aye…' McTiernan was nodding, she could see his shadow '…now that's a nice, tidy scheme, Mr Stanier.'

'I suggest you get skiffs out, harry the ship from both sides to drive it, otherwise there's too much sea for it to escape into,' Nathan continued.

Sick, Clemence pushed away from the mast and went to the galley which seemed, just now, like sanctuary. And she had started to believe that Nathan was a good man at heart, that he might be on the side of the angels— even if only for the thought of the reward.

McTiernan might be a pirate, but at least he wasn't two-faced. Nathan had absolutely no need to have put that strategy to the captain. McTiernan would have been quite happy with a report on the frigate. His only motive could have been to ingratiate himself, and, presumably, to share in the plunder until such time he could find an opportunity to betray this ship with some chance of escaping with a whole skin.

How could her instincts be so at fault? How could she have this bone-deep certainty that he was not all he seemed, when every time she let herself believe in him, he did something that proved her wrong?

'Look where you're going, boy!' She skipped back just in time to avoid the two men with the slop buckets of swill for the prisoners below. One of them dropped a cloth holding ship's biscuits and swore.

'I'll bring them, you've got your hands full.' She

snatched up the bundle and fell in behind them, heart thudding. Now she would discover where the men were kept, perhaps see the door opened, catch a glimpse so she could assess their condition.

Down they went, down again, the decks becoming lower, the light from lanterns less bright, the stench of the bilges stronger. Finally the men grounded their pails and one lifted a key on a chain from a hook.

'What the—?' The foul language swept over Clemence, made worse somehow by the icy calm with which the rant was delivered.

'I was just helping, Cap'n,' she stammered when McTiernan was finally silent. Behind him, on the lowest step of the companionway, she could see Nathan's shadowy form.

'If I catch you down here again, brat, I'll have the flesh off your back. You hear me?'

'Yessir.'

'And that goes for anyone I don't tell to come here. Anyone. Is *that* clear?'

'Yessir.'

'Then get the hell out of here.' She tried to slide past him, but he lashed out at her as she did so, sending her into the bulkhead as though she weighed nothing. Clemence bounced off and into Nathan who grabbed her, none too gently.

He shoved her on to the steps. 'Idiot boy.' Clemence stumbled up, her head spinning, until they reached the deck where their cabin was. Nathan took her ear and dragged her towards it, keeping up a stream of angry reproof. 'You do as the captain says, always, do you hear me? Or you'll feel my fist even before he gets to you.'

The shove he gave her sent her sprawling onto his bunk as he slammed the door. Clemence tried to rub as many painful spots as she could at once—ear, head, shoulder—and glowered at Nathan.

'Ow!'

'Serves you right.' He leaned back against the door panels and regarded her with a look that held everything of the angry ship's officer and absolutely nothing of the tender man from the pool. 'Just what did you hope to achieve with that ridiculous start?'

'To see how the men were secured, whether they were chained up or free inside the hold, how many there are and if I knew any of them.'

'That *would* have been helpful if they recognised you—*good day, Miss Clemence,*' Nathan mimicked savagely. 'Even the dimmest member of the crew is going to suspect something if their captives started falling on your neck with happy cries of recognition.'

'It was so dark down there, you could hardly see, and anyway, they would never dream it was me,' she retorted. 'If we get into a fight, I was going to slip down and let them out. At best, they could attack the crew, at worst they wouldn't be trapped down there if we are holed.'

'Brilliant,' Nathan said.

'Thank you.' *At last, he realises that I am capable of doing something to help.*

'Brilliant, if you want to end up dead,' he continued grimly, 'You are not dealing with your uncle here, you are dealing with a murderous, insane, cunning, suspicious brute and you will give me your word you will not set foot on any deck below this one.'

'No.' Clemence rubbed her ear resentfully. 'You hurt me.'

'It had to look real. Swear, Clemence, or I'll lock you in this cabin for the duration.'

She had never broken a promise in her life. Oaths were sacred, but was a promise to a renegade binding? Was her conscience worth more than the lives below deck?

'I promise,' she said. *I promise to let those men out, I promise to do everything in my power to sink this ship.*

Nathan had obviously dealt with equivocal promises before. 'What, exactly, do you promise?'

'I promise not to go down to the orlop deck again,' she said between gritted teeth.

'Good, now stay here out of McTiernan's sight until he finds someone else to divert his attention.' He went out, closing the door behind him with such deliberate care that he may as well have slammed it.

'Yes, Lieutenant, or Captain or whatever you were, Stanier,' Clemence said mutinously to the empty air. 'Whatever you say, *sir*.' It did not help that she knew, deep down under her simmering frustration and anxiety, that he was only trying to protect her. She rubbed her ear again, wincing as she circled her shoulder to ease the bruises where McTiernan had flung her against the bulkhead, and made a conscious effort not to sulk.

Nathan leaned on the rail of the poop deck and watched Clemence seated below on an upturned bucket, peeling sweet potatoes for the next day by the light of a lantern. When he had let her out of the cabin, judging McTiernan's mood to have lifted a trifle, she was silent, stiff-shouldered, but not, thank God, prone to pouting.

She seemed to feel safe with the cook, so he did not

interfere when she went to the galley and offered her services. At least he could keep an eye on her and she had stopped rubbing her sore ear. He felt bad about that, but he could hardly have taken her by the hand and led her off under McTiernan's bloodshot gaze. The urge to tell her who he was, what he was about, was an almost physical pressure that had to be resisted for her own safety. Clemence, when her emotions were engaged, was not the best actress in the world.

'We'll skulk for one more day,' the captain was saying to the first mate and the bo'sun. 'Let that bloody frigate get well away, then at first light the day after tomorrow we'll slip out and see what we can catch. Mr Stanier, show them your trap.'

Nathan turned to the chart and began to explain. When he looked back, Clemence and her bucket of potatoes had gone. With any luck she'd be asleep when he went down.

'You'll take the second watch, Mr Stanier.'

'Aye, aye, sir.' Time to snatch some sleep himself, in that case. Nathan touched two fingers to the brim of the wide straw hat he wore, noting inwardly how deeply the habits of respect to a captain were ingrained, and made for the cabin, collecting a mug of the well-stewed coffee from the galley stove as he passed.

'Good lad of yours, Mr Stanier.' Street loomed out of the shadows.

'He is that, most of the time. Boys will be boys.' Nathan eyed the big cook. He was a rogue, but not, he judged, a vicious one. 'Keep an eye out for him for me, eh? If we get into a scrap and I'm…not around.'

'Aye.' Street nodded, impassive. 'I'll do that.'

That was probably all he could do in the way of insurance. Nathan opened the door softly on to the dark cabin, noting the hump in the opposite bunk that was Clemence's sleeping form. He took off his shoes, un-buckled his sword belt and lay down, silent in the still-ness so as not to wake her.

Then the quality of that stillness hit him and he held his breath. No one was breathing. When he pulled back the bedding he found not a young woman, but a roll of blankets. He did not waste any time swearing. There was only one place she could be, in defiance of her promises.

He did not take a lantern, feeling his way through the shadows, down past the gun deck with the occupied hammocks swinging to the motion of the ship and small groups of men dicing in pools of candlelight, down like a silent wraith into the stinking darkness of the orlop.

Only it was not dark. There was a figure holding a half-shuttered lantern, hand raised to the keys on their hook. As his heel hit the deck she swung round with a gasp and the keys dropped.

'You little fool.' He went down on one knee to retrieve the keys. 'I trusted you. Why is it impossible for a woman to keep her word?'

'This is more important,' she hissed back, her face white in the lamplight. He must have scared the wits out of her. 'This is my duty. Let me open the door and see who is in there, speak to them.'

'Duty!' He got to his feet. He knew where duty got you. 'Get back up. *Now.*'

They both heard the sound of feet on the deck over their heads at the same instant, saw the spill of light from a lantern. He had never hit a woman in his life, had never dreamed that he would. Nathan clenched his fist and caught Clemence a neat uppercut under her chin. She went down like a stone. He had just enough time to push her under the steps before McTiernan and Cutler appeared in the hatchway above.

'Well, well, well. What have we here, Mr Cutler?' The drawl sent a cold finger down Nathan's spine, his hand closed on empty air where his sword should be.

'It seems we have a navigator who doesn't obey orders, Captain,' the first mate answered, his eyes sliding warily over Nathan. 'You want to explain what you are doing here, Mr Stanier?'

'Curiosity.' Nathan hung the key back on its hook.

'Curiosity flayed the cat,' McTiernan said, coming slowly down the steps, his eyes never leaving Nathan's face. '*With* the cat.' He smiled thinly at his nasty pun. 'I don't make idle threats, Mr Stanier.'

'I imagine not.' Nathan felt relief that his voice was steady. His stomach churned. Out of the corner of his eye he saw Clemence stir and willed her to be still.

'A dozen?' Cutler suggested, something like a smile creasing the corner of his mouth.

'Eight,' McTiernan corrected. 'I want him on his feet in thirty-six hours. We'll have it done now; call all hands and tell the bo'sun.'

'With your permission, I'll stop off at my cabin and change,' Nathan drawled. 'This is a decent pair of trousers, I don't want to get blood on them.'

'…blood on them.' Clemence managed to focus her spinning brain and process the words that she had been hearing for the past few moments. *Blood.* They were going to flog Nathan. She had got him killed.

Three pairs of feet climbed the wooden steps over her

head. Clemence dragged herself out and managed, using her hands, to climb after them. Her jaw throbbed, her ears were ringing, but that was as nothing compared to the utter terror gripping her. She saw Nathan move away from the others, go towards their cabin. At least they had not tied his hands. Could he get through a porthole? No, too small.

'Nathan.' He was stripping off his trousers as she hurtled into the cabin, breathless with fear. He dropped them on the floor and pulled on a pair of old loose canvas ones, not bothering to tuck the shirt back.

'Are you all right?' He pulled her towards him, his hands firm on her bruised jaw as he explored it with calloused fingers. 'I didn't have time to argue with you.'

She ignored the question, jerking her chin out of his grip. 'Nathan, tell them it was me, that you were only following me.' She hung on his arm as he turned to the door.

'Clemence, if they take you to flog you they will find you're a girl, then they'll rape you.'

The cabin spun round her. 'I know, but it was my fault, I broke my promise, you can't be flogged for something I did.'

'And if they try to rape you,' Nathan continued inexorably, 'I'll have to try to stop them and they'll kill me. Eight lashes will not kill me. Now, do you want to get me killed in order to salve your conscience?'

'No! Nathan, I'm so sorry…' Eight lashes with a cat-o'-nine-tails. She couldn't even begin to imagine the pain, then she remembered the screams of the man who had dropped the fid from the mast and the room went dark.

'Listen.' Nathan had her by the shoulders, shaking her. 'You can't faint on me, you must not cry. Do you hear me? If you do, you'll give yourself away and this is for nothing.' She nodded, her eyes locked with his, something of his strength seeping in to give her courage. 'Come on, let's get it over with.'

Silent, feeling as though her blood was congealing in her veins, Clemence followed him. He must feel fear, and yet he did not show it. She could never put this right, but at least she could make sure it didn't get any worse, she resolved. She would be quiet, she would not weep and she would look after him when it was all over. He might, she supposed, forgive her one day. She thought she could never forgive herself.

Blinking, she stumbled out on to the lamplit deck, the hands all crowded round, the babble of excited voices. Nathan pushed her towards someone and a meaty hand took her shoulder and pulled her back behind him. Street.

'No. I've got to watch,' she stammered. 'My fault.' Listening to it happen would be even worse, she sensed. The cook shrugged, but let her stand in front of him. Nathan had tossed his shirt aside and stood, in front of one of the hatch grills that had been upended, bare feet braced on the scrubbed white planks. The bo'sun came forward with lashings, tied his wrists and ankles so he was spread-eagled against the frame, his face turned from her.

The man walked back, picked up a bag and drew the cat-o'-nine-tails from it, running his fingers through the knotted strings to shake out the tangles. Clemence's stomach clenched. She forced her eyes wide.

The crew fell silent, waiting. Their faces, she saw, were not showing any pleasure at this spectacle. Nathan was liked, or, at least, respected, and they knew that with this captain it could be their turn next. The first lash landed with a noise that made her flinch back against Street's great belly. He put one hand on each shoulder and held her. 'Steady, lad.'

Two. Three. The blood was running now. Four. Five. So much for Cutler's nice white deck, Clemence thought wildly. Nathan was silent, still, braced for the next blow, the muscles of his back and shoulders rigid and stark in the light. Six. He sagged, then recovered. Seven. She realised she was praying, her lips moving silently, although she hardly knew what she was asking for. This time he hung from his bonds, unmoving.

'*Thank you, God,*' she murmured, realising what she had been asking for. He had fainted.

Eight.

Street pushed her to one side and strode forward, catching Nathan's limp body as the lashings were cut. He slung him over one shoulder as if he was a side of beef and stomped back to the companionway. 'Bring water, boy. Salt and fresh.'

It took a moment to make her legs work. Clemence felt as though she were watching someone else through a thick pane of glass. Water splashed everywhere as she filled buckets, hands shaking. 'Here, I'll take those.' It was Gerritty, the sail-maker, taking a bucket and thrusting a bundle of soft rags into her hand. 'You'll need these.'

'Thank you.' She followed him down. There was no doctor on board. What should she do? What did you do for a man whose back was cut to ribbons?

She pushed past the men, stripping back the blanket on Nathan's bunk, taking away the pillow. 'Put him here.'

The big man laid the limp body face down, grunted and went out. 'Salt water first, while he's out of it,' the sail-maker advised. 'Cleans it out. Then the fresh.'

Street came back and thrust a bottle into her hand. 'Here, brandy.' That appeared to be all the advice she was going to get.

The door closed behind them, leaving Clemence on her knees beside the bunk. Acting on instinct, she fumbled under Nathan's heavy body for the fastenings on his trousers, then pulled them down, leaving him naked on the bed. It never occurred to her to feel any embarrassment. Keeping him as comfortable as possible was all that mattered.

She rolled towels and pushed them along his sides and flanks, then started to wipe the blood off all the un-damaged skin. She draped another sheet over him from the waist down, then made herself really look at his back for the first time.

It was as though someone had been tracing the pattern for a crazy patchwork quilt on his back in red ink, careless of how it ran. Salt water, Gerritty had said, and quickly, before he began to come round. Sponging, rinsing, she worked doggedly, not realising she was crying until something tickled the sore point of her chin and she rubbed the back of her hand across it.

There. She looked doubtfully at her still-bleeding handiwork. Now fresh water. And then what? Should it be bandaged, or left to the air? At least there were no flying insects here.

In the end she wrung out a large piece of soft clean cotton cloth and draped it over the wounds, then went to mix birch-bark powder into a mug of water. With nothing left to do, she went back to sit by his head to wait.

She wanted to put her hand over his as it lay lax on the pillow, but somehow she felt she had forfeited the right to touch him like that, even when he was unconscious.

The long hiss of indrawn breath had her alert in an instant. 'Nathan?'

His lips moved. Lip-reading, she came to the conclusion it was curses. She reached for the mug, then realised he could not drink in that position. 'I'll be back, just one moment.'

'Mr Street!'

The cook turned from his game of cards. 'Aye, lad? How's he doing?'

'He can't drink lying on his stomach. Have you got a clay pipe? A new one?'

He got up and lifted a long churchwarden pipe from a rack on the wall, its stem a good foot long, and knocked the bowl off with a sharp blow on the tabletop. 'That's good thinking, boy. He's come round, then?'

'Just. He's swearing a lot.'

'That'll do him good. You all right, Clem?'

'Yessir, thank you.' She could have hugged him, grease and all.

Nathan was moving his head, restless, when she got back. 'Clem?'

'I'm here.' She restrained the impulse to ask how it felt, how he was, all the other useless, automatic questions. Instead she dipped one end of the pipe stem in the mug of birch-bark powder and water and sucked until she could taste the bitter liquid in her mouth. She turned his head gently on the pillow and slid the stem into his mouth. 'Suck.' He grimaced, twisting away, but she held his head firmly. 'That's an order, Mr Stanier,' she said, making her shaking voice hard. Nathan gave a small gasp that she realised with surprise was a laugh, and did as she said.

When the liquid was almost gone she trickled brandy into the mug, sighing with relief when he slid back into unconsciousness again. Then she sat down on the deck by his shoulder, rested her head back against its hard edge and settled down to wait.

Now, with nothing to do but think, it was hard not to slip into complete despair. She was falling in love with Nathan Stanier; she could no longer delude herself that it was gratitude or desire or infatuation. And something was telling her to ignore the evidence of his presence on this ship and trust him with the rest of her life, if he wanted her.

But now she had broken her word to him and he had been punished, brutally, for her defiance. He might have desired her, he was too much a gentleman to stop protecting her, but he was never, after this, going to love her.

Chapter Ten

'Clemence?'

She was awake and twisting round on her knees in an instant. 'Yes? Nathan, what do you need?' His forehead was hot and sweaty under her palm, the cloth over his back darkly stained in the lantern light. 'Something to drink? Try more of this, there's brandy and water and the bark powder.'

He sucked greedily and his voice, when he spoke again, was stronger. 'What's on my back?'

'A damp cloth. I washed the wounds in salt water, then fresh, and covered them.'

'Good. There's a jar of salve in my pack. Green salve.'

Clemence found it, sniffed. 'It smells very odd.'

'It will help the healing and stop the cloth from sticking.' He lay still while she lifted the cloth away. 'How does it look?' He was by far the calmer of the two of them; she could hardly stop her hands from shaking.

'Um.' *Dreadful.* 'There's some swelling. It has stopped bleeding.' *More or less.* 'Do I spread the salve on the cloth?' The thought of having to touch that raw flesh, cause even more pain, made her dizzy.

'Yes.' There was silence while she worked at the table, trying to spread the evil-smelling stuff as evenly as possible. Then she lifted it by two corners and came back to the bed. 'Clemence, are you crying?'

'Yes,' she admitted.

'It stings when you drip.' Again that impossible hint of a laugh.

'Sorry.' She laid the cloth back in place, trying to ignore the indrawn hiss of breath. Then she sat down again, close to his head so he did not have to move to see where she was. 'I'm so sorry.'

'More salt water, good for it.' He had closed his eyes again.

'I mean I am sorry for this. For breaking my promise, for doing this to you.' She grabbed one of the cloths and blew her nose, furious with herself for showing her emotions. Nathan did not need tears and self-recrimination. He needed calm and sleep. She dipped a cloth in cold water and began to bathe his forehead.

'You did what you thought was right. You didn't ask me to get involved.'

'But I knew I could rely on you,' she admitted. 'I doubt I'd have had the nerve to do it at all without knowing that.' He seemed to have forgiven her—she could hardly believe it.

'You trust me, then?' Nathan's eyelids parted to reveal a glimmer of deep blue.

'With my life.'

He murmured something else that she could not catch. But he had drifted off again.

At some point she must have dozed and slid down to curl up on the floor, Clemence realised, waking to find herself stiff and cramped. She rolled over and sat up, wincing at the discomfort in her jaw and the aches in her joints, blinking at the light coming in through the porthole. It was morning. The bunk above her was empty. 'Nathan!'

'Here.' He came out of the privy cupboard, the sheet swathed round his hips.

Furious with relief and anxiety, Clemence scrambled to her feet, scolding like a fishwife. 'What do you think you are doing? How do you expect to get better? Get back to bed this instant!'

Under his tan he was flushed and he was moving like an old man in the grip of arthritis, but Nathan made it to a chair and sat down. 'There are some things a man cannot do lying on his front,' he pointed out, ignoring her *tsk!* of exasperation. 'And I need to keep moving.'

'Why?' Clemence demanded baldly, moving behind him to peer at the cloth.

'Because I need to be on deck and I can't navigate the ship flat on my stomach.'

'Why have you got to be there? I'll tell Captain McTiernan that you have a fever—which you have, don't try and deny it—and are in no fit state to help him harry any shipping tomorrow. It is his fault. If the man wasn't insane, he wouldn't flog valuable officers.'

'You'll explain that to him, will you? And after he picks you up and drops you overboard for insolence, who is going to bandage my back and get me my breakfast?'

'You should be lying down, resting. *Please*, Nathan.'

In answer he placed his elbows on the table and leaned forward, letting his forearms take the weight. 'Like this, I am resting. I need to eat and drink and the fever will go down. If you bandage my back, the salve will work. Believe me, I know what I'm doing.' He sounded as though he was hanging on to his patience by a thread, but she was too worried to heed that.

'How do you know? You've never been flogged before, I've seen your back.'

'But I've seen men flogged.'

Clemence backed away and sat down, hard, on his bunk. She found she was shaking her head.

'Please will you bandage my back?' he asked. 'And bring me food and help me get back up on deck?'

'Why should I?' she whispered.

'Because this is painful and I need the help? Because I'll feel better for eating?' he suggested. 'Because if I'm on deck at least we'll know what is going on? Because if I'm mobile there is some hope of getting those men below out of there?'

Clemence bit her lip. If he was lying down, he would be resting. Conventional wisdom said that you starved fevers. If he was not navigating, perhaps McTiernan would not make such a good job of hunting his prey.

'Because you trust me?' Nathan asked softly.

With my life. But not with head and not with my heart, oh, no. Not with those. 'Very well.' Clemence found the spare set of clean linen strips she had made to bind her own chest.

He sat up gingerly as she approached and raised his arms, making beads of sweat start on his forehead. But he sat still, with an effort she could feel vibrating through her fingers as she wrapped the bandages round, bringing a pass up over each shoulder to keep the strapping in place so she did not have to make them too tight.

'Thank you.' He leaned back on to his forearms.

Clemence went in search of food, coffee and the strangely comforting bulk of Mr Street.

Nathan set himself to ignore the exhausting pain in his back and thought about Clemence. Tomorrow, if everything went according to plan, he would take the *Sea Scorpion* into a trap. If he survived the resulting action and if the ship was captured and if he got Clemence off safely— He stopped, contemplating that long list of *ifs*. Assume all that. Then he would take her back to Jamaica and do something about her uncle and cousin. And then what?

This adventure would have ruined her, he knew that. It made not a jot of difference whether he seduced her or not, the assumption would be that she was no longer a respectable marital proposition.

He didn't give a damn about that. All he knew was that he wanted her, physically and, increasingly, for all sorts of other reasons as well, the overriding one of which was the strong need he felt to protect her. And now marriage was the only thing that would save her from whatever fate awaited the ruined orphan daughters of small merchants within a claustrophobic island community.

Would she have him? She was as stubborn as a mule. She said that she trusted him, although he doubted that trust was wholehearted—she was too intelligent for that. How was she going to react to the extent of his deception and what he must tell her about his past life? And then, if he persuaded her to say *yes*, others would most certainly have something to say about such a match. His mother, for one, the rumour-mongers for another. For himself, he didn't care. He was never going to fall in love again, that was over and done with;

marriage to Clemence would do very well. But could she cope with the reality of life with him?

She was very young, very inexperienced in the hard realities of life away from her comfortable middle-class existence. If she married him, her world would be turned on its head yet again. Would that be better than the alternative? It had to be. Although, looked at from the viewpoint of this cabin, at this moment, he was not much of a catch; his prospects just now appeared negligible.

Nathan shifted in his seat and swore. The pain was going to be better tomorrow, he knew. Agony though it had been, eight lashes got nowhere near the dreadful damage a prolonged flogging would inflict.

He was going to have to get up again in a minute and move around. By tomorrow, he had to be at least fit enough to keep on his feet, hold a pistol and look after Clemence or all of this agonising over her future would be pointless.

Gritting his teeth, he stood and moved to where she had folded his clothes so neatly. It made him smile, the way she attacked the hated task of keeping the cabin clean and tidy and the rueful way she acknowledged that she had been fortunate in the past to have had servants. She didn't grumble about her changed circumstances, just coerced the dirt and disorder into submission and got on with the next thing. He wanted, Nathan realised, to pamper her and shower her with luxury and that was ridiculous. She would not be the woman he thought she was, if she would find that kind of existence acceptable, even assuming he could afford it.

No, marriage to him would be hard work and something utterly different from anything Clemence was used to. She was so very young, ten years younger than he. Was he being fair to even think of asking her? Probably not, but that was not going to stop him, if he survived. Fairness didn't come into it; making the best of a bad situation and doing his duty to look after her was all that mattered.

He sat down to put on his shirt, relieved to find that he was not as weak as he feared. The widespread damage to his back was painful, but it did not, from that number of lashes, have the deep impact a sword or bullet wound had, shocking the entire system and costing pints of blood. Already the green salve that he had purchased from a herbalist when he had been briefly stationed on Corfu was working its magic. It was going to be a while before he slept on his back though, he thought, pushing his feet into his shoes and standing with caution to buckle his sword belt low on his hips so it did not chafe.

Clemence found him as he made it to the deck and stood catching his breath. 'You idiot!' she hissed, stabbing him in the chest with one very sharp finger. 'What are you doing? You told me you were resting.'

'You are behaving like a nagging wife,' he murmured, observing with interest the way she coloured up. Interesting that she should react so. Was it possible that she had been thinking of herself in those terms?

She dropped her hand and glared, shrugging, a sulky boy again for the onlookers. 'You'll bleed on your shirt and I'll have to wash it again,' she said.

'Cheeky brat,' he said with a simulacrum of irritation. 'Go and get me some food.' He resisted the temptation to follow her with his eyes as she left, focusing instead on the challenge of negotiating the ladder to the poop deck, with McTiernan waiting at the top of them.

'You're a hard man, Stanier,' the captain observed

when he joined him at the wheel. 'Perhaps I should have added a few more lashes.'

'There's just so much I can take of staring at my cabin walls.' Nathan almost shrugged, then thought better of it. Exercise was one thing, violently agitating his back muscles, another. He hitched a hip on to the hatch cover. 'What's the plan for tomorrow?'

'One of the skiffs has just come in.' McTiernan jerked his head towards the little craft bobbing alongside. The crew were furling the lateen sail and securing the lines. 'There's a nice little merchantman making ready to sail with a most interesting cargo.' Nathan raised an eyebrow. 'Chests—and an armed escort at the dockside.'

'Bullion?'

'Could be. All very secretive, the idiots. If they'd taken no precautions, they wouldn't have stood out.' Nathan suppressed a grin. *Bluff and double bluff.* 'If the winds hold as they are, it will be passing tomorrow before noon. We'll get the skiffs out and the lugger with a couple of light guns on it to herd it back towards your sand-bar.' He ran a cold eye down Nathan's carefully still body. 'You up to the chase?'

Nathan contemplated the likely results of saying *no*. 'Aye, Captain.' Down on the deck he could see Clemence balancing his meal in one hand with two tankards gripped in the other and exchanging mild insults with two of the hands. 'I'll get some food,' he observed, concentrating on not wincing as he stood up. She was getting too confident, he worried, then saw her put the food down on a barrel and swing up into the rigging, climbing like a monkey to the first spar, apparently just for the hell of it. No, perhaps she was right. Who would suspect a merchant's daughter could be capable of scrambling about twenty foot above deck?

* * *

'Get down here, Clem!' Clemence peered down through the lattice of rigging at Nathan's upturned face. He wasn't going to let her fuss over him, that was plain. She began to descend, revelling in the freedom that climbing gave her. Her muscles were working again, she had an appetite, she felt fit and happy and terrified, all at once, and the source of that happiness was standing eating the cheese she'd brought him, a scowl on his face.

Nathan was only pretending to be angry, she was almost certain. Sometimes she thought that she was beginning to understand him, could read the expression in his eyes. And then he reacted in a way that surprised her, or the amusement turned to something still and secretive and she realised she didn't know him at all. And although he knew her lethally dangerous secret, she was convinced that he was confiding in her only what was absolutely unavoidable.

She dropped to the deck and trotted over. 'Sorry.'

'No, you are not.' He pushed the food towards her and shifted his position as if getting comfortable.

Instinctively Clemence followed his gaze around. Yes, there was no one within earshot. 'What is it?'

'I don't know whether I'll get another chance to talk to you—McTiernan is planning and we could be on deck all night. Tomorrow there will be a fight. They've spotted the ship they want, and very tempting it is, too. We'll drive it on to the sand-bar and then the plan is to board it.'

'Yes?'

'But the crew of the merchantman will board us instead and when that happens I want you to get down to the orlop and let those men out. Tell them that the navy is up top and show them the weapon chests on the gun deck—and then get into the cabin and stay there. Do you understand?'

'The navy? How do you know?' Understanding and an enormous sense of relief flooded through her. 'You've planned this all along, haven't you? The crippled merchantman...that was a trap that went wrong. You aren't just an opportunist, seeing if you can find a way to get a reward if the chance arises, are you?'

'No. You'll do as I say?'

She ignored the question. 'Who are you?'

He met her eyes, his shuttered. 'Nathan Stanier.'

'You are still in the navy, aren't you?' *Please say yes, please tell me that I can believe in you.*

'I'm working with them. I've told you all you need to know.' He hesitated. 'If anything happens and I'm...not around, go to Street. He's the best of a bad bunch.'

The cold seemed to sink down from the crown of her head to her toes, despite the heat. 'You mean, if you are killed?'

'It is going to get confused. I might not be in the right place at the right time, that's all.'

'How can you fight with your back in that state?' she asked through tight lips.

'I shall endeavour to use a pistol and not engage in any strenuous hand-to-hand combat,' Nathan said lightly, as though they were discussing a friendly fencing match and not a pitched battle with murderous pirates.

'Nathan.' She had to say this now, in this moment of stillness before the storm, or she might never have the opportunity to say it again. Something in her tone reached him, his eyes narrowed on her face. 'Nathan, I am sorry I did not trust you at first. I do now.' Somehow, she couldn't say the other thing, utter the three words that filled her heart. She did not have the courage.

But he knew there was something behind her sudden admission, even if he did not understand it. He kept his face under control with an effort that was visible to her, but Clemence had no way of telling what emotion he was concealing.

'Clemence, you are very young,' he began and her heart sank. 'What you think about me is...confused.'

'I had to start growing up extremely fast the day my father died,' she countered. 'I know what I feel. It took me some time to trust you—and you didn't help!—but I liked you, almost from the start.'

'We have been thrown together, intimately. You have come to rely on me. It is not so very surprising that you think you may—' He searched for a phrase. 'That you have come to like me more than is wise,' he persisted patiently.

He did guess she felt more than liking for him. A wave of humiliating heat swept over her. Perhaps he even thought she had formed a *tendre* for him. 'I didn't say I liked you too well,' she said with an attempt at hauteur, but knowing that she was blushing furiously. 'Goodness, I know you are a rogue, navy or not, and your life must be full of loose women. I'm not such an idiot that I'd think you *wanted* me, or anything like that.' *Oh, Lord, how did I get into this muddle?* 'You think I'm an annoying brat, even if you do want to kiss me occasionally, but I expect that's just being male.' She stopped. 'I just wanted you to know I do trust you.'

'I see.' Nathan studied her flushed face. 'What has changed?'

'I don't know. I shouldn't trust you, even now. You won't tell me what you really are.'

He grimaced. 'I tell you what it is safe for you to know. And you are right, men want to kiss pretty girls, it is one of the failings of the sex. And I think you are a handful, although I don't think I'd describe you as a brat. You don't have to make declarations of trust, Clem, I'll do my best to get you out of this, and, when I do, we'll see what the Governor can do to make things right.'

She shook her head, not at all comforted by the thought of the Governor's assistance.

'Try not to worry—if he cannot hush this up, then I'll marry you. I don't think I'm much of a bargain, but marriage to me is probably better than life as a ruined woman.'

'Marry you?' A bucket of cold sea water wouldn't be much more of a slap in the face. Clemence bit her lip and struggled to preserve some dignity after that comprehensively well-meaning and damning proposal. She had told him she trusted him, against reason, and he thought she was asking him to take care of her when all this was over. And, of course, that meant marriage, so the wretched man was being noble about it.

'Thank you, Mr Stanier, but no. I doubt a young lady could expect a less romantic offer of marriage. I told you that I trusted you, not that I was looking for a husband. Please be assured that I will not put you to the trouble; I would walk the streets of Kingston, rather, than marry a man like you.'

'Clemence, damn it—'

She ducked away from his outstretched hand. 'Excuse me, I'll just go and check I know where all the weapon chests are below deck.' *And find a corner in the dark to have a good weep.*

'Clem!'

She ran. Behind her she heard McTiernan. 'Mr Stanier! When you have quite finished failing to control that boy, perhaps you would be so good as to join us?'

Chapter Eleven

Nathan was still cursing himself hours later when he went down to the cabin to snatch a few hours' sleep. The pain in his back as he eased cautiously down to lie on his stomach on the bunk was an almost welcome distraction. From across the cabin came the sound of Clemence attempting to breathe as though she were asleep and not lying there confused and wounded by his tactlessness.

A demon of temptation whispered that he should go over there, take her in his arms and make love to her. His conscience told him that doing that could only make things worse; besides, he was in no fit state to make love to a virgin as she deserved to be loved. Which thought produced the inevitably uncomfortable result.

Damn, there went any hope of sleep. The one thing he had been resolved upon was that he must protect her, not hurt her, and instead he had leapt to conclusions and in trying to reassure her he had managed to both wound her and shatter the confidence between them. And come daybreak she was going to need that confidence.

The fact that her violent repudiation of his proposal made him not irritated, or relieved, but disappointed, was not lost on him. If she were not having unwise feelings, then he most certainly was. But increasingly the idea of marriage to Clemence, young as she was, ignorant, too, of the realities of life to a man who made his living at sea, was becoming strangely tempting.

He lay, dozing fitfully, part of his mind noting the ship's bell counting the hours, vividly aware of the pattern of Clemence's breathing as she finally slept.

When a thin light began to show through the porthole he got to his feet, methodically working the protesting muscles, wincing as the healing lash marks stuck to the bandages.

It was better than he had feared and once the action began he would not be so aware of it. He'd fought with a bullet in his upper arm and a sabre slash down his thigh before now. Nathan laid out his pistols on the table and quietly began to strip them down and clean them. More than his life was going to depend on them today.

When he could not leave it any longer, he went to her bunk and laid the back of his hand against her cheek. 'Clemence.'

'Mmm?' She turned her face against his hand like a cat, a smile curving her lips, eyes closed. Nathan saw the exact moment when she recalled where she was and what had happened yesterday. He took his hand away and turned back to the table, unwilling to see her eyes on him, for her to see him lift his own hand against his cheek for a fleeting moment.

'Time to get up. Stay near the head of the companionway and then, when we're about to grapple her, go down to the orlop.' He wanted to say *take care*, for all the good it did, but his voice seemed to be failing him and he needed to be out of there.

The door handle was in his grasp when she spoke. 'I just want to say, I *do* trust you. And, good luck, Nathan.'

He should turn, talk to her, but he found he could not. Something was tight in his throat—it felt, impossibly, like his heart. Somehow he got the door open. 'Thank you.'

Superstition maintained that when something was going absolutely to plan, then disaster could not be far away. By that reckoning, he was in for a bad time, Nathan decided, watching the merchantman *Bonny Lass* tack and turn ahead of them, harried by the light guns of the skiff blocking the open sea. The gap between the islets beckoned, temptingly. Unless they had a man in the top-mast crow's nest, then they would never see the danger shimmering beneath the waves, not if they were the ship McTiernan believed them to be.

Closer and closer they drew, gaining on their prey. 'Terrible sail handling,' Cutler remarked as *Bonny Lass* lost more way.

'Panicking,' Nathan suggested, one wary eye out for Clemence, loitering by the dark mouth of the companionway. *Don't overdo it*, he thought urgently as though he could reach James Melville, his old friend, captaining the decoy in his shirtsleeves with no gold lace to betray his true identity.

Long minutes passed as the two ships closed. He could see them in his mind's eye as though from the peak of Lizard Island, two elegant toys skimming across the green-blue ocean without a hint of the carnage that was about to be unleashed.

Bonny Lass slid into the trap. Nathan felt himself hold his breath. Had he miscalculated? Was the smaller ship going to clear the sand-bar? And then it struck as though it had hit a wall and *Sea Scorpion*, responding to the helm, swung round to come up alongside it.

Nathan spun on his heel; the mouth of the companionway was empty. Clemence had gone. He drew his pistol and turned back, one target in mind, but McTiernan was already down the steps, dodging amidst the mêlée. Cursing, Nathan followed Cutler, searching for a clear shot.

Clemence was buffeted by the men running up from the gun deck to join the hand-to-hand fighting above. That one last glimpse she had of Nathan, pistol in hand, seemed burned into her mind as she stumbled down, snatching a lantern as she went.

The key was still on its hook and behind the closed door she could hear shouts. As she tried to unlock the door something heavy hit the inside, sending the key tumbling from her fingers. Doggedly she tried again and it came open, bringing with it the men who had been trying to break it down.

One of them lunged for her throat. 'Johnnie Wright! It's me, Clemence Ravenhurst!'

She hardly recognised him. The mate of the *Raven Duchess*, his face white and pinched, his eyes wild, stared at her, hands still raised. 'Miss Clemence?'

'Yes. No time to explain, Johnnie—we're alongside a naval vessel. Can any of you fight? I know where there are weapons.'

'Aye, we can fight, can't we, lads?' There was a roar from behind him, then they were tumbling out of the hold, bearded, stinking, out for blood. Clemence turned and ran up the companionway, her scarecrow army at her heels.

'Here.' She gestured at the open weapon chests. *'Hurry!'*

They stampeded past her up to the noise of shouting, shots, the grinding of the two ships against each other. Panting, Clemence pulled her knife out of its sheath and followed.

She couldn't see Nathan, but she could see McTiernan, Cutler at his side, fighting surrounded by bodies. There were blue naval uniforms, officers fighting hand to hand, seamen she didn't recognise who must be part of the decoy's crew. Splinters flew up from the deck at her feet and she saw marines in the rigging, firing down. A hand descended, pulled her back through a door.

Street wiped blood off his meat cleaver and showed his teeth. 'Your Mr Stanier's not what he seems, boy. Told me to look out for you. You reckon I ought to heed him?'

'He'll help you, if you do,' Clemence promised, craning to see past the cook's bulk. 'He said you're the best of the bunch. You can't want to follow a man like McTiernan, surely?'

'He's my captain, I don't turn my coat, leastways, not while the bastard's alive and breathing.'

A shadow fell across the doorway, a sailor, pistol in hand, the barrel pointing directly at Clemence. Trapped against the stove, she threw up her hands in a pointless gesture of defence; after all this, she was going to die here, now. It seemed impossible to feel such terror and still be conscious. She wanted to live, she wanted Nathan and now it was all going to end in noise and blood and smashed bone and agony—

The gun went off, the sound loud in the confined

space, her heart seemed to stop, beside her an earthen-ware pot shattered. He had missed. In the second it took her to realise she was still alive, Street raised his hand wrapped around a long-barrelled pistol. The man took the shot in the face, falling back, dead before he hit the deck as Clemence, sickened, reeled back with a sob of terror, her vision filled with the image of what the bullet had done to human features. That had been a man. That had almost been her.

Then there was a scream, lost in a tremendous crashing, the sun vanished and the whole mainmast of the decoy ship began to fall. Clemence ducked away from Street's hand, dived through the door and saw Nathan in the stern as the mast came down between them.

Clemence's slight figure was lost in the descending mass of spars and canvas. Nathan began to move forward, parrying a descending sword. 'Hulme!' he shouted into the face of the lieutenant wielding the weapon.

The man pulled the stroke. 'Sir!'

'Pass the word, there are captives from the hold fighting on our side.' He raised his pistol, fired and a man about to stab a midshipman fell off the rail with a scream. 'I'm going forward.'

'You're going to hell.' It was Cutler, blood dripping down his face, his cutlass in his fist. 'You bloody spy.' He gestured with one hand, beckoning Nathan forward like an alley bruiser with a victim. 'Come on and die, Stanier.'

Nathan had no loaded weapons left, his cutlass had broken off five minutes before as he sliced at a pirate and hit a cannon on the down stroke.

'Sir!' Hulme was holding out his own sword.

'Thanks, but I've no time for this.' The dagger came

out of its sheath as though it were oiled and his eyes were still locked with the first mate's when the blade thudded into the man's chest.

Nathan yanked it out and was running before the big body collapsed on to the deck, dodging through the knots of fighting men. The fallen mast blocked one end of the deck from the other as effectively as a wall—a shifting, treacherous wall full of traps and tangles. He turned aside, swung out into the rigging and began to climb.

The pain flashing across his back was like fire as he reached and stretched but he kept going, heading for the ropes dangling from the first spar. He couldn't see Clemence, but he could see McTiernan, cold as ice, his blade cutting down men all around him.

Then a scarecrow of a man pushed his way through to confront the captain. What he was yelling, Nathan couldn't hear as he climbed, bullets flying past his ears, but he saw the contemptuous ease with which McTiernan felled him with a sideways sweep of his cutlass, raised the weapon for the death blow.

And out of the smoke and confusion Clemence appeared, a broken spar in her hands. She swung it, even as Nathan shouted her name, and McTiernan's blade stuck into the wood. The man yanked it towards him and she went with it, into his lethal embrace.

He was still below the dangling rope. Nathan jumped, reaching with a yell of pain as the wounds on his back split open, but he had it, swinging across the barrier of the fallen mast. At the height of the swing he let go and hit *Sea Scorpion*'s limp foresail, one hand scrabbling for a handhold, the other slicing into the canvas with his dagger. The weapon held him for a moment and then began to cut down. All he could do was hang on, trying to control his descent with his feet as he slid towards the deck.

Below him was a blur of movement, but he could hear Clemence screaming defiance at McTiernan, and then he saw her, her hands locked around the man's sword hand with desperate strength, while he shook her back and forth like a terrier with a rat.

Nathan landed, staggering, behind them and launched himself at McTiernan's back just as the man swung Clemence round, taking Nathan off his feet. He seized her as he fell. 'Let go!' She fell with him and he dragged her up and behind him, turning to face the pirate with the realisation that the only weapon he held was one small dagger and the man was too close for a throw.

'I'm going to slice you open and drag your guts out in front of your eyes,' McTiernan hissed, lowering his cutlass to weave a dizzying pattern.

'Clemence, run.'

'No.' She edged further round and he realised that she was effectively trapped. If McTiernan took him, she had no escape.

The man lunged, the point of the weapon slicing through his shirt, across his belly like a whiplash. Nathan recoiled back, shifting his balance, searching for an opening, aware that if he had to, he could take the blade in his body to give Clemence a chance to get free.

'Stanier!' It was Melville.

Nathan looked up in time to catch the thrown sword and drive McTiernan back with one slashing stroke. He took Clemence's arm and almost hurled her through the opening.

'Melville! Catch!' There was no time for more as

McTiernan leapt forward with a roar, Nathan's foot slid on the bloodsoaked deck and he went down, flat on his back.

'Nathan!' Clemence bit, screamed, struggled, but the burly man in the blue uniform simply wrapped his arms round her, hauled her to the side and thrust her at a marine.

'Get him below. Guard him.'

She did not make it easy, and the marine, confused about exactly who he had got hold of, was not gentle. There was a sickening moment when she hung over the gap between the two ships as they ground together and then more hands took her, bundled her below, thrust her into a cabin. She heard the lock turn and hurled herself at the door, hammering at the panels. 'Nathan!'

The explosion hit her before she heard it. A great blow, like a hurricane striking, then the side of the cabin blew in, at first very slowly, as if in a dream, and then, as the noise came, with a thundering crash. Something hit her head, she was aware she was falling, then, nothing.

'Miss Clemence! Miss Clemence, wake up do, miss!'

Eliza? She must have overslept; Papa would be impatient if she was late for breakfast. Clemence made an effort, then realised that the drum beat thudding through her was a monumental headache.

'Eliza?' She managed to open her eyes a crack. There was the familiar face of her maid, her face contorted with worry. Perhaps she was ill. But she was never ill. Something was wrong.

'Miss Clemence, there's so much trouble and grief, you must wake up!' Yes, something was wrong. Uncle had dismissed Eliza. Papa was dead. Nathan was—

'Nathan?' Hands took her shoulders as she sat up, pillows were heaped behind her. 'Where am I?' This wasn't her bedchamber, this wasn't the cabin.

'The hospital, Miss Clemence. And there's a guard outside and they do say you were one of the pirates' women, and it's only because you are a female that you aren't in the gaol with the rest of them that got captured.'

'I'm not,' she managed, before Eliza held water to her lips. 'What happened? Is the *Sea Scorpion* taken?'

'Sunk, Miss Clemence, and most of that crew of scum with her, two days ago. I'm working for Mrs Hemingford now and she does charitable work in the women's wards once a week and I saw you being carried in, yesterday.' Eliza, her dark face anxious, shook her head. 'I didn't think it was wise to say I recognised you, not with Mr Naismith about. I don't trust him, the way he made me go without letting me see you. I knew you'd speak to me first if you wanted to dismiss me.' She helped Clemence drink again. 'I said I'd like to come down and help some more, and Mrs Hemingford, she's a good Christian woman, she said I could.'

Clemence struggled to absorb it all. Nathan was either dead or in prison. If he was free, he'd have looked for her. Now she would have to look for him. She tried to ignore the clammy feeling of fear in the pit of her stomach and looked down at her body. Her bindings and all her clothes had gone and she was clad in a coarse cotton nightgown.

'Eliza, can you get me clothes? I must wash and dress and go to the Governor.'

'How are you going to get out, Miss Clemence?'

Then the maid grinned and got to her feet. 'I know, don't you fret, I'll not be long.'

Somehow Clemence managed to keep calm until Eliza returned half an hour later. 'It's not decent, her in those men's clothes,' Clemence heard her saying to someone outside. 'You let us in and we'll have her looking like a God-fearing woman, at least.'

The lanky white woman with her hair in a turban was carrying a bundle on her shoulder while Eliza lugged in a pail of water. 'My friend Susan,' she said with a jerk of her head to her silent companion. 'Can you get up and washed, Miss Clemence?' She began to rip the sheet into strips. 'These'll do nicely to tie up poor Susan.'

Comprehension of what Eliza intended swept over her, propelling her out of bed despite her headache and her shaky limbs. 'Oh, thank you! I'll do my best to repay you, just as soon as I can.'

'That's all right, miss.' The other woman smiled. 'Eliza here's done me no end of favours these last few weeks, with my children being so sick. Don't you worry about me none.' She was shedding her clothing down to her shift as she spoke, and after a hasty wash Clemence dressed herself.

Skirts and stays and stockings felt very strange after days in trousers. She wrapped her head in the turban while Eliza tied up Susan on the bed, pushing a hand-kerchief carefully into her mouth as a gag. 'You start thrashing around and kicking in ten minutes,' she said. 'Look odd if you don't. Pretend we hit you on the head.'

With the bundle of clothes on her shoulder, Clemence walked past the dozing guard, down the long shady corridor and out into the sunshine. The ground beneath her feet seemed to shift uneasily. 'I haven't got my land legs back yet,' she said, holding on to Eliza's arm. 'How are we going to get inland to the King's House?'

'No need.' The maid guided her around a pothole. 'He's down for the trials, wants to preside over the hangings, so they say. Here we are.'

Gaining admission to the Governor's town residence dressed as a washerwoman was not easy until the disturbance Clemence was creating brought out Mr Turpin, the Governor's confidential secretary.

'Miss Ravenhurst! We thought you were dead!' He stood staring at her over his spectacles as though he had seen a ghost. 'Come in, come in, the Governor will be most happy and relieved to see you.'

He ushered them into a reception room and went out, only to return a few minutes later. 'Well, this is providential,' he said mysteriously, opening a door and showing Clemence through. It closed sharply behind her, leaving Eliza on the other side. The Governor stood up from behind his desk, as did two gentlemen who had been sitting with him.

'Clemence,' said her uncle's reproachful voice. 'You poor misguided child, thank God you are safe.'

Chapter Twelve

'No!' The shock was like a blow. All that had happened, all the danger and for *nothing*. She was back in this man's power. Clemence turned to the Governor, desperate to find the right words. 'They are trying to take my inheritance, force me to marry—don't let them—'

'My dear Miss Ravenhurst, please.' The Governor held up his hands. 'No hysterics, I beseech you. Your poor uncle has been with me time and again since your disappearance and a more concerned relative you could not hope to see. I am sincerely sorry that you have chosen to distress him so.'

'*What?*'

'The shame of it, your Excellency,' Uncle Joshua lamented. 'You may well understand that we gave out that she was dead rather than admit that the poor, wanton creature had run off with a lover.'

'I did not! I ran away from you.' Clemence stabbed a finger at the Naismiths. 'And I was captured by pirates—'

'Dear Heaven! The abandoned female in boy's

clothing taken on the *Sea Scorpion*. Thank God your poor father was spared this news.' The Governor regarded her with horrified fascination.

'The shame!' Uncle Joshua moaned. 'I had no idea she had sunk so low. We will take her home. Even now, Lewis may do the noble thing for the sake of the family name and wed her.'

'No!' Clemence made a break for the door, but her cousin was before her, scooping her up in his arms. He was stronger than she would ever have guessed, or perhaps she was weaker. Kicking and fighting, Clemence found herself being carried through the house and out of the back door.

The yard was full of men, marines in their scarlet, some naval officers and, chained together in the middle, a huddle of familiar figures. Street, Gerritty the Irish sail-maker, half a dozen of the hands. Next to the cook, a bandage around his head, his shirt in bloodstained tatters, was Nathan.

Nathan had seen her, thank God, for she had no idea whether to shout his name would make things better or worse. Almost sick with relief that he was alive, Clemence began to struggle as hard as she could manage, creating as much disturbance as she could. When it came to the reckoning, no one was ever going to say she had gone with the Naismiths willingly, but when she craned back over Lewis's shoulder, no one had moved to help her.

They were all staring, guards and prisoners alike, and as the turban fell off her cropped head she saw the recognition on the men's faces. Nathan, his eyes blazing, mouthed something. *I'll come for you*—is that what he had said? But how could he? The very fact that he was there with the captives showed his gamble of turning informer had not paid off and her desperate hope that he was still a naval officer had been just wishful thinking.

The yard gate slammed behind them, the big carriage was standing waiting. Lewis flung her into the carriage and climbed in after her before she could reach the handle and get out the other side. 'Sit still or I'll tie your hands,' he snapped.

'You can't get away with this.'

Her uncle settled himself comfortably opposite them, folded his hands across his belly and beamed at her. 'You have behaved like a mad whore in front of the Governor, his confidential secretary and an assortment of naval officers. Really, Clemence, I could not have hoped for better. No one will now question your seclusion at Raven's Hold and all will honour Lewis for his selfless sacrifice for the family name when he eventually weds you.

'Of course,' he added thoughtfully, 'we'll need to make certain you aren't breeding a pirate brat first.'

Clemence opened her mouth in furious denial and then shut it again. If she did not tell them she was still a virgin, then that would keep Lewis from her bed for a few weeks, at least. It wouldn't be much of a reprieve. Marie Luce, like all the female staff, would know her cycle as well as she did herself, but if she was not free within two weeks she could abandon hope.

No, never that. She would never give up, even if they hanged Nathan, even if Lewis forced himself on her; one day she was going to bring them to justice.

Clemence gave a little sigh and slumped into a

feigned faint. She had to think, to shut their hateful faces out of her mind. But all that filled it was the image of Nathan, battered, bloody, chained. *I love you, I love you.* She reached out with her will, trying to touch his consciousness, but nothing came back to her, there was no feeling of connection. She had lost him.

To her surprise, the Naismiths took her to her own room. Her thoughts must have shown on her face, for Lewis strode across and turned the key in the doors to the balcony.

'The trellis and the climbers will be gone by night-fall,' he informed her, putting the key into his pocket. 'Then you may take the air again.'

'You aren't worried that I might throw myself over in truth?' Clemence enquired bitterly from the chair where the coachman had deposited her.

'That would be a tragedy, of course. And we would be subject to society's reproaches for not having understood just how demented you had become,' her uncle agreed. 'But our grief would be assuaged by our thankfulness that you had made a will in our favour, weeks before this madness came upon you.'

'I made no will,' Clemence said slowly, cold fingers running up and down her spine.

'You sign so many papers, my dear.' Joshua went to give the balcony doors a precautionary shake. 'And you have such a nice, clear signature.' He ran his eye over her, his mouth compressing in irritation. 'Now, turn yourself into something resembling a gentlewoman.' He turned to Marie Luce, who had slipped in behind them and was waiting silently, hands folded. 'How long before we can be certain she's not breeding?'

'Best say four weeks, master, to be certain sure. She'll look like a lady again by then.'

'See to it.' Joshua stalked out, Lewis at his heels, already discussing business matters, already dismissing her as yet another tiresome problem solved.

Ignoring Marie Luce, Clemence got to her feet and walked to stand in front of the long pier glass. The woman that stared back at her looked as though she had escaped from Bedlam, filthy, tattered, sunburned, her hair a ragged thatch, her eyes wild. The bruises on her face had gone, only to be replaced by a fresh crop of scrapes, and there were scratches all over her hands and arms.

No one was going to take her seriously while she looked like this, Clemence realised. She had no idea how she was going to escape, but when she did, she was going to be Miss Ravenhurst, granddaughter of the Duke of Allington, and someone was going to have to take her very seriously indeed.

'Fetch me hot water, creams, someone who can dress hair,' she said to Marie Luce, who stood watching her with an expression of smug insolence on her face. 'Or do you want me to tell Mr Lewis that you are jealous and do not want to help me look like a lady again?'

That at least wiped the smile off the woman's face, but it was a petty victory. It did not give her the key to the door or news of Nathan, yet defiance made her feel stronger, kept the lethally sapping despair at bay.

Clemence made herself bathe, used every one of the aids to beauty a young lady was permitted, had her ragged hair transformed into a smart, if eccentric, crop and forced down a large supper while behind the shutters there was the noise of men tearing down the trellis and the climbers, her staircase to freedom.

Then, alone at last, she sat straightening hairpins and trying to recall everything she had ever read in sensation novels about picking locks, ready for the small hours when she could try to open the door. It shouldn't be hard, she comforted herself. In such a hot climate internal doors and their locks were lightweight and the household relied for security on external watchmen and bars on the windows.

Raven's Hold had fallen silent by degrees until all she could hear was the chirp of crickets, distant dogs barking and the sea below. Clemence knelt down, took her strongest hairpin and began to probe the lock.

The thud from the balcony was so sudden in the silence that the pin jerked in her hand, scoring a deep scratch into the polished wood. Clemence scrambled to her feet as, with a rending noise, something was forced into the lock and the double doors burst open to reveal a tall figure.

He stepped into the room, his eyes fixed on her, and for a blank moment she stared back. 'Nathan?'

'Clemence?' He sounded even more stunned than she felt. 'My God, you look—' He broke off. 'You look like a lady.'

'And you look like a gentleman,' she replied, finding her feet rooted to the ground with shock. A somewhat dishevelled one as a result of whatever acrobatics it had taken to arrive on her balcony, it was true, but a gentleman none the less with cropped hair, clean shaven, in fresh linen and well-cut breeches. 'You're free,' she added, inanely. 'I thought they were going to hang you.'

She still could not move, half-convinced he was an illusion, but he recovered from his shock sooner than she and came across the room to take her in his arms and she knew he was no phantom. She hugged him tightly, then remembered, as her hands felt the strapping beneath his shirt, that he was hurt.

'Nathan, your back, I'm sorry…'

'Shh.' He pulled her back against him and she let him hold her, her hands sliding down to rest at his waist. 'It will all be well now.'

It seemed, resting her head against his chest, that it might be, because he was alive and here.

'What were you doing?' he asked.

'Picking the lock so I could get out and rescue you,' she admitted. 'It sounds very easy in Minerva Press novels.'

'I see.' He was shaking somewhat; she had the lowering suspicion that he was laughing, but she had no intention of letting go to find out. 'And having picked the lock, how did the rest of the plan go?'

'I wasn't wasting time planning. I needed to get away from them first, then I could think. Find my maid Eliza, that was the first step.'

'She's waiting for you.'

That did bring her out of her daze. 'Eliza? How?'

'Let's get out of here—there's too much to tell you.' He hunkered down and studied the lock.

'But how did you get in here?' Clemence ran to the balcony. There was a grappling hook biting into the carved stone and a rope dangled down into the darkness. 'Who is on the other end of that rope?' she asked, coming back into the room, all too aware of Lewis's room and his open windows.

'Street, one bemused midshipman and the crew of the frigate *Orion*'s jolly boat.'

'Street!' He merely nodded, his concentration on the lock. 'And you are navy? Truly?'

The door clicked open and Nathan got to his feet. 'Captain Nathan Stanier, at your service, Miss Clemence.' The relief took the strength out of her legs. Clemence sat down with a bump on the nearest chest. 'Come on, we haven't got time for sitting about.' He snuffed all but one candle and took that to the balcony, shielding it and uncovering it with his hand before blowing it out. 'Right, now we've got to get to that cove quarter of a mile along to the east and I think we can relax.'

Clemence pulled herself together and pushed the questions that were clamouring for answers to the back of her mind. 'This way. If we go out of the dining-room windows on to the veranda and then along to the kitchen yard, we'll miss the watchman at the gate.'

Nathan followed her, soft-footed on the wide polished boards as she led him through the rooms, as familiar as the palm of her own hand in the darkness. The loose window latch opened easily and then they were out into the fragrant, sound-filled night.

Old One-Eye gave a soft *wuff* of greeting as he scented her and came padding across, the links of his chain rattling. 'Damn,' Nathan murmured beside her and she saw his hand go to his knife.

'No!' she hissed back. 'And I'm taking him with me; he's old, I'm not leaving him with them.'

'We can't take a geriatric guard dog in a jolly boat,' Nathan protested as she fumbled for the catch on the dog's heavy studded collar, but she just tugged One-Eye towards the gate and he followed, muttering. She thought she heard *totty-headed woman*, but she couldn't swear to it, and anyway, he sounded amused.

The cove was a favourite picnic spot and Clemence did not need the occasional flash of a shielded lantern ahead to follow the path through the brush and down the cliff path to the beach. One-Eye, who seemed to take this unorthodox walk in his stride, growled low in his throat as figures appeared out of the darkness and the shape of the beached boat became clear.

'Quiet, One-Eye. Friends,' Clemence ordered, although as one of the silhouettes turned into the unmistakable bulk of Street, she was not so sure.

'You all right, Clem?' he asked, his voice grumbling out of the darkness.

'Yes, thank you. But what are you doing here?'

'Joined the navy, haven't I?' he said. 'Mr Stanier said I'd got a choice, that or the gallows, seeing as how I looked after you.'

'Better get in the boat, sir.' A young man, she assumed the bemused midshipman of Nathan's description, was edging them towards the water. 'Er, are we taking the hound, ma'am?' What he thought of being sent out with a pirate ship's cook on a clandestine mission on English soil, to rescue a woman and an elderly dog, she could not imagine.

'Certainly we are.'

Only one sailor was bitten, and the midshipman drenched, getting the very reluctant animal into the boat, and Nathan's shoulders against hers were rigid with what she could only assume was suppressed laughter, but they were at sea at last.

'Where are we going? To the Governor?'

Clemence let herself lean into Nathan's side and he put his arm around her, no doubt an action harmful to naval discipline, but he did not appear to care.

'No. I fear his mind is unlikely to be elastic on the subject of young women who run away from their guardians. I'm quite certain we can convince him in time, but tonight I think you rest, then we can assemble our case and I'll deal with him tomorrow with you safely out of the way.'

'Very well.' It was sensible, although her fantasy of confronting Uncle Joshua in front of the island's Council, finger pointing dramatically at the miscreant, was too satisfying to easily give up.

'Captain Melville has a house in Kingston that we've been using as a base. We'll go there—no one knows that the navy is the tenant.'

'Spying,' Clemence murmured, almost asleep. 'I knew you were a shady character.'

She woke up as Nathan handed her out of the boat to Street, who seemed more than a little put about to have an armful of young woman who sounded like the boy Clem, but who was clad in fine lawns and silk ribbons. Clemence found herself bundled back into Nathan's arms with unseemly haste.

'I can walk,' she protested, wide awake.

'Quicker like this.' Nathan strode off, with Street and the dog at his heels, leaving the boat party to row back out to where she assumed the frigate must be anchored. They were in the streets of middling houses in the west end of town, dwellings hanging on to respectability by their fingernails, an area where the shabby-genteel residents kept themselves to themselves.

Nathan turned into a passageway, then into a yard. The back door opened with alacrity and there was Eliza. 'Oh, Miss Clemence! He's got you safe. Oh, thank you, sir!' She flung the door wide and ushered them in. 'And One-Eye. Who's a good dog, then?' She made a fuss of the hound, who leaned panting against her leg before turning to glower at Street, lurking uncomfortably in the doorway. 'And you, you great lummox—what are you doing here?'

'Bodyguard,' he growled.

Nathan set Clemence on her feet. 'Eliza, you'll show Miss Clemence to her room.' He looked at her. 'You'll want to sleep.'

'I couldn't sleep a wink,' Clemence said. 'Not until I find out what has happened. And, Eliza, you should get to bed.'

'I'll just show you your room, Miss Clemence,' the maid began.

'It is all right, Mr—I mean, Captain Stanier can show me.' There was a gasp from the maid. 'Eliza, I've been sharing his cabin for nights, it is all right.'

Without waiting she turned and climbed the stairs. After a moment she heard footsteps behind her and smiled. Thank goodness, she had been afraid he was going to treat her like a society lady the moment they were free.

'The door on the right.' It was a simple room, but clean and the wide bed with its white mosquito net sat serenely in the middle of an expanse of polished floor.

'Oh, a real bed. Bliss.'

'Then sleep.' Nathan was standing in the doorway, watching her.

'No. Not until we talk.' She held out a hand and he came in and took one of the rattan chairs. Clemence curled up in the other, noticing with a pang of anxiety that he stayed sitting upright, not letting his back touch the chair. 'Tell me who you are and how the men from the hold are.'

'We've lost some of them, but the survivors are, on the whole, all right, although some have fevers and all are badly malnourished. There are eight of your men safe. As for me, I am part of a mission to eradicate pirates in the Caribbean.' Nathan steepled his fingers and looked as though he were about to present a formal report. 'We deprived McTiernan of his navigator in a brothel about a week before he took me on; it took a while to spread the rumours about me, enough for him to get interested, but not suspicious.'

'The *Orion* is your ship?' She imagined the elegant, white-sailed frigate, Nathan on the quarterdeck.

'No, Melville's. I haven't a ship at the moment, I was detached for the mission. You can guess the rest—the disabled merchantman was the first intended honey-trap. When that didn't work, we set up the sand-bar trap with a supposedly secret bullion ship as bait.'

'How did you communicate?' Clemence watched him, noticing the cut in his hairline, bruises on his cheek, the edge of a bandage showing beneath one cuff.

'It was pre-arranged, most of it. Contingency plans for every eventuality we could think of. I knew about the sand-bar, I only pretended to find it when we were up on the headland. While you were setting out the food, I was signalling with a mirror.'

'It all seems very efficient,' Clemence observed, wondering as she looked at him now, with his austere manner and his spare reporting, how she could ever have thought him a suspicious rogue. 'I must have been a nuisance. Why didn't you tell me the truth?'

'I wanted you to react to things as naturally as possible.' He shrugged. 'And instinct told me that the less you knew, the safer you were.'

'I see. And when I saw you this afternoon?'

'Yesterday by now, I would guess.' He glanced at the clock. 'Yesterday I had been helping salvage what we could of *Sea Scorpion*, searching for survivors, which was why I looked as I did. I wasn't chained in the middle of those men, but I was talking to them, trying to sort out the ones it was safe to try and have reprieved. There are some good seamen amongst them.'

'And when you saw me?'

'I did not know what was going on, the Governor's men were armed. I couldn't risk shooting starting. When Eliza came tumbling out into the yard after you, I got the whole story out of her.'

'So what was I doing in the hospital?'

'That was a mistake, no one knew who you were. Melville just grabbed you when I threw you at him, and anyway, he got knocked unconscious when that cannon went off and I didn't speak to him again until after I had seen you.'

It seemed that all she had to concern herself about was her own future. 'It is all under control, then? All shipshape and navy fashion?' He nodded, smiling, and got to his feet. 'And what about me?'

'I'll talk to lawyers tomorrow, and then the Governor. We'll get your inheritance back, Clemence, never fear. We'll find you somewhere to stay safely until it is all over.'

She stood up. 'And when it is?'

'I meant it, Clemence. With the best will in the world, I don't think your reputation is going to survive this scandal. We'll go back to England and I will marry you.'

'Out of the goodness of your heart?' she enquired, trying to keep the bitter edge out of the question. No, it would not happen. He was going to put all this into the hands of lawyers, sail off and leave her, and she would never see him again. Because marrying a man who proposed to you out of decency and kindness was impossible, even if—especially if—you loved him.

'Because I would like to.' He frowned at her as though the sincerity in his own voice had taken him by surprise. 'Clemence, you have come to matter to me. You know I desire you, that has never been in doubt. I'm too old for you, of course—'

'Nonsense!' The protest was jerked out of her before she realised how betraying it was. Nathan looked down into her face and took her hands.

'Ten years and a great deal of experience older than you, sweetheart.'

'I don't consider that,' she murmured, suddenly shy. 'Isn't there anyone else?'

'No one, I swear. England will be difficult, I know, but you will come to like it, make friends. Won't you take pity on me?'

'Take pity on *you*? Your friends will say you are the one to be pitied for marrying a ruined woman who had been on a pirate ship.'

'No, my friends will love you.'

And will you love me? she wondered, her hands curling into his. Would he learn to love her? She would make him a good wife and perhaps he would, in time. She had never been able to envisage the man she would marry; now, here was one she desired, one she liked and she loved. It seemed he shared the desire and the liking. Was that enough? It was more than many couples had, she knew.

'If… Yes. Yes, I will marry you,' she said, suddenly as dizzy as if she had thrown herself from the peak of the mainmast.

Chapter Thirteen

'Clemence.' It was a sigh, and on the breath Nathan kissed her, his mouth certain, his grasp that of a man claiming what was his. Passive, unsure of what he expected, she let him explore her mouth, his lips shifting over hers, his tongue fretting over the join of her lips until she parted shyly for him. And then that shaft of desire pierced her, just as it had when they had kissed in anger and passion on the ship and she opened for him, drew him in, tasted and savoured and arched herself against the maleness that was going to be hers.

His hands cupped her behind, lifting her to him on tip-toe so she was in no doubt of how aroused he was as he shifted against her, setting up a rhythm that made her moan against his mouth.

Her hands went to his head, her palms tingling with the friction of his unfamiliar, short hair, traced down the tendons of his neck, then up, skimmed lightly, tenderly, over the wound on his forehead, found the strong whorl of his ear and played for a moment with the lobe, wondering hazily at her own desire to take it between her teeth and nip. There was so much to learn and Nathan was going to teach her and the lick of fearful anticipation only added a delicious edge to that thought.

The half-awakened sensuality Nathan had stirred in her, her own imaginings, the heat and strength and sureness of him were coming together to transform her body that she thought she knew so well into an aching, urgent, desperate thing of liquid heat and tingling nerves. And this, this dizzying sensation, she knew was only the beginning.

Slowly, he lowered her so her feet were flat on the ground and freed her mouth. Clemence opened her eyes and found his, looking as dazed as she felt.

'I think,' Nathan managed, sounding like a man who had been running, 'that we may find we are very compatible in bed.'

'Isn't it always like that?' Her fingers had curled around his forearms, seemingly of their own volition, but he did not seem in any hurry to move away.

'Not in my experience,' he confessed. 'Clemence, I must go.'

'Must you?' she murmured, unable to free either her hands or her eyes.

'If I do not go now, I will not be able to.'

'Then stay.' The blue of his eyes darkened, whether with doubt or desire she was not sure. 'Nathan, we are going to be married and I do not want to be alone tonight.' She managed a smile, a quite successful one under the circumstances, she thought. 'I am used to sleeping with you now.'

The way her lower lip quivered into a smile undid him. It was all there in that smile and in her green eyes, locked with his. Innocent passion, trust, the need for comfort. Who was he protecting by rejecting her, leaving her to face her memories alone while he walked off to his room in the smug certainty that he had done the right thing, the virtuous thing?

Nathan wrestled with the doubt that he was justifying doing what his own desires were clamouring for. He had got the strength to walk away, he decided. If he wanted to.

He freed her hands from their grip on his arms and went to the door. 'Good night,' Clemence whispered behind him.

'I hope so,' he said, turning the key in the lock and coming back to her, seeing her face light up. 'A very good night, I hope.'

The sudden doubt flickered behind her eyes. 'I don't know what to do. I'm afraid you'll be disappointed.'

'Well, fortunately I do know, and I do not think you could disappoint me, Clemence.' It was more his fear of disappointing her, Nathan thought wryly, finding the buttons either side of the waist of her gown. One virgin in a personal history of long periods of abstinence at sea interspersed with intense relationships with expensive, but highly skilled *chères amies*. And that virgin, his wife, had been a confident, passionate little temptress without, he was convinced, a nerve in her body.

And not one woman before had looked at him with such trusting expectation, which only made the pressure worse. *Slowly*, he told himself, easing the gown from her shoulders, bending to kiss the tender skin exposed just above the small breasts her corset lifted to him, like a gift.

She gave a little gasp and managed to find room to begin unbuttoning his shirt. Then she found the bandaging beneath and remembered, pulling her hands away.

'Nathan, I'm sorry, I forgot your back. How could I have been so thoughtless? Forgive me.' She tried to edge away, but he held her, his palms cupping her shoulders.

'I will be fine, Clemence, I promise. Look.' He shrugged out of his shirt, turning to show her. 'See, no more bleeding.'

'And there's a cut on your arm, and your stomach and bruises. Nathan, you should be in bed, resting, not—'

'Not making love to a beautiful woman?' He smiled at her blush and the definite shake of her head in denial of the compliment. 'Isn't the warrior deserving of a reward?'

The look she gave him in response to that question was pure Clem, but she stood still for him to unlace her corset, standing in her shift and stockings, her hands clasped shyly as though afraid to touch him now. 'The mosquitoes are getting bad,' she murmured 'Perhaps we should get under the net?'

Fighting one's way under a mosquito net, working all round trying to tuck it under the mattress from inside, and then pursuing the one buzzing menace that had managed to get in with them, might not have been the most erotic prelude to lovemaking, but it broke down the last vestiges of reserve.

Clemence came into his embrace willingly as he lay back on the soft white covers and curled up, her head on his shoulder. *Let her set the pace*, his instinct told him, *let her relax*.

'Oh, the bliss of a proper bed,' she sighed, her exploring fingers wrecking havoc with his pulse rate as she stroked the skin exposed by the bandages over his shoulders.

'Your uncle certainly gave you a beautiful bedchamber,' Nathan remarked, set on talking until she was at ease. Discussing furniture seemed as good a way as any to keep his own arousal in check. He ran his fingertip along the upper edge of her shift, watching the betraying little peak of her nipple hardening beneath the fine lawn. 'And the house was far finer than I had expected, from what you had told me about him.'

'But Raven's Hold is my house,' she said, lifting her hand and stroking lightly over his evening beard, her fingertips running along the edge of his jaw in a way that made him shiver. 'Uncle Joshua and Lewis moved in when Papa died and just took over.'

'Raven's Hold?' Memory was stirring, claws of apprehension tightening in his gut. He knew he had heard her name before.

'Called after the family castle in Northumberland,' she was saying, now seemingly engrossed in tracing the line of his collarbone.

Nathan jolted up on his elbows, forcing her to roll onto her back. 'Clemence, what is your surname?'

'I told you, Browne.' She was teasing him.

'No, your real name.' Something in his tone reached her and she sat up, her eyes puzzled and wary.

'Ravenhurst.'

Nathan closed his eyes for a moment. 'The Duke of Allington is your cousin?'

'Yes,' she said smiling. 'Do you know him? I haven't met any of my cousins. I was going to London for next year's Season when Papa died. But I'll meet them now we are going to England.'

'I met *Lord* Standon and *Lady* Dereham, whose husband is an old friend, in London when I was on leave, before I sailed for the West Indies. They were expecting *Lord* Sebastian Ravenhurst and his wife, the *Grand*

Duchess Eva, to join them in a few weeks. I have not met the *Duke*, no, nor your uncle the *bishop* nor any of the rest of them—they were presumably too busy occupying their niche at the pinnacle of society at the time.'

'Nathan? You are angry—what is it?'

'I told you who I am—were you not listening? I am the younger son of an impoverished baron. I am a career naval officer with no land of my own, no prospect of a title and advancement other than what I can earn myself in a dangerous profession. I thought you were the daughter of a modestly well-off merchant and that, by offering you marriage, I would save you from the consequences of the situation you found yourself in, that the life I could give you would not be materially worse than you were used to.'

'Yes, but I would not be worse off! You are saving my reputation, you are taking care of me and we have my inheritance—when the lawyers manage to untangle it.'

Nathan sat up, trying not to wince at the strain on his back. Ignoring wounds when sexually aroused was one thing—now every laceration and bruise seemed to be alive and protesting. 'Just what, exactly, does your inheritance consist of?'

'Six merchantmen—it was seven before *Raven Duchess* was taken.' She began to count them off on her fingers. '*Princess*, *Lady*, *Baroness*, *Marchioness*, *Belle Dame* and *Countess*. Then there are the warehouses, Raven's Hold, the house in Spanish Town and three penns, all with free labour, two in Port Royal parish and one in St Andrew. They supply food for the household really, not income.' She was studying his face now, her expression anxious. 'And the investments, of course.'

'Of course,' Nathan echoed. 'The investments.

Clemence, listen to me. You do not need to marry me, all you need to do is to arrive in London, put yourself under the protection of the Ravenhursts and everything will be all right. They'll send out lawyers who will eat the Naismiths alive and so cow the Governor that not a whisper of this will escape—their influence in society is such that your name will be completely untarnished.'

'But, I would *like* to marry you, Nathan.'

'You said yourself that there was no one to whom you were attracted on the island, so no wonder you are willing to marry me now. When you get to London you will have the choice of every eligible man in society. You do not need to throw yourself away on me,' he added harshly.

'But I wouldn't be! How could I throw myself away on a good, courageous, honourable man?'

He hugged those words to himself for a second, then put them away somewhere to recollect when she was gone. 'Because you can do better,' he said harshly.

'Nathan—' Whatever it was she had been about to say was cut off. Clemence shook her head, as though arguing with herself.

'Clemence, I have only the money that I earn myself—my pay and prize money. I was, seven years ago, so well off from prize money that I felt it safe to take a wife.'

'A wife? You have been married?'

He nodded. 'She is dead. I did not take enough care of her. And she was very expensive—the money is gone.' There, now she knew.

'Did you love her?'

'Yes.'

'So you are a widower, you can marry again.'

'I am trailing the scandal of her death,' he said tersely

and something in her expression showed she recalled a conversation they had had before.

'The duel you fought?'

'With the man who intended to become her lover,' he said, heedless of the blow to his pride that admission caused. 'You see how desirable I am? If we lived quietly, that would hardly matter, but you have a position in society. I do not relish taking on the mantle of the fortune hunter who brought about the downfall of yet another well-bred virgin.'

'So you do not wish to marry me at all, really?' Clemence slid back so she was against one of the bedposts. 'You were just doing the honourable thing to save my reputation.' She waved a hand at the rumpled white bedding. 'And I suppose, at least, once you had taught me to be less ignorant, you would not have minded bedding the wife you took out of kindness.'

Nathan wanted to protest, to tell her he wanted, not just to bed her, but to discover her in his bed every day. That far from forcing himself to do the honourable thing, he now found he was having to use all his will-power not to act dishonourably and take her, here and now, and keep her. Because Clemence Ravenhurst had got under his skin and into his heart in a way that he had thought would never happen to him again. If he were not careful, he would find himself fancying that he was in love with her and that was only a delusion, for that part of him was dead.

'You are too young,' he tried. 'If you had more experience of the world, you would understand…'

'I am too young, too rich and too well connected. I see,' Clemence said, her voice flat. 'What it boils down to is that you do not care to face my relatives and risk what they might say of you. What I am, as a person, does not count in this equation. Very well, I understand that a man's honour is a very touchy and particular thing. And I am so very sorry about your wife. Please…' she gestured towards the door '…please do not let me keep you from your rest.'

'Clemence.' They stared at each other. He was exasperated with himself for his inability to explain this without hurting her, and under that he found he was hurting, too, far more than he would have believed possible for a man whose emotions had been cauterized seven years before. And Clemence, he knew perfectly well, was as upset as he, for her own reasons.

She had been through enough. She did not deserve to find herself persuaded into marriage with a man she had come to trust and depend on, have her innocence disturbed by his lovemaking and then to be told she was alone after all, except for her important relatives, far away. Yes, of course she wanted to cling to him and the security that marriage, however inappropriate, would give her.

'Nathan, please will you get off my bed and out of my bedroom? As it appears that I am not about to lose my virginity tonight, I would rather like to get some sleep.'

In the face of that, there was not much else to do than fight his way out of the mosquito netting, find his shirt and shoes and remove himself. He sincerely hoped she was going to get more sleep than he expected to.

It was all too much to take in, but one thing was clear: he had loved his wife and he blamed himself for her death. She had to be thankful they had not made love,

Clemence told herself, staring at the indentation Nathan's long body had made in the bedding. She was rich, she was eligible, she was well connected and those three highly desirable characteristics were enough to drive away the man she was in love with. *Loved*, she corrected herself.

The marriage would not have taken place, of course; he would have discovered her name before that. She recalled, with a stab of guilt, that on the ship she had deliberately not told him who she was, afraid the temptation of such a hostage would be too much for the rogue she suspected he might be.

What had just happened proved he was every bit as honourable as she could have hoped—and that very honour was stopping him marrying her. That and the fact that he did not love her, of course. It was important to remember that, to remember that he had offered only to protect her because, otherwise, surely he would have made that declaration?

He had loved his wife. Did he love her still? Was the bitterness in his voice for her, for himself or for the man with whom he had fought that duel? What had happened to provoke that calamity?

And what would Nathan have done if that conversation about Raven's Hold had taken place after they had made love, not before? Would he have married her then?

A high-pitched buzzing at last stirred her from her position against the bedpost. It took ten minutes to tuck in the net and to hunt the mosquito, by which time she was beyond tiredness, beyond even feeling miserable. Taking her remaining clothing off was too much trouble. Clemence curled up in the middle of the bed and sank into sleep.

* * *

'Miss Clemence?' It was Eliza. 'It is eight o'clock. The gentlemen say they are sorry not to let you sleep longer, but they need to speak with you. They say, will you take breakfast with them?'

This time Clemence had no trouble recalling where she was and why. She sat up, pushing her short hair back from her face, thankfully aware that a few hours' sleep had restored her body and her wits to something like normal.

Inside there was a dull ache of loss, but there was a bitter energy, too. She could not rely on anyone but herself, it seemed. So be it.

She had only yesterday's muslin to dress in, with salt-water stains around the hem and the marks of One-Eye's affectionate slobbering on the skirts. That would need to be remedied and she would need to borrow the money, somehow, to send Eliza out shopping for her.

Three men in naval uniform rose as she entered the shabby dining parlour at the front of the house. Nathan, a burly captain she seemed to recognise from somewhere and a tall lieutenant with a wide smile that suited his chubby face. Her eyes on the captain, Clemence made a slight curtsy. 'Gentlemen.'

She saw him glance at Nathan, then he seemed to realise he was being asked to take command of the introductions. 'Captain James Melville of the *Orion* at your service, ma'am. This is Lieutenant Conroy. Captain Stanier you already know.'

'Good morning.' Clemence shook hands, forcing herself to allow her fingers to rest in Nathan's grasp for a reasonable length of time. She sat beside Captain Melville, Mr Conroy opposite her and Nathan at the foot of the table, and managed a social smile. 'I must thank you, Captain, for sending your men and the midshipman to rescue me last night.'

'The least we could do, Miss Ravenhurst.' Eliza came in with platters of fruit and meats and Melville broke off while she set out the food and put the tea and coffee pots by Clemence's right hand.

'Miss Ravenhurst, we have been joined by two other frigates and a cutter bearing orders for *Orion* to sail for England as soon as I have been able to hand over command of this operation to the senior officer commanding. Captain Stanier has apprised me of the deplorable actions of your uncle and I can only agree with him that the resources of the Ravenhursts would best bring this matter to a speedy conclusion. It is also of the first consideration to remove you from any danger and I understand that the Governor may take some persuading of this.' He drank coffee, watching her over the rim of the cup to gauge her reaction. Clemence nodded.

'It appears to us, therefore, that the sooner you can be united with your family in London, the better, ma'am.'

'Indeed. If it had not been for my father's death I would have sailed some weeks ago for a long-planned visit.' Clemence ate, her attention on Melville. That way, despite her internal agitation, she could at least try to ignore Nathan's silent presence at the end of the table.

'It seems impossible to secure you passage on a merchantman, given the delicacy of your situation here.' Melville passed her fruit and began to peel himself a pawpaw. 'How soon could you and your maid be ready to sail on the *Orion*?'

'On the frigate? I—' Clemence made herself focus. 'I do not know if Eliza will wish to make such a journey, she is a free woman; in fact, I do not know how she is able to be here, for she has another employer now.'

'She tells me she has resigned her position and is willing to sail with you,' Melville said. 'What else is required?'

'Clothes—every necessity, in fact,' Clemence admitted. 'And I have no money, I will need to borrow from somewhere before Eliza can shop for me.'

'That we can take care of.' Melville waved the difficulty away. 'Conroy, you accompany Miss Ravenhurst's maid—we do not want to place her in any difficulty if the Naismiths see her and realise what she is about.'

'And we need to lay a land mine under the Naismiths,' Nathan said, making her jump. 'I suggest that while Eliza and Conroy are out, you, Miss Ravenhurst, write an account of all their actions following the death of your father, including their most recent imprisonment of you. Melville and Conroy will witness it and we will leave it with our agent here against the time the Ravenhursts' lawyers take action.'

'Thank you,' she said, finding that she could meet his gaze and smile, after all. This was the man with whom she had nearly lain last night, this tall, distinguished, serious-looking officer. It did not seem possible. And then he smiled and she saw the rogue with the dice sitting in the dockside tavern who had made her feel safe in the middle of terror. The man whose look made her tremble and ache.

'It will give you considerable satisfaction to be able to continue the campaign against the pirates with more ships, I imagine, Captain Stanier,' she observed in her best drawing-room manner, accepting his empty cup to refill it.

'It would do, Miss Ravenhurst, if I were not to be returning on the *Orion*,' Nathan said, reaching with both
hands to catch the cup as it slipped out of her suddenly
nerveless fingers.

Chapter Fourteen

'Miss Ravenhurst, are you faint?' Both Conroy and Melville were on their feet, looking at her anxiously. 'You have gone quite pale,' the captain continued, reaching for the bell.

'No, not at all. I thought I saw a centipede, over there, by the sideboard,' she improvised. 'They are venomous, you know. But I think I was mistaken.'

Nathan's hands were still cupped around hers. 'Nothing spilled,' he observed, lowering them after a moment.

'No, indeed, not even milk,' she joked, managing a smile for her own feeble wit. Nathan, on the *Orion*? To be with him on a frigate for six, perhaps eight weeks? She would not have to say goodbye to him for ever in a day or two—yet the painful pleasure of being close to him could only make that eventual parting worse.

And the intimacy of their shared danger and deception aboard the *Sea Scorpion*, living with him, so closely—there would be none of that. Instead she would be under the scrutiny of others the entire time, having to treat him just as she would any of the other officers.

'Are you sorry to be leaving the Jamaica station?' she asked, handing him back his filled cup. 'Do you know where you will be posted next? Or are you not to speak of such secrets?'

'I must await their lordships' command,' Nathan said, so lightly that she suspected he was as uneasy about this development as she was. No wonder—he must have thought the difficulties she had brought him would be over within days.

'You will excuse us, Miss Ravenhurst?' Melville was on his feet. 'Conroy will wait until your maid is ready to go out, but Stanier and I have to go on board. We will leave you to compose your statement in peace.'

'Yes, of course.' Clemence watched them go out, then heard the lieutenant talking to Eliza in the kitchen. She tried to think of all the things she would need for two months at sea, heading into a cooler climate. It would still be summer in England, late August perhaps, when they landed, but she had heard too many of her father's tales of English summers to place any confidence in being able to manage with light lawns and fine silks until she could replenish her wardrobe.

And where would the Ravenhursts be? she wondered. In England, so she understood, no one of fashion would remain in London during the summer. What would summer fashions in England be like? Would Nathan like her in a modish gown, perhaps following the latest French trend? Would he visit her, perhaps strolling beside some landscaped lake in a verdant English park, while the breeze blew cool and the flowers bloomed on the banks?

'Shall we make a list, Miss Clemence?'

'Oh, Eliza, you made me jump.' *And just in time, too.*

*Of course he will not visit, he would not expect the
exalted Ravenhursts to invite him. But he says he knows
Cousin Gareth...* 'I was wondering what on earth we
will need, because it will be perhaps two months at sea
and then English weather. You'll need warmer things,
too, and clothes for wet weather.'

Eliza was bustling around, finding ink and paper,
looking remarkably cheerful for someone about to be
uprooted and sent across the oceans at about two days'
notice. 'Are you sure you don't mind coming with me?'

The maid smiled. 'Oh, no, Miss Clemence. I never
thought I'd get such a chance. What an adventure!'

When she and Lieutenant Conroy finally left, the
house seemed eerily quiet save for the rumbling snores
of One-Eye stretched in unaccustomed comfort on the
hearth rug. The men had gone off, apparently without
any fear that the Naismiths might find her. And of
course, they were quite right and she was being foolish.
She took up a penknife and began to sharpen her nib,
telling herself firmly that daydreams about Nathan were
equally foolish.

The sound of footsteps in the hallway had her on her
feet, the little knife clenched in her hand as the door
opened. 'Street!' The cook looked abashed.

'Sorry, Miss Clemence, I just came in to see if you
was all right.'

'I…I'm fine, thank you. I didn't realise you were
here, that's all.'

'Wondering if you can trust me, miss?' He cocked an
eyebrow at her, more like his old self despite the absence
of his bloodstained apron and villainous meat cleaver.
'I'm Mr Stanier's man now. Saved my neck, he did. And
you're his lady.' He grinned and it was as if she was back

in the galley again. 'Never thought young Clem would scrub up so well, miss, begging your pardon.'

'Thank you, Street. But I'm not Captain Stanier's lady, you know.'

'What? Won't he marry you? That's bad, that is. He ought to—'

'No, indeed, Street.' The big man looked ready to march off and lecture Nathan on his responsibilities. 'There's absolutely no need for him to and I'm going to my relatives in England and they'll look after me.'

'If you say so, miss. I still think…' In the face of her complete lack of response his voice trailed off. He looked at the hound, feet twitching as it chased rabbits in its sleep. 'What you going to do with that when we sail, miss?'

'He's coming, too,' Clemence said firmly, wondering how hard it would be to convince Captain Melville to house a large, elderly and, it had to be admitted, smelly hound in his smart frigate.

The unfortunate Lieutenant Conroy escorted Eliza round every lady's emporium in Kingston in an effort to spread her purchases and not cause gossip. Then, when he finally delivered her and a carriage-load of parcels back to the house, he found himself conscripted along with Street to wash One-Eye.

'Street and I have tried,' Clemence explained. 'But it needs another man to get him into the hip bath.'

'I can see that, ma'am,' he said, rolling up his sleeves as One-Eye curled back a lip from the opposite side of the yard.

'If I hold his collar, he won't bite, but even Street couldn't lift him when he struggled.' She pushed the hair off her damp forehead while Eliza, clucking, went for another bucket of hot water, the tussle so far having emptied the bath.

'Right,' Conroy announced, advancing on the hound. 'I've fought pirates and lived, I can do this.'

Twenty minutes later the four humans were soaked and faintly hysterical with laughter while One-Eye, a paler shade of brown than Clemence could ever recall seeing him, was sulking in the scullery.

'Oh, dear, look at you, Lieutenant!' Clemence handed him a towel while Eliza and Street carried the bath back inside. 'And you haven't got a clean shirt with you. Never mind, we'll sit here in the sunshine and dry off.'

'Miss Ravenhurst.'

There was no reason why she should feel guilty to be discovered, flushed and smiling, sitting next to a good-looking young man in a sopping wet shirt that clung in a most becoming manner to his torso. Indeed, there was nothing in Nathan's tone or expression to make her feel so. But it did.

It appeared to work powerfully on Conroy, too, who was on his feet, reaching for his coat, despite the state of his shirt.

'Sir! Bathing the dog, sir.'

'Indeed? That required both of you to get in the bath with it?'

Clemence glared, embarrassed, cross with herself for being so, and with Nathan for making her feel that way. 'Yes. Actually, it required four of us to get completely soaked, but at least I will not be taking a dirty dog on to Captain Melville's frigate.'

'Or at all, I imagine.'

'One-Eye goes, or I do not.' The old hound and Eliza were all she could take of Jamaica into her new life and she wanted them both, she realised.

'I'll be getting back to the ship, ma'am, if you don't need me any more?' If a naval officer could be said to sidle out of a gate, the lieutenant was managing it now.

'Thank you so much, Mr Conroy,' Clemence said with warmth. 'I am sure Mr Stanier will be joining you directly.'

Nathan waited until the other man was out of earshot, his arms folded across his chest. 'You are not Clem now, you must not indulge in that sort of behaviour.'

'What sort?' Clemence folded her own arms just as assertively. 'If Eliza and I had been bathing the dog with only Street to help us, you wouldn't have said a thing. Simply because Mr Conroy is an attractive man, you react like my brother. Well, you are not.'

'I am well aware of that! Clemence, you have your reputation to think of now.'

'Nonsense,' she snapped. 'I can dress as a boy, run away to join the pirates and sleep for *nights* with a man and yet my smart relatives can magic all that away, according to you. I am sure mixed dog washing can be excused as a very minor sin for the rich, well-connected Miss Ravenhurst.'

'Just because I will not marry you does not mean you have to start flirting with every young man you come into contact with! Wait until you get to London and the chaperonage of one of your aunts, at least.'

Clemence was not quite certain which part of that comprehensively inflammatory statement she most took exception to. She closed the four-foot gap between them, index finger extended. 'If you are suggesting that I am *flirting* with Lieutenant Conroy—' *prod* '—because my nose is out of joint—' *prod* '—because you will not marry me, Nathan Stanier—' *prod* '—then you have a more swollen head than I could have imagined!'

He grabbed her hand and held it an inch away from his chest. 'I am suggesting that you are unused to not getting your own way, Miss Ravenhurst, and that you want to show me that you do not care that I am taking a more mature view of this.'

'Mature?' Clemence drew in a long, shuddering breath. 'We are back to my age again, are we? Might I point out that a mature response on your part would be to ignore a perfectly normal episode of domestic life and avoid embarrassing poor Mr Conroy.' Nathan's face darkened in a most satisfactory manner, so she cast around for oil to throw on the flames. 'Of course, I appreciate that your temper will be uncertain this morning after last night's frustrations.'

'Frustrations?' The blue eyes glittered dangerously. 'Allow me to demonstrate what frustration involves, Miss Ravenhurst.'

The yard was neglected, like the house, but at one time someone had constructed an arbour, screened with climbers. They were overgrown now and the seat within was rickety with age. It creaked ominously under their weight as Nathan scooped Clemence up and threw himself down on it, holding her across his knee with one hand despite her furious wriggling.

He is trying to frighten me for my own good, she thought, suddenly still, suddenly understanding. *But I am not frightened and I want him to want me, want him to understand what he is giving up.*

Her mouth was open under his as he thrust into the moist, soft interior and she let him, passive for a moment while she learned the rhythm, then her tongue joined his, touched, probed, fenced and her body curled against his, finding the places where they fitted together, feeling his erection under the curve of her buttocks, wriggling against it in wanton invitation.

Everything that his gentle caresses of the night before had aroused sprang into hot, urgent life again. Nathan growled, freeing her mouth, bending his head to see what he was doing as his free hand pulled down the loose neck of her damp muslin gown so that the newly burgeoning curves of her breasts were exposed to his gaze and his hot, avid mouth.

They ached and tingled and seemed to grow as he licked and nibbled and then his thumb rubbed under the corset edge and found her nipple and she arched, panting, her head thrown back on his shoulder, utterly unable to do anything but surrender to the impossible pleasure.

And then he stopped. He pulled up her gown, tied the ribbons, got to his feet and placed her on to the seat, then stood there regarding her as though absolutely nothing at all out of the ordinary had happened in the last few crowded minutes.

Nathan's breathing was fast; she could see the rise and fall of his chest under the shirt ruffle, the vein in his temple standing out, but his voice was controlled and his bow, immaculate.

'That, Clemence, is what frustration feels like. I am but a short walk from the highly skilled means of relieving it, just as I was last night. You, I regret, must learn the consequences of teasing a man, and especially, of teasing me.'

'You...' At least days on the *Sea Scorpion* had enriched her vocabulary; she searched for the worst word she could recall.

'Tsk.' He shook his head in reproof. 'Ladies do not swear. Good day, Clemence. We will come to collect you and your baggage tomorrow morning at six.'

'…bastard,' she finished in a whisper as he picked up his cocked hat and strode out of the gate. He would not hear her, but she felt better for it. Her body was on fire with new confusing sensations, her pulse was all over the place; if he had intended to utterly wreck her composure, he had succeeded a thousand-fold.

'Eliza!'

'Yes, Miss Clemence?' the maid called from the door.

'A cold bath, if you please. I have become intolerably overheated.' And then, to crown it, to be told he had gone to a brothel after leaving her bed and was going to one now! She hoped he had his pocket picked and his boots stolen and drank bad rum and felt like hell in the morning. Because that was how she felt now.

'Miss Clemence? You're crying, Miss Clemence.' Eliza was patting her hand.

'Only because I am so angry with that wretched man, Eliza, that's all.' But anger had never made her cry before. Never.

Nathan strode along the harbour front, his expression enough to send anyone in his path diving to the side. How that outburst over Conroy had happened he had no very clear idea. Of course Clemence was not flirting with the lieutenant, let alone contemplating any more shocking behaviour. They were two attractive young people who had been having strenuous fun in the company of a perfectly respectable lady's maid and one disreputable ex-pirate.

But the sight of her in that light muslin gown, wet and

clinging to those lovely long legs, the way it had draped, tantalising, at the junction of her thighs, the way her breasts, sweet as apples, had curved above the demure neck of that gown, had driven him insane. The fact that he could tell, even if she was too innocent to realise, that Conroy had been equally inflamed by the sight had been the final straw.

The man had been behaving perfectly properly, he had no doubt. Conroy was a gentleman. And, damn it, so was he and a gentleman had needs and he was going to find that high-class brothel that Melville had recommended. His conscience stirred at the recollection of Clemence's face when he had taunted her with the implication that he had gone there last night.

He wished now, as he stood in front of the shady porch, the white muslin curtain blowing in the breeze and the scent of flowers drifting from the garden behind the high fence, that he had done. Which saint had said it was better to marry than to burn? He couldn't recall, but he was certainly burning and here was the remedy.

Half an hour later, reclining in a hammock in that fragrant, shady garden, a glass of planter's punch to hand and a pair of very lovely ladybirds slipping slices of fruit between his lips, he ruefully concluded that the flames might be doused a little by alcohol, but they were certainly not extinguished.

Confronted by Madame's selection of highly skilled girls, he had realised that he did not want any of them. None of them was tall and slender and green eyed. None of them looked at him with a clear, innocent gaze that seemed to go right inside him and turn his brain to mush. His body wanted them, it would be impossible to deny the very visible evidence of that, but however willing the flesh, the spirit was decidedly disinclined.

'Thank you, Madame,' he had said, looking out at the hammock swinging between two breadfruit trees. 'But I am hot, tired and in need of little refreshment, that is all.'

And now he was comfortable, cool, refreshed and feeling every bit the bastard Clemence had called him. But short of going back and making love to her—after which he would have effectively tied her to him—there was nothing to be done about it. Nathan closed his eyes and wondered just how many weeks it was going to take to get back to England and safety.

Chapter Fifteen

'I really do appreciate you taking my dog as well, Captain Melville.' One-Eye settled, hackles raised, into a corner of the cabin, showing none of the becoming gratitude his mistress was attempting to convey. The three sailors it had taken to get him up the gangplank had retired, grinning. She must remember to tip them later.

Captain Melville, with only the faintest suggestion of gritted teeth, waved away the remark. 'Not at all, ma'am. Captain Stanier has explained that you are very attached to the animal and that, given that this is the first time you have been from home, it is important that you retain your, er…pet.'

'Indeed?' Clemence slid a sideways glance towards Nathan, who was further down the same deck, directing sweating sailors loading cannon balls. 'How very thoughtful of Captain Stanier,' she said sweetly, 'but I know I am depriving one of your officers of his cabin. Who should I thank for this comfort?'

She had a very good idea, having seen a valise with the initials R.C. being carried out. She and Robert

Conroy had rapidly progressed to first names as they'd struggled with the wet dog yesterday.

'Mr Conroy, Miss Ravenhurst. He takes the Third's berth and so on.'

'And some poor midshipman ends up in a cupboard?' Clemence said with a smile. 'What happened to the Second Lieutenant?'

'He has given up his cabin next door to Captain Stanier.'

That was useful to know; she must remember to be very discreet in what she said to Eliza. And it was distinctly disquieting to think of Nathan sleeping only the thickness of the thin partition away. They had exchanged the minimum number of polite phrases that morning. He showed no signs of suffering from an evening of dissipation, from which she could only conclude that either he had not indulged in one or had a remarkably hard head. Or had been otherwise engaged than in heavy drinking.

Whatever he had been doing, she had most certainly not forgiven him for yesterday afternoon and he showed no signs of remorse, so the sensible thing would be to stop thinking about him. Or at least, to try, which was not easy when her body still appeared to be remembering the whole incident in graphic detail. Clemence put her new reticule on the lower bunk and surveyed her new home.

This was, in fact, an inferior cabin to the one she and Nathan had shared, less than half the size with the two bunks one above the other and only a flap-down table. And no privy cupboard, either; they would have to improvise with a chamber pot and a corner-curtain. Nor was there a porthole; their only ventilation came from louvres in the door. This was home for possibly two months; it was a good thing they had so little luggage.

Eliza was already putting things away as the captain took himself off with a bow and an invitation to dine with him and his officers that evening.

'Under there, dog.' The maid pointed to the space beneath the lower bunk, but One-Eye simply ignored her.

'I think we'll have to chain him up outside the door,' Clemence said, popping her head outside. 'There's a hook.'

'Fred says he'll take him for walks and deal with that sort of thing.' Eliza stood in the middle of the small space, a pile of underthings in her hands, turning round and round as she tried to find somewhere to put them.

'Fred?'

'Street.' Eliza looked decidedly self-conscious. 'These will have to stay in the bags under the bunk, that's all,' she pronounced.

'Eliza?' The only response was a wiggle of her hips as the maid got down on hands and knees. 'Are you and Street walking out?'

'He should be so lucky,' the maid remarked, straightening up. 'I've only just met him. Still, he's a fine figure of a man.'

'He is certainly that.' If one judged by sheer expanse. No doubt a responsible mistress would forbid her maid-servant from associating with a man of bad character—even if he had recently reformed. But this was hardly a normal situation. Clemence tried to imagine arriving at whichever stately home was the Dowager Duchess of Allington's current residence and introducing herself with her entourage of one mulatto maid, one ex-pirate, one decrepit hound and one small trunk.

For the first time Clemence started to wonder just what this unknown relative might be like and just how different life as one of the Ravenhurst clan would be from the one she was used to. The apprehension was almost enough to displace the dull ache of unhappiness about Nathan. But not quite.

But still, unpacking and making the best they could of their new quarters did pass the two hours before Midshipman Andrews presented himself with the captain's compliments and the suggestions that Miss Ravenhurst might wish to see the departure from on deck.

'You must never go on to the poop deck where the officers are without an express invitation,' Clemence warned Eliza. 'And we must do our best to stay well clear of the men working and not wander about the ship.'

'Don't see how we're going to get any fresh air, then,' the maid grumbled, clambering up the companionway. 'This thing goes up and down a lot.'

'It will be worse when we are at sea, so you must grow accustomed. But we can certainly take exercise; I'll ask the captain at dinner where we may place chairs and where we may promenade,' Clemence said soothingly, hoping that Eliza would prove immune to seasickness. A reproachful bark sent her back to untie One-Eye's leash. 'And as for you, behave yourself!'

She had seen the island so often from on board a ship that she had not expected it to be any different this time. But somehow the vista of hills and mountains, the buildings on shore, the jumble of shipping in the harbour seemed like a painting, something unreal and distant. This was no longer home.

Clemence stood, one hand gripping the rail, one tight on the hound's leash, and stared, trying to fix the scene in her memory along with the smells that the soft off-shore breeze brought across the water. A hand removed the leash from her hand and replaced it with a large handkerchief before she was even aware that silent tears were rolling down her checks.

'You will come back one day,' Nathan said, looking not at her but at the island.

'I know.' Clemence dried her eyes, but held on to the white linen. 'It is just that I cannot imagine what I am going to or what my new family is like or what they will think of me.'

'They are good people, the ones I know,' he said. 'People with a strong sense of family who will love you because you are theirs and then, once they know you, because you are you.'

'Oh!' Charmed out of all self-consciousness, Clemence turned to face him. 'Oh, thank you.' She smiled and for a moment the blue eyes that smiled back into hers held the expression she had surprised in them sometimes aboard the *Sea Scorpion*, the look that had lingered on her face as they hung together in the cool waters of the pool. And then the shutters came down and it was the polite smile of a gentleman who had offered a minor compliment to a lady.

'It is merely the truth,' Nathan said, handed back One-Eye and walked abruptly away towards the poop.

By the time Clemence's eyes were focusing properly again, the ship was sailing east along the coast and Nathan was nowhere to be seen.

After two weeks out at sea life had settled into a routine. To Clemence it sometimes felt as though this was real life and everything else was a dream. She and Eliza had made themselves as comfortable as they could in their cabin and Eliza, at least, now knew the ship from stem to stern thanks to Street and his excuses of either needing to take One-Eye for a walk, or asking advice on his mending or cajoling the maid into joining him and the ship's cook in the galley.

'I hope he intends to make an honest woman of you,' Clemence said severely one morning after Eliza had come back to the cabin in the small hours.

'He will, if I'll take him,' Eliza had chuckled, her fingers busy whipping a hem.

The awning that the men had rigged over the chairs, table and hammocks that had colonised the 'ladies' corner' of the main deck flapped idly in the light breeze. Clemence fanned herself and rocked in her hammock, too idle to sew or read one of the books she had borrowed from the officers.

The Straits of Florida were proving hot and humid and they were experiencing an uncomfortable combination of heavy squalls interspersed with virtual calms and the officers, Nathan included, appeared to be able to think of nothing other than navigation.

They all made polite conversation at dinner, of course, scrupulously avoiding matters relating to the running of the ship, but Clemence never lingered, certain they greeted the sight of her retreating back with relief so they could relax and get back to talking of naval matters.

She adjusted her pillow now and tipped her straw hat over her nose, secure in the knowledge that she could peep through the gaps in the coarse weave and scrutinise the comings and goings on the poop deck unseen.

Nathan was up there now, in deep conversation with the officers on watch as usual. He was so scrupulously polite and reserved in her company that anyone who did not know would assume he had never met her until she had boarded the *Orion*. She had hoped, for the first week, that he would think better of his attitude towards marriage, but the respectful way she was treated by his fellow officers only confirmed what he had said—as a Ravenhurst, it would take more than an adventure on a pirate ship to ruin her standing.

And the more she thought about his late wife, the more convinced she became that he still loved her. There was more behind his refusal to wed her than the fear of being thought a fortune hunter, Clemence was certain. She was certain, too, that if she could only get close to him again he might come to realise that, precious though his lost love was, there was another waiting for him, one that was alive and warm and wanted him.

But a frontal approach was not going to work, he was armoured against that, she told herself, lying awake at night and hearing him moving around in his cabin. But what would happen if she waited until all was still and then slipped next door and into his bed? One night she had got as far as putting one foot out from under the sheet and then had snatched it back with the thought of just how humiliating it would be when he rejected her again.

As she thought about it the bo'sun appeared, the two youngest midshipmen at his heels. 'Sir, I've got Mr Markham and Mr Stills for their navigation lesson, like you said, sir. I'll be more than grateful if you can get these two sorted, they're beyond my powers.'

Nathan came down the steps. 'I gather that you two are finding your mathematical studies a challenge.' There was an exchange of sheepish looks and two nods. 'Right, well, take your notebooks and the theodolites over there and we'll see if we can keep this vessel off the Grand Bahama.'

The bo'sun knuckled his forehead and took himself off, the boys ran to do as they were bid. And Clemence, still watching furtively, saw Nathan stretch his shoulders and flex his back with a grimace that spoke of more than stiffness. His back must be healed by now, surely, but the skin must be taut and tender.

Concerned, Clemence swung her legs out of the hammock and stood up. The hound opened his eye and looked hopeful. 'Oh, come on, then. I'll just take a stroll along the deck,' she said, waving Eliza back to her sewing. 'Where's Street?'

'In the galley, I dare say, that's where he usually is.' Eliza bit off her thread and folded the petticoat. 'I'll just have all these finished by the time we get to England,' she grumbled. 'And then you'll be wearing them three at once on account of the snow.'

'Not in early September, surely?' Clemence queried, watching Nathan's progress along the deck to the waiting boys. No, he wasn't moving as well as he had before the flogging.

By the time she drew level with the hatch cover that Nathan was using as his makeshift classroom, one midshipman was being put through his paces with the theodolite while the other stared glumly at a page covered in figures.

'Difficult?' Clemence queried softly, peering over the boy's shoulder while One-Eye sat down panting beside them.

'Yes, ma'am,' he admitted glumly. 'There's something wrong, but I can't see what.'

'It's Mr Stills, isn't it? I'm very interested,' she

offered. 'Why don't you work down the page explaining it to me and perhaps you'll spot the problem?' She leaned over the notebook. 'Come along, start at the top.'

She knew exactly when Nathan realised she was there and what she was doing; she felt his gaze on her like a physical weight, but she kept her head bent over the book, her finger tracing slowly along the lines of figures.

'I don't understand this,' she prompted.

'That's the angle of the headland to the bows,' Stills began confidently, 'and you have to take it away from this one and that—'

'Doesn't make sense,' Clemence finished for him, running her finger back. 'Where is the error, do you think?'

A moment's heavy breathing and Stills pointed triumphantly. 'There, ma'am, I added it twice.'

'Well done, Mr Stills,' Clemence praised. 'I think it all makes sense now, don't you?'

'Which is more than it does to me, Miss Ravenhurst,' Nathan said, coming up to stand between them and placing one hand on each shoulder. Clemence made herself relax and resisted the temptation to sway towards him. 'You are fortunate, Mr Stills. Miss Ravenhurst is a better mathematician than you, but better yet, she can read your appalling handwriting. It is no wonder you make mistakes. You may write out *Thank you, Miss Ravenhurst* fifty times in your best hand in your own time.'

'Sir!'

Clemence smiled at the unfortunate youth. 'Excuse me, gentlemen.' She strolled on, feeling the three pairs of masculine eyes resting on her as she unfurled her parasol, raised it and gave it a coquettish twirl. Nathan had not seemed angered by her interruption of his lesson, but it was a very small step towards re-establishing their easy relationship.

Street was at home in the steamy confines of the galley, swapping Creole recipes for Mediterranean specialities with the ship's cook.

'Street, may I have a word?'

'You shouldn't be down here, Miss Clemence.' He wiped his hands on his apron and came out on deck with her, slyly passing a bone to the dog as he did so. 'What can I do, ma'am?'

'Have you seen Mr Stanier's back, Street?' she asked without preamble. 'He doesn't look comfortable to me and it's more than three weeks.'

'No, ma'am, not without his shirt, I haven't. Needs oiling, I'll be bound—a massage to get the skin supple again.'

'What with? Goose grease?'

'There'll be palm oil in the galley.' Street went back inside and reappeared with a jug. 'Thought so.'

'Then you'd better have a word with him,' Clemence said. 'And massage his back tonight.'

'Me, ma'am? With these hands?' He spread his great calloused paws out, palm up. 'I'd take the new skin off, not make it better. You should do it, ma'am.'

'Me? Street, that would hardly be proper.'

He gave her a quizzical look. 'That's out of the question, then. You won't want to do anything that wasn't proper, Miss Clemence, now would you?'

'You—' She subsided, knowing full well that Street's suggestion was exactly what she wanted to do. 'Thank you, I'll see what I can think of,' she temporised, taking the jug and calling One-Eye to heel.

* * *

Nathan was sharing watches, although he could have simply sat back and become a passenger. But it was not his nature to be idle and it gave him far too much time for thought. And with Clemence swaying in her hammock by day and gracing the wardroom or the captain's cabin in the evening, he needed all the distraction he could get.

He had thought her attractive before, despite bruises, cropped hair and with her natural curves lost to grief and poor diet. Now with rest and air and good feeding she was blossoming, her hair growing into waves and curls, her figure becoming what it was meant to be.

She would never be buxom like Julietta with her lushness, but that was part of the problem, how very unlike his late wife she was. There was nothing about Clemence that reminded him of that turmoil of infatuation, love and hate.

A book fell to the floor, knocked by his coat as he eased it off. Damn, but he was feeling clumsy. Nathan untied his stock and began unbuttoning his shirt, conscious of the sensitivity of the skin as the cotton fabric moved across it. It was healed, but stiff and tender, and the continuing nagging discomfort was almost as tiring as the pain had been.

He threw the shirt on a chair and kicked his shoes across the room, followed by his stockings, hearing in his mind Clem's *Tsk!* of irritation at his untidiness. She was so close, only a thin bulkhead away. He spread his hand on the wood at the point where he guessed her bunk would be, imagining her lying in a thin nightgown, sheet discarded in the steamy heat, the perspiration dewing her brow and making that thick, short hair curl into sensual disorder.

God, but he missed her. Those brief moments when she had strolled along and helped Stills with his calculations and he had found an excuse to touch her, stand close enough to inhale her unique scent; those stood out like one coloured woodcut amidst a book full of black and white.

He tried to tell himself that, even if there were not the disparity in their fortunes, he was still not the man for her. Clemence needed love, even if she might think she was willing to settle for a marriage of convenience and friendship touched with desire. And he was not at all certain that he even understood what love was any more.

The draught of air across his back and a sharp indrawn breath were the only warning he had that he was not alone. Nathan stood very still as the door clicked shut. It was her, no one else would have entered without knocking or speaking, no one else brought the faint sensual drift of frangipani and roses on the hot air.

'Oh, your beautiful back,' she breathed in distress.

Nathan took a deep breath, telling himself that it was all to the good if she found his scars repellent, and turned.

Clemence was standing there, not in the thin nightrail of his imaginings but a most proper wrapper concealing her from chin to toe. He let out the breath, then almost choked as he saw the bare toes peeping from under the frilled hem.

'Clemence, what are you doing here?'

'Your back needs oiling, it will help relax the scarring and make it more comfortable.' She put down a jug on the table beside his logs and began to roll up her sleeves. 'Lie down.'

'What!' In the nick of time Nathan recalled the thinness of the walls and got the volume down to a hiss.

'You cannot come in here with me half-naked and massage my back!'

'But I can't do it when you've got your shirt on,' she said in the voice of someone humouring a fractious child. 'It will do it good.'

He knew it would, he could feel the cool slide of oil across the tender skin even as she spoke. 'I am sure you are correct, but you aren't going to do it.'

'I am.' In the lantern light Clemence looked very determined. She held up her hands. 'See? Smooth. Smoother than anyone else's on board. It is important for your work that you are fit—don't be a prude, Nathan.'

A prude? He had never felt less prudish in his life, which was half the problem. 'Very well, then.' He drew his belt through the trouser loops with a crack of leather and tossed it on to his shirt, then lay down on his bunk, buried his face in his arms and surrendered to whatever she wanted to do to him.

Chapter Sixteen

Nathan lay trying to follow Clemence's actions with his hearing alone. There was a rustle of fabric, over by the chair. Her wrapper? Then the soft pad of her bare feet back towards him, the sound as she put the jug on the floor beside the bunk. At least it was narrow; that would restrict her reach somewhat.

Then there was pressure alongside his right thigh, then the left, and weight came down on his buttocks. 'Clemence!' Nathan tried to buck her off, but she came down with both palms flat on his shoulder blades, flattening him back to the bed.

'Lie still, this is the only way I can do this properly.' He wriggled. 'I can't be too heavy.'

With a faint groan Nathan surrendered. At least the tickle of fabric at the top of his trousers told him that she was still wearing something, which was a mercy.

Then she bent down to pick up the jug and her weight shifted and her thighs tightened to help her balance and he realised that there was nothing merciful about this whatsoever.

'The oil might feel cool,' she warned. It dribbled into the small of his back, making him draw in a reflexive breath and shiver with sensual anticipation. 'Sorry.'

He did not feel up to explaining that this was already verging on more pleasure than he felt capable of taking. In an effort to control his own reactions he said harshly, 'I wonder you care to look at my back, much less touch it.'

'They are honourable scars,' Clemence said softly, putting the heels of both hands into the small of his back and pressing lightly as they slid upwards. 'How could I be repelled by them? I know how much courage they represent.'

It silenced him, humbled him, too. 'Clemence—'

'Shh. Just relax.'

It seemed impossible. How could a man relax with that soft feminine weight pressing his loins into the firm mattress, shifting and clinging as she worked? Her hands were firm and gentle and she seemed to understand exactly how much pressure to apply to the new skin, just where the underlying bruising was still tender.

Gradually he found he was drifting, the rhythm of her hands and the shifting balance of her body almost mesmeric. The noises of the ship working around them faded and he slid into something that was not sleep—a trance, perhaps.

This was sensual in a way he could not have imagined contact with a woman could be. Clemence was not teasing or enticing, she had no intention of using this as a prelude to lovemaking, she was too much of an innocent for those sort of games. She was doing this for him in the same way as she had tended to him after the flogging.

Under her hands his back muscles relaxed as they had

not since the moment he had realised that the punishment was inevitable. As the oil sank into his skin the soreness vanished and all that was left was a heightened sensitivity, a feeling of dreamlike power, the fantasy that they were part of one another.

Her hands slowed, slid up either side of his spine in one long sweep, then moved down until they were on the mattress, on either side. She bent forward and Nathan hung there in his sensual trance as her nipples brushed his back through the soft lawn of her gown and her breath feathered the nape of his neck.

'Are you asleep?' she whispered.

No. No, I want to roll over and take you in my arms and make love to you until you faint with pleasure, that was the honest answer. With will-power he did not know had, Nathan lay still, breathing deeply. After a moment she smiled, her mouth so close to his skin that he could feel the change in her breathing, then she straightened up and climbed carefully off his shattered body.

As the door closed softly behind her Nathan lay still, eyes closed on reality, and let himself drift into fantasy, just for once, just for that night.

'You going to get up, Mr Stanier, sir?' There was a thump and the sounds of clothes being shaken out. 'Only it's eight bells and the Bahama Keys are fine on the port bow.'

Nathan blinked and saw the bulk of Street, moving around the cabin like a pantomime housemaid. There was a tray on the fold-down table with what looked like bread and coffee. 'Your back looks better,' he added, picking up the oil jug and heading for the door. He sounded not one whit surprised.

'Street!' Nathan twisted round and sat up. *Damn it, it* was *better.*

'Yessir?' The ex-pirate was not cut out for looking innocent.

'What do you know about that?' He pointed at the jug.

'If a certain party were to have asked me for some oil for your back, sir, I'm sure I'd have forgotten about it this morning. Amazing how stuff gets left lying around, isn't it?'

He went out, hands full, leaving the door to swing behind him.

Nathan turned the chair to face the table and began to eat, his mind spinning. It seemed he was forgiven and Clemence would tolerate his company once more, a dangerous indulgence, but an irresistible one. The click of claws was all the warning he got before a wet nose nudged sharply into his ribs, effectively focusing everything on the fact that one large dog was after his breakfast.

'Miss Eliza!'

'Yes, Mr Stanier, sir?' The lilting island accent came from right behind him.

'Get this hound out of here.' He did not turn round, realising his shirt had vanished along with Street.

'Yes, sir. My,' she remarked to an accompaniment of claws being dragged across the deck, 'you've a fine set of muscles, sir, that you have. Enough to dazzle a lady. Pity to waste that, I'd say.'

When he swung round she was gone, the door latch falling.

'Oh, there he is! Bad dog, running off!' Clemence looked up from her book as Eliza dragged a reluctant One-Eye on deck. 'Where was he?'

The maid tied the leash to a ring on the rail and flopped down in the shade. 'Phew, I thought it would be nice and breezy on a ship.' She waved an embroidery pattern to and fro in front of her face. 'He was in Mr Stanier's cabin trying to steal some breakfast. Sitting there with no shirt on, Mr Stanier was; he's a fine figure of a man, I'll say that. I'll wager he strips well.'

'Eliza!' Clemence hissed, blushing all over at the thought of just how well. 'Someone will hear you.'

'And what if they do? There's nothing wrong with my eyes, or yours, either, Miss Clemence. Why aren't you marrying the man?'

'Because he says he's not good enough for me,' Clemence confessed. 'Apparently my having a duke for a cousin and owning a small fleet of merchantmen would make him a fortune hunter.' She sighed. 'And he's still in love with his late wife.'

'Man's a fool, then.'

'Eliza, that isn't fair. I think his scruples are honourable, if infuriating, and as for his wife, I think it is very romantic—or, at least, I would do if it wasn't for the fact it affects me.'

'So you want him, then?' Eliza picked up some of the endless hemming, but left it lying on her lap. Her brown eyes were wide with curiosity and concern.

'Being a normal female in full possession of my faculties,' Clemence said tartly, 'yes, I do.'

'What are you going to do about it?'

'Short of alienating all my relatives and giving away all my money, there isn't a lot I can do,' Clemence said, staring out to sea.

'You in love with him, Miss Clemence?'

'Yes,' she confessed. Eliza opened her mouth to

speak. 'And, no, don't ask why I don't tell him. Even if could bring myself to be so brassy, all it would achieve would be to make him feel sorry for me.'

They relapsed into thoughtful silence, Clemence pretending to read a very dull book of sermons the Third Lieutenant had offered her, Eliza idly basting the hem of a shift. One-Eye barked a greeting and a long shadow fell over them.

'Ladies.'

'Mr Stanier.' Clemence schooled her expression into one of polite greeting and tried not to remember the feel of Nathan's body gripped between her thighs, the heat of his skin under her palms, the strange feeling of power when he had lain quiescent under her.

'May I join you? I find myself at leisure for an hour or two. With these light airs we will be tacking back and forth for a tiresome while longer, I fear.'

'Please.' The ship's carpenter had rigged them up a table and an awning as well as fetching up chairs and the hammock.

Nathan dropped into one of the low chairs and stretched out his legs. He had shed his uniform coat for a light linen one and he had a wide-brimmed hat like the planters wore on his head. 'My back is very much better this morning, Miss Ravenhurst.' Clemence saw Eliza's sharp gaze focus on their faces.

'My suggestion that an oil massage would help proved successful?' she enquired as though her own hands had been nowhere near either back or oil.

'Miraculous,' Nathan said, his lids lowered so she could not see what was going on in those blue eyes. 'Extremely therapeutic. In fact, I can safely say I have never felt anything like it.'

'Will it be necessary to repeat it?' she asked, attempting to sound nonchalant.

'It would perhaps not be wise.' And then he did look fully at her and the heat blazed like firelight behind sapphires and the breath caught in her throat.

'Eliza, I think this would be a good time to give One-Eye some exercise,' Clemence announced.

'Yes, Miss Clemence,' Eliza said primly, folding her work and getting up. 'Come on, lazy hound, let's see what Street's got in the galley for you.' As she passed behind Nathan she caught Clemence's eye and pursed her lips in an exaggerated kiss.

'Clemence? What has occurred to put you to the blush?'

'Eliza, drat the woman,' she confessed. 'She reads more into what I did last night than…'

'I read only kindness,' Nathan said softly. 'And, considering recent events between us, considerable powers of forgiveness and trust.'

'If we are speaking of forgiveness, I can still not forget how you came to be injured in the first place,' Clemence protested. 'And as for you refusing to marry me, I suppose I can accept that your scruples are honourable, although I find them misguided. If I had known about your wife, how you feel about her still, then of course, I would have refused immediately.'

'How I feel?' he queried, frowning at her.

'You told me you loved her. And there was such emotion on your face when you spoke of her. You fought a duel over her, put your career at hazard to defend her honour—you do not need to explain any more, and I should not be intruding into those feelings in any case. I would not want to be a second wife under those circumstances, to know that my husband could not help but compare me to his first wife.'

After a moment he said, 'You are right, my feelings for you are very different from what I now feel for Julietta.' Clemence felt the cramping misery inside at the shadow that passed over his face as he spoke.

'Well,' she said with an attempt at lightness, 'we may be friends again, may we not?' There were weeks still to go, days to become accustomed to being with him and knowing that now she could never become any closer, figure any larger in his life.

'Friends?' Nathan reached out and lifted her hand, which lightly clasped the edge of the hammock. 'Yes, we may be friends.' The kiss he dropped on her fingertips was feather-light, but Clemence felt it as though it had caressed her lips. Then he picked up her book and grimaced at the open page and the moment had passed.

'You are enjoying this?'

'No, it is deadly dull, but Mr Jones gave it to me and I do not like to hurt his feelings. I thought I could read one sermon at least and then discuss it with him at dinner.'

'The trials and tribulations of being a well brought-up young lady,' Nathan teased, settling back in his chair and tipping his hat over his eyes.

'I am sure my manners will fall far short of what is expected in English society,' Clemence worried.

'You will enchant them with your freshness. Anything that is different to prevailing manners in Jamaica you will quickly learn; besides, your relatives are sure to be in the country or at the seaside, so you will have plenty of time before you have to worry about the rigours of the Season.'

'Will you go to sea again soon?' she asked, endeavouring quite successfully not to sound wistful. Nathan must never guess how she truly felt about him.

'I would hope to. I have no desire to languish on half-pay.'

'No, indeed not. I imagine that must be most frustrating. And I suppose, too, that with the end of hostilities there must be fewer opportunities.'

'Yes,' he agreed, his mouth set, and she mentally kicked herself for tactlessness.

'Papa wished to go into the navy. He was the youngest son, so that was quite acceptable. But then they found his eyesight was so very poor he was ineligible.'

'Is that why he became a merchant and built his fleet?'

'I suppose so—he did love the sea,' Clemence mused. 'Personally I am becoming thoroughly bored with it and this intolerable dawdling progress.'

'Don't wish yourself a storm.' Nathan pushed back his hat and got to his feet. 'The wind is changing now—can you feel it? We'll be clear of the Straits soon and into the Atlantic and all its swells and winds. Then we'll see how bored you are! And cold,' he added, pausing by the hammock and running the back of his hand fleetingly up her bare arm, sending delicious shivers down her spine. 'You will disappear under layers of everything you possess.'

'Forty-two days out,' Clemence observed, looking up from the diary she was keeping of the journey. 'Is it always this slow?'

'No.' Nathan glanced up from his own notes. 'We've had more contrary winds than I would have expected. Are you warm enough? I fear we will have to move our customary morning journal meeting inside soon.' From the day after what Clemence always thought of as their truce, they had been meeting in the morning to write their journals. It was companionable, yet entirely proper, and gradually she sensed that both of them had relaxed into friendship. Nathan was careful not to touch her and she resisted any inclination to flirt. It answered very well in daylight, but at night she still ached for him, lying awake listening to the sounds of him moving about in his cabin, trying to imagine what he was doing.

'Oh, no, I enjoy this.' Clemence smiled over the top of the warm scarf Midshipman Stills had bashfully offered her when he overheard her commenting on the cold.

'Three weeks perhaps, sooner with any luck,' Nathan added, looking up at the mainmast and then down to his notebook. 'We're a good two hundred miles off the Newfoundland Banks now.' Clemence glanced across to see what he was doing and smiled at the sketch of one of the hands clinging on like a monkey that he had achieved with only a few pencil lines.

'That's good.' Her own journal was so scrupulously devoid of any personal remarks or feelings that she could have heard it read at Sunday service from the poop deck without blushing and Nathan appeared as unconcerned about her reading his.

'Midshipmen are taught to sketch as part of the training.' He looked across at her, grinned and executed a swift caricature of her bundled up in her scarf and borrowed pea jacket. *I wish I could draw*, Clemence thought. *When we part, I will have nothing tangible to remember him by.*

'What is the first thing you are going to do when you land?' Nathan asked.

'Buy warm clothes! And then find out where Aunt Amelia is.'

'Which one is she? I lose track of your vast clan.'

'Lord Sebastian and Lady Dereham's mother. I have been studying the family tree in an effort to learn them all—I just hope I meet them one at a time or I will be quite overwhelmed.'

'You will cope,' Nathan said easily, closing his notebook and getting to his feet. 'I have every confidence that next Season you will be the toast of London society.'

'Oh, good.' Clemence sighed inaudibly as he smiled and left her. 'I cannot wait.'

Chapter Seventeen

'Land ho!'

'Eliza! Eliza, wake up!' Clemence scrambled off the bunk, thrust her feet into her slippers and pulled on her wrapper. 'Land!'

There was the sound of feet outside as those with cabins on their deck ran to see.

'It's the middle of the night,' Eliza complained sleepily, opening her eyes. 'Miss Clemence!' She sat bolt upright. 'You cannot go out like that—look at you.'

'Oh, bother it.' Clemence snatched up a scarf and wrapped it around her neck. 'It cannot be that cold, close to land; it is early September, after all.'

'I mean you aren't decent—' Eliza's voice vanished as Clemence ran up the companionway into the early morning light. And there it was, land at long last, low wooded cliffs, rolling hills, the line of grey that seemed to be an endless shingle bar.

She clung to the rail, staring across the grey water to her new home. No scents reached her nostrils, no vivid colours broke the tranquillity of grey and brown and muted green. Would the people be as cool and muted, too?

'Welcome to England. We are off Weymouth, not so very far from Portsmouth now,' said Nathan's voice in her ear. She turned against the rail and found him close, shrugging out of his heavy coat. 'Here, put this on. You'll catch your death and you'll corrupt the innocent midshipmen before their time otherwise.'

Smiling, Clemence did as he said and found herself enclosed in warm, Nathan-scented wool. For a moment it befuddled her half-sleepy senses and she found herself looking up into his face, smiling, her face unguarded, the carefully polite smiles of friendship forgotten. 'Thank you.'

'I had made myself ignore what a kissable mouth you have,' he said, pulling her gently into a secluded corner. 'But we are nearly there now. What harm can one English kiss do?'

An English kiss, from Nathan, was, if anything, more inflammatory than a Jamaican one, perhaps because of the contrast between the cool air brushing her face and the heat of his body and his mouth. Or perhaps it was the effect of weeks of living so close to him and behaving with utter propriety.

Her lips parted and he took her mouth with the same implacable gentleness that she had learned to expect as she wrapped her arms around his neck and the coat slid unheeded to the deck.

This was the last time he would kiss her, her last chance to fill her senses and her memory with the feel and scent and taste of him before he became unobtainable, the man she would measure all the others against. The one they would never match.

His eyes were dark and hazed as he lifted his mouth from hers and stood looking into her face. 'It has not gone away, then, that connection when we touch,' he said, his voice husky.

'No.' *Does it not tell you something?* she wanted to ask him, but that was impossible without saying that she loved him, spoiling their last hours together with regret and embarrassment and pity. Instead she smiled and lifted her hand and touched his lips lightly, then bent to pick up the coat. 'Take this, I must go below.' And she ducked under his arm and down the steps before the tears had a chance to show.

That was a mistake, Nathan told himself, shrugging back into the coat and not even attempting to pretend to himself that he was not burying his nose in the lapels to drink in the perfume of sleepy woman. A mistake and an indulgence, but also another memory of Clemence that he could store and bring out on some long, lonely watch to warm himself with.

He was conscious of another, bulkier figure close by and turned to see Melville leaning on the rail beside him, his telescope on the small sailing boat beating out to meet them. 'That's flying the ensign, they'll have been on watch for us from the harbour battery and will be bringing orders, I've no doubt.'

'I thought you were making for Portsmouth.' Nathan realised he had thought no further ahead than landfall. His own orders were to report to the Admiralty in Whitehall.

'Aye. I hope they haven't changed that and we've got to beat round to Chatham.'

The lieutenant scrambling on board with the oilcloth-wrapped packet of orders saluted smartly. 'The admiral's compliments, Captain Melville. If you would be so good as to proceed to Chatham with all speed.'

Melville caught Nathan's eye, but made no comment other than to thank the man and take the orders. Clemence, Eliza at her side, came back up on deck. The maid looked miserable, hunched in her layers of clothes as her eyes fixed hopefully on the shore, and Clemence looked paler, more weary than she had when she had left him just a little while before. As Nathan watched, Clemence put her arm around Eliza's shoulders and hugged her to her side.

'Are you both all right?' he asked.

'Tired and cold and impatient,' Clemence admitted with a rueful smile. 'Seeing land and not being able to disembark brings it home how long we have been on this ship.'

And now they would have the delay while they sailed along the entire south coast, round into the Thames estuary. He walked back to Melville. 'We could put the women off here, send them back in the boat with the lieutenant.'

'What, by themselves?' Melville looked across. 'Although they do look as though they would like to get ashore, I must admit.'

'I'll go with them. I can find them a respectable lodging, discover where Miss Ravenhurst's aunt is, send her off in a hired chaise and post up to London myself. My orders are to report to the Admiralty, not stick to the *Orion*.'

'True enough. And you won't be much later, if at all, that way. Lieutenant! Hold hard there.' He strode away across the deck, leaving Nathan to speak to Clemence.

'Would you like to go ashore here at Weymouth, now?'

'Now?' Clemence blinked at him.

'It is that or stay on board until we reach Chatham. Better to land now.' She was looking doubtful, daunted no doubt by the thought of coping alone in a strange country. 'I'll come, too,' he added. 'I can find you lodgings and organise a post chaise to take you to your aunt.'

'But your orders?'

'This will probably be faster,' he said. 'The roads are a little different from what you are used to and I can be in London in hours from here.'

'Then if it is not an inconvenience to you, I would be most grateful, thank you.' She said it with cool good manners, a remote young lady, no longer the warm soft creature, half-tumbled from sleep, responsive in his arms. She was wise, no doubt, to distance herself like this. When he had kissed her, when she had responded to him, they had expected to be parted within hours. Now it could be a day or two.

'You had better hurry and pack, I'll send some men down to carry your things on deck.' Even Eliza roused herself at that, hurrying below to leave him to explain to the lieutenant that he was returning with three passengers, a pile of luggage and a cantankerous old hound.

Nathan stood for a minute, contemplating what he had just let himself in for. But she was tired and anxious and needed to be with her new family; to make her endure any more time, within sight of land yet in limbo, was too cruel. He just needed to extend the self-control he had been exercising for a little longer. No doubt it was good for his soul, Nathan thought with a wry smile as he followed the women and went to fetch his belongings.

Clemence clutched the rail of the skiff with one hand and her hat with the other and squinted against the stiff breeze. 'What a fabulous beach!' Golden sand arced around a wide bay before the coast lifted into cliffs and the wide expanse was dotted with figures and strange small huts.

'See the bathing machines?' Nathan stood at her elbow, his fingers clenched in One-Eye's collar. 'You could go for a swim.'

'No, thank you! I can recall everything you told me about flannel bathing dresses and large women who dunk you under.' And although the beach might be golden, the sea was grey and cold and there were no palm trees waving in a warm breeze. She shivered. This cool foreign land was home now so she'd better get used to it.

They were into the harbour channel now, steep slopes crowned with fortifications to the left, the busy quayside to the right. Clemence craned to see while Eliza at her side was wide-eyed. 'It's so different, Miss Clemence, so square and grey.'

Nathan was talking to the lieutenant who had brought the orders out to them. 'The Golden Lion? Remember, I have ladies with me—is it respectable?'

'Eminently, the senior officers always lodge there with their wives. And you can hire post chaises from them.'

Clemence felt she should take a hand in the decisions being made, assert herself and not rely upon Nathan. Soon, very soon, he would be gone and she must learn to manage. 'That sounds perfectly satisfactory, thank you.' Then a thought struck her. 'Nathan,' she whispered. 'I have no money!'

'Here.' He opened his pocket book and handed her some unfamiliar bank notes. 'This is the change from the one hundred guineas Melville drew against our official expenses. I am sure your aunt will be able to arrange to have it repaid to him.'

'Thank you.' She took the money and folded it carefully into her reticule, relieved that she was not having to borrow it from Nathan. How expensive would the inn be and how long would they have to stay? What if…? Clemence drew a deep steadying breath and told herself to stop worrying. She could cope, of course she could.

The Golden Lion proved comfortable, if rather dark and overpowering with thick hangings and a heavily be-curtained bed. 'It all smells odd,' Eliza complained as they set out on foot for Harvey's Library and Reading Rooms where the porter had assured Nathan they would find all the news-sheets they could possibly want.

'Shh, and don't stare so,' Clemence chided.

'They are all staring at us,' the maid retorted.

It was hardly surprising, Clemence thought. A young lady bundled into layers of decidedly unfashionable garments, attended by a maid in a colourful head-wrap and escorted by a naval officer and a vast man with an ancient and belligerent hound on a leash. Yes, they certainly stood out amongst the crowds going about their business and the fashionable strollers who sauntered down the pavements closer to the centre of the town.

'Here we are,' Nathan said, sounding as nearly rattled as she could recall hearing him. 'You wait outside, Street.' Under the eye of a matron with a vast bonnet and an eye glass, he swept them into the entrance of Harvey's Library.

An attendant showed them into the newspaper reading room, found them a table and chairs and brought them the *Morning Post* and *The Times* from the beginning of June.

Clemence applied herself to scanning the columns in search of any reference to the Ravenhursts, but it was hard to ignore some of the other news.

'It says here,' she reported, 'that Mr Kemble remains at Stanmore Priory under the severe visitation of what Dr Johnson styles *arthritic tyranny*, vulgarly called the gout. Poor man, having that printed. And there is famine in Transylvania, wherever that is.'

'I have found a list of the prices at the Pantheon Linen Warehouse,' Eliza contributed. 'Coloured dresses for only seventeen shillings and six pence.' She frowned. 'Is that expensive?'

'I have no idea,' Nathan said repressively. 'Concentrate, or we will be here all day.'

They had arrived at the first week in July before Clemence found it. 'Here! *It is understood that Lord Standon daily expects a most fashionable house party to assemble at his country seat in Hampshire, the distinguished company of Lord Standon's illustrious relatives to include, it is rumoured, Lord Sebastian Ravenhurst and the Grand Duchess of Maubourg.* Thank goodness.' Although a house party did sound somewhat daunting.

Nathan was already on his feet, checking the *Peerage*. 'Long Martin Court, principal seat of the Earls of Standon. And it is not far from Romsey, which means I can escort you and then take the chaise on to London.'

'I had better write.'

'You would arrive on the heels of the letter if we leave first thing tomorrow,' Nathan said, unfolding a map he had found on the shelves. 'Look, we are here, there is Romsey. Now we know where you are going and when, would you like to look at the shops?'

What she wanted was to retreat to her fusty, dark room and panic quietly about her arrival at Long Martin Court. It was almost worrying enough to distract her from the dull ache inside at the prospect of parting from Nathan for ever. Clemence fixed a smile on her face. 'That would be delightful.'

It was seven years since he had been shopping with a lady, Nathan realised, watching the tension gradually fade from Clemence's face as she browsed amongst the shops lining the more fashionable streets. He wanted to take her somewhere quiet and hold her, stroke those lines creasing her brow until they vanished, kiss her until the worry disappeared from her green eyes.

With Julietta all his energies had been devoted to keeping her out of the scrapes her impulsive nature sent her tumbling into. Emptying his wallet as she shopped had been one way of doing that, even if the silks and taffetas, the pearls and bangles, had all been deployed to attract attention and aid her in flirting with any man who paid her heed. He closed his eyes for a moment against the pain. That was all she had ever meant to do: flirt. And yet it had killed her.

But Clemence did not flirt and she did not once open her reticule, although he saw her lips curve at the sight of a shop window full of nonsensically pretty hats and look wistfully at a display of fans and shawls. He wanted to buy it all for her, see her eyes light up and hear her laugh. But he should not give her something as intimate as a garment, he knew that.

Eliza had found a shop full of small antiquities, old paintings, statues and trays of second-hand knick-knacks.

She rummaged enthusiastically while the shopkeeper stared at her dark skin and her colourful head-wrap.

To distract himself from watching Clemence, Nathan picked up fans from a shelf, almost at random. One small one caught his eye. Painted with a group of young women in the centre, it was surrounded in verses in French. It wasn't new—in fact, it was slightly scuffed—but it intrigued him. The women were taking papers from cherubs who appeared to be operating some kind of lottery or lucky dip. It was hard to read in the subdued light as he skimmed the words, then he saw the name in the last verse. Clémence.

'I'll take this.' The shopkeeper wrapped it for him and he thrust it into his breast pocket as the two women tore themselves away from the trinkets and came to join him. 'Finished?'

'Yes, thank you. You must be so bored.' Clemence smiled up at him. 'Should we go back to the inn?'

'I think so. I will hire a chaise for tomorrow.'

She grew quieter and quieter as they neared the inn and Nathan found himself suddenly devoid of conversation. 'You'll take dinner in the private parlour?' She nodded. 'I will not join you. I have business to attend to.' He stopped at the door. 'I will send a note with the time for us to leave.'

'Yes, of course,' Clemence said politely, her eyes troubled. His memory brought back the look in them when he had refused to marry her. He felt, obscurely, that he had let her down, and yet, surely by now she knew he had made the right decision? 'We will be ready.'

Almost there, he thought as he strode off down St Edmund's Street towards his non-existent business. *Almost free of the need to watch every thought and every word. Almost time for the safety of loneliness and of not having to worry about another human being.* Because that was all it was, all it could be, this odd ache inside him. He had missed feminine company and Clemence was such an original female it was hard not to be attracted by her. He had been trained to care for those under his command and he supposed that was why he felt such a need to protect her. And he wanted to make love to her and that, of course, was impossible. So the sooner he could return to his bachelor existence, the better.

It had been easier to sleep in the cramped cabin, Clemence concluded after a restless night in the high bed, alternately stifled and cold. Everything seemed to be moving still, yet the familiar shipboard noises had been replaced by cartwheels on cobbles, shouts from the harbour, heavy feet on the landing outside and heavy snores from the chamber next door.

Nathan did not snore. Clemence rolled over and buried her head under a pillow, but all that the comparative peace provided was more tranquillity in which to think and to worry.

Somehow she would get through the meeting with her family, she knew that, despite her anxious anticipation. But what then? They would expect her to become part of their world, to take her place in society and to find a husband. And how could she when the only man she loved didn't want to marry her?

Those days together on the *Orion* had given her a glimpse of what their life together could be, the companionship, the shared amusements, the spark of temper and the fun of making up. Everything, that is, except the nights spent in each other's arms. Her body ached as she let herself remember the feel of those slim hips between her thighs as she had massaged his back, the ripple of muscle under the palms, the spring of his hair, the scent of hot masculinity.

Stubborn, stubborn man! And yet, now, she could understand his scruples. And it was not as though he loved her, after all. He knew she was safe now so he had no need to fight for her.

Clemence screwed her eyes tightly shut and refused to let herself cry.

Chapter Eighteen

'We have arrived.'

The chaise swung through between tall gate posts. Clemence caught a glimpse of a quaint cottage and a man holding the gate, then they were into parkland, great sweeping grasslands dotted with trees, the glint of distant water, a small temple artfully placed on a mound. Elegant, artificial and yet deeply satisfying.

'What are those odd cattle?' Eliza pointed.

'Deer.' She knew that, she had seen pictures. Clemence tightened her grip on her reticule, her elbow rubbing against Nathan's. A hired chaise was hardly big enough for a hound and four people, not when one of them was Street. Street, Nathan had decreed, was staying with her, although in what capacity he had not said. Her imagination baulked at the thought of the ex-pirate in footman's livery.

The carriage drive seemed endless, but at last they came to a halt and Nathan opened the door and handed her down. 'Courage,' he murmured as he offered her his arm. 'You faced down Red Matthew McTiernan, one duchess will be child's play.'

The footman who answered the door was too well trained to express surprise to find himself confronted by an unexpected member of his master's family on the arm of a naval officer, although his eyes widened at the sight of their entourage, one of whom was snarling at a peacock. The butler, materialising as they entered, was above showing even that degree of surprise and ushered Clemence and Nathan into a salon. 'Your staff will be comfortable in the servants' hall, sir. I will ascertain if her Grace is receiving.'

'Clemence! My dear child, I had no idea!' The human whirlwind who appeared five minutes later, sweeping past the butler, clasped Clemence to her bosom and kissed her on both cheeks. 'You poor lamb, I was devastated to hear about your papa and then your uncle said you were unwell—we had no thought you might be able to make the journey.'

Clemence found herself seated beside the lady she supposed must be her aunt. She was tall, although not as tall as Clemence, dark haired, long nosed and remarkably handsome. At first glance she seemed daunting, but there was humour in her large blue eyes and kindness in the clasp of her hands around Clemence's own cold ones.

'I was not unwell, ma'am. My uncle Naismith is determined on seizing my inheritance by forcing me to marry my cousin Lewis. I ran away,' she added, then ran out of words. There ought to be some way to gently lead up to what had happened, but it escaped her.

The duchess raised her eyebrows, took a deep breath, then turned her eyes on Nathan. 'With this gentleman?'

'Captain Nathan Stanier, your Grace. Royal Navy.

Miss Ravenhurst's fight took her into the hands of a pirate crew of which I was, at that time, the navigator.'

'On a naval mission, I trust? Your present occupation does not represent a sudden change of heart?' Despite her sharp words, her expression as she turned back to Clemence was gentle. 'My dear, I am sure you would like to tell me all about this alone in my boudoir.'

'No, thank you, ma'am. There is nothing I cannot discuss in front of Captain Stanier. I was disguised as a boy. There was a battle and it was all very unpleasant. But, through it all, Captain Stanier knew and protected me. He was hurt because of me. Nothing…untoward occurred.' At least her aunt was not having hysterics, or had shown her the door or any of the other unpleasant scenarios that had been running through her mind.

'Call me Aunt Amelia, child.' The duchess squeezed her hands. 'You will want to rest a while and take some tea. Captain, may I trouble you to pull the bell? Thank you. Ah, Andrewes, please will you show Miss Ravenhurst to the Blue suite and send my woman to her. And a tea tray.'

'Aunt Amelia—' She was being got out of the way while her aunt interrogated Nathan, which was unfair. She should stay and defend him.

'I will just have a word with Captain Stanier, my dear,' the duchess continued, confirming her fears. 'I will come and see you shortly.'

Nathan met her eyes and mouthed, *Go*, so Clemence got to her feet, bemused. She could hardly cling to his coat and insist on staying.

'Perhaps you had better say goodbye now,' her aunt added with finality.

Clemence swallowed. She had not expected the

parting to be so sudden and she had no words beyond, 'Thank you, Na… Captain.' He was studying her, like a painter looking at a subject before he laid chalk to paper. She tried again. 'You saved my life, at no little risk to your own. I thank you and I wish you well. Goodbye.'

'It was a pleasure to be of service, Miss Ravenhurst.' He reached into his coat and pulled out a slender package. 'A trifle. A keepsake. I saw your name on it, but I have not stopped to translate it, I fear.'

He bowed, she curtsied and took it, an unimportant thing when all she wanted was him, and then she was walking away from the man she had thought, for a few blissful moments, would be her destiny.

'Well, Captain Stanier?'

Despite the distinct feeling that he was up before the admiral on charges, Nathan felt a twinge of appreciation. The duchess was formidably unshaken by the unexpected arrival of her niece and, he could see, was more than capable of looking after Clemence.

'There is no doubt, your Grace, that Miss Ravenhurst is quite comprehensively compromised. She has spent nights in my cabin, during only one of which was I fooled into thinking she was male. But I can give you my word that, although she has been exposed to violence that no young woman should ever see, her virtue has not been outraged.'

'You relieve my mind,' she said drily. 'But as you say, my niece is compromised. It does not occur to you to offer her the protection of your name?'

'It did. That was my intention—before I knew who she was. I am unequal to one of her birth or her fortune. I am the younger son of the third Baron Howarth and I live on my pay. When I prevailed upon Clemence to tell me her name, I realised that the power of the Ravenhurst family would both protect her good name and effectively crush her uncle and his schemes. She has no need to marry me—she may marry who she chooses, as high as she chooses.'

'That is true.' The duchess sat studying him. Nathan looked stolidly back at her. If she thought she was going to push him into babbling on, she was mistaken. 'What do you know about her uncle?' she asked at length.

'That when Clemence ran away her face was swollen from the blow he had dealt her because she had refused his son. Their intention was for the young man to come to her bed and force her until she was with child. They assumed this would compel her to give in for the sake of the baby, thus giving them permanent control of her fortune.'

He had thought he could get through this without emotion, but it was an effort to control the anger in his voice. The duchess's eyes widened in shock, but she did not speak. 'The navy has legal representation on Jamaica. We have left a deposition with them against the time when you wish to act.'

'Then I must thank you, Captain Stanier. It seems Clemence owes you her life—I am not sure how we may repay that debt.' He made an abrupt gesture of rejection and she nodded. A perceptive woman with more sensibility than her forthright appearance had led him to expect. 'What are your plans now?'

'To report to the Admiralty as soon as I reach London. The post chaise is waiting.'

'Then all I can do is thank you.' The duchess rose and held out her hand. He bowed over it and turned. 'Tell me, Captain Stanier,' she said softly as he was halfway to the door, 'do you love her?'

It halted him in mid-stride, the truth of it like a blow. Nathan stood, his back to the tall woman, staring into the glass that hung on the wall, reflecting his image and hers into the overmantel glass and back again. He saw his own face, endlessly repeated and the sudden shock of knowledge on it, and he saw, too, the pity on hers.

In front of him the door handle turned and the door opened a fraction. It was Clemence, he knew it by instinct. She had not wanted to abandon him to her aunt's questions; now she had come back to defend him.

'Do I love Clemence?' he repeated, his voice clear and cool, his intent driving the words through the wooden panels as though they were a rapier thrust. The door stopped opening. 'No,' he lied, shocked at how the word hurt. 'No, but I would have done my duty by her if that was the right thing, naturally. I confess, it is a relief not to have to take that step. I have been married once, your Grace. I have no desire to be burdened with a second wife, however sweet and young.'

The gasp was so soft he hardly heard it—perhaps he imagined it. He felt as though he had hit her. By why should he feel so badly? She did not love him, even if she felt friendship, gratitude and perhaps, still, some half-aroused desire. At worst, she had formed a *tendre* for him and that would soon vanish in the admiration and attention of a dozen young aspirants for her hand and heart. The door closed softly. *Click.* There, it was finished.

'Good day, your Grace.'

The hall was empty when he stepped out into it, although the butler appeared with the usual supernatural efficiency of his kind, Nathan's hat and gloves in hand. 'I have found accommodation for Miss Raven-hurst's maid and *man*.'

'Personal cook and bodyguard,' Nathan explained, finding some faint amusement at the expression that crossed the butler's face.

'As you say, sir. Doubtless we can outfit him suitably. The hound is in the stables.'

But not for long, I'll warrant. 'Thank you.' There was nothing for it now but to walk out of the wide front doors and get into the chaise and drive back to London and to duty and the whims of their lordships of the Admiralty and to learn to pretend that the last three months had not happened. To come to terms with the fact that his feelings for Clemence Raven-hurst were not simply liking and friendship and desire, but love. Thank God he would never have to see her again.

Clemence stood on the landing, a foot back from the balustrade, and watched Nathan's back until the doors closed, something hot and painful lodged in her chest. What had she thought, what had she dreamed? Surely not that he would change his mind at the last moment, ignore the wealth and magnificence of her cousin's home, the dignity and station of her aunt and discover that he loved her after all?

Yes, of course that was what she had dreamed. A fantasy of Nathan on his knees, clasping her hands, telling her he could not live without her and his scruples were as nothing compared to the force of his love and adoration for her.

So, now she knew. He would have done his duty and she was sweet and young. But it was a relief not to have to marry her, he had said, with the air of a man explaining why a horse was not of the right conformation to suit him.

Something was hurting her hand. She looked down to find it clenched around the slim hard package he had given her. Clemence retraced her steps to the bedchamber that had been allotted to her and sat down at the dressing table to unwrap it.

It was a fan. Not new, slightly scuffed, with plain sticks and a printed design on one side. Feeling as though she was watching someone else through a window, Clemence opened it and studied the design. Six young women clustered around a table on which stood a revolving drum and above their heads little Cupids fluttered, taking papers from the drum and giving them to the girls. The verses were in French, the print small. Clemence began to read. It was, it seemed, a lottery for a lover.

Here is Love, putting the charms
Of all these beauties to the test.
The prizes, he has promised, will be
The true qualities of men…
A constant friend, a faithful husband,
Are both a lottery.

It was horribly apposite. Clemence made herself continue to translate. Isis, despairing, had drawn a blank, Aglaé a man with no merit; Aglaure, though, was more fortunate, winning a man both constant and handsome. Mélise finds she has a man with three good qualities— he will be generous, handsome and sensitive. Clemence began to see the pattern: the next girl would win a man with four virtues and, indeed, Aline's lover was destined be a man with wit, beauty, good heart and fidelity.

And finally, there remains but one.
It is for the lovely Clémence.

That was what Nathan had meant—he had seen her name. She read on, the fragile object trembling in her hand.

Her destiny is wonderful, but rare.
It surpasses all her hopes.
A stout heart, a quick mind,
Virtue, courage and a handsome form.
Her lover is blessed with them all.
She has won the fivefold prize.

He had not translated it, she had to believe him. He would not be so cruel. He had bought the pretty thing for her simply because of her name upon it, never guessing the irony. Clémence's promised lover was everything Nathan was in her mind, everything she loved him for.

She closed the fan until all she was holding was the slender length of it between its polished brown guard sticks. Her hands closed on it, tightened. It would break so easily, just like her heart.

After a long while she laid it down and drew a silk handkerchief from her reticule, wrapped the fan in it with care and slid open the drawer beneath the dressing-table mirror. It fitted as though it had been made for it, just as Nathan had been made for her. Clemence slid the drawer shut, consigning it to darkness.

When both Eliza and a housemaid with the tea tray arrived she was standing by the window looking out over the sweeping lawns that ran down to a lake. Several couples were strolling in the sunlight, a boy was throwing a ball to a tall man and two nursemaids followed on behind, their arms full of squirming bundles.

She turned, eyes dry and aching, and smiled at Eliza. 'I expect those are some of my cousins down there. What a lot of people to get to know.'

'A good thing, a big family,' Eliza observed, hands folded primly in front of her crisp white apron. The minute the other maid had gone she threw up her hands, dignity forgotten. 'This place is huge, Miss Clemence! A palace! The King's House on Jamaica is nothing to this—and the *staff*. My knees are knocking, they're so grand, believe me. And they stare so.'

'They are not used to seeing many people of colour,' Clemence explained. 'They do not mean any harm by it and you will all soon become accustomed to each other. How is Street getting on?'

'That butler, Mr Andrewes, has taken him off to find him what he says are suitable clothes. And poor old One-Eye is chained up in the stables, though Fred says he'll look after him.'

'You are one of the upper servants here,' Clemence warned her. 'But I am a very junior member of the family and you will take my precedence. Do you understand? I am sure the housekeeper will explain how to go on.'

'Yes, Miss Clemence. I'll unpack your things.' She turned to the trunk, but Clemence heard her murmur, 'An upper servant! Me!'

Clemence had not realised how tensely she had been awaiting her aunt's questions until the tap on the door brought her to her feet.

'Are you rested, my dear?'

'Yes, Aunt Amelia. This is a very lovely room, thank you.'

'You must thank Jessica, your cousin Standon's wife, as she is your hostess. But that can wait until dinner time. If you can spare your maid now, perhaps we should talk.'

It was quite plainly an order, however pleasantly put. 'Yes, Aunt Amelia. Eliza, you may leave us now.' She sat down, hands folded, trying to remember her deportment lessons.

Her aunt regarded her steadily. 'Can you tell me what has happened, from the time your papa died? Is that possible without distressing you too much?'

'Yes, I can do that, ma'am.' Clemence took a deep breath and began, in as orderly and dispassionate manner as she could, to set out what had happened to her ever since the news of the loss of *Raven Duchess* had reached them and her world had fallen apart. She told the older woman everything except the intimate passages with Nathan—those she could hardly bear to think of, let alone speak about.

There was silence when she reached the end of her narrative, then the duchess gave a little sigh. 'That is a terrible story. You have been very brave, my dear. Now, are you quite certain that nothing has occurred that you have been unable to tell me of?'

Her meaning was quite clear to Clemence. She felt the colour mounting in her cheeks, but she said quite steadily, 'Did you not believe Captain Stanier?'

'Yes, I did. No, I mean was there anything that happened that you were not able to confide in him?'

'No.' Clemence was beyond feeling shy about discussing this. 'Cousin Lewis found me too scrawny to attract him unless he absolutely had to bed me and no one on the ship knew my sex.'

'Good. Then that is one less thing to worry about,' her aunt said briskly. Clemence relaxed, forgetting she was facing an experienced questioner. 'Are you in love with him?' the duchess asked casually.

'Y— No! Good heavens! No, of course not.' Was she believed? The duchess was far too skilled at hiding her feelings for her to tell.

'Excellent, although you do surprise me—he is a most attractive young man.' The duchess's mouth curved into a positively wicked smile. 'But there are other handsome men out there and ones with titles and fortunes beside. So all we need to do now is to provide you with a fitting wardrobe and to introduce you to society. You will need to tell Mr Wallingford, our solicitor, all about your inheritance and he will make sure the Naismiths are dealt with.'

'Good,' Clemence said with some feeling, wishing it were possible to send both father and son to sea with Red Matthew McTiernan for a few months. Keelhauling was too good for them.

'And now, my dear, it is time for you to change for dinner while I tell you all about your new family.'

Chapter Nineteen

Nathan stood in the waiting room outside the admiral's office in no very compliant frame of mind. His nerves felt raw since he had left Hampshire and distance did not seem to help. If anything, the more time he had to think about Clemence and the awful truth that he had fallen in love with her, the worse he felt.

He had risen through the navy, always accepting his orders without question, even when they had seemed eccentric and inexplicable. Now he found himself resentful and ready to argue. They had sent him out to Jamaica to fight pirates; he had done so—with some success, if he said so himself—and now they were hauling him back before they even knew how he had prospered.

If they had left him where he was, he would never have realised he was in love with Clemence. He could be happily hunting buccaneers at this very moment, if they had just left him be. The admiral's secretary opened the door. 'Captain Stanier?'

'Sir.' He arrived on the rug in front of the desk,

saluted and stared stonily at the weather-beaten and irascible face glowering back.

'What's the matter with you, Stanier? Unhappy because we've called you back? Hah.'

'I am entirely at your lordship's disposal. Sir.'

'You most certainly are. What do you think we sent you out there for?'

'To fight pirates, my lord.'

The admiral narrowed his eyes, unable to fault the tone or the words. 'I recall at the time telling you to assess the situation and develop a strategy to fight pirates.'

'My lord.' And what the hell did they think he and Melville had been doing?

'So you've had a look. Tell me what needs doing. And stand at ease, man, you look as if you've a poker up your breeches.'

'I was about to send despatches, my lord.'

'Not good enough. I need you to convince their lord-ships of the need to put more resources out there because I'm damned if I can. This needs stamping out, once and for all before these freebooters and scum become useful allies for our late colonists. And I don't trust those Americans an inch—too much competition for trade in that area, however friendly they seem to be.

'We didn't deal effectively with the Barbary pirates and they are still a thorn in the flesh of every law-abiding merchantman in the Mediterranean. You've been out to the West Indies, you've seen the situation, now I want you to work on a strategy and we'll get the ships and money we need.'

Nathan felt himself relax. That at least sounded logical. 'And then I can go back out there?'

'Yes, you and Melville. I need you both to meet with

Commodore Lord Hoste. You know where his office is? Well, get yourself along there and get organised.' He waved a hand in dismissal. 'And, Stanier—he'll need a vice-commodore to take control out there. Do you understand what I am saying?'

'But Melville—'

'Melville is a good fighting captain. You are that and a strategist as well.'

Feeling somewhat as though he had been hit over the head, Nathan found Lord Hoste's office. *Vice-commodore?*

Melville was already there, both men bent over charts, a secretary scribbling in the background. Hoste, an elegant man in his early forties who cultivated a deceptive manner of caring for little except the cut of his coat and the mix of his snuff, raised a languid brow at Nathan's arrival.

'How long do you need to get yourself equipped for two weeks in the country, Stanier?'

'My lord?'

'I was promised to a house party; you had better both come, too, because I'm damned if I'm going to stick in London, it's as dead as a graveyard and as stuffy as hell. We can work there as well as here. A couple of extra men are always welcome at these affairs and we'll have every excuse for shutting ourselves away when they want us to listen to some simpering ingénue thumping the piano, eh?'

'Your hostess—'

'Done, sorted, all agreed.' He waved a hand towards the secretary. 'Tompion's coming, too, with his cipher books and the charts and so forth. Can you be ready by Tuesday?'

Two days? 'Yes, my lord.'

His brother Daniel's valet could drag his stuff out of storage and beat the moths out of it, he supposed. It wouldn't take more than a day to replenish his stocks of linen and call on his bootmaker. His brother was still at the town house, pleased to see him and confiding wearily that staying put throughout the summer was the cheapest option. 'Priscilla's gone off with the children to stay with her mother at Worthing,' Lord Howarth had said with the air of a man off the leash. 'Too unfashionable to stay in town at this time of year. Don't like to argue with her, not now. She's increasing. Again.'

The downing of a number of bumpers of strong drink to celebrate the forthcoming arrival of another little Stanier would doubtless help him pass this evening, at least. Nathan pulled his attention back to the charts spread out on the wide map table and joined with Melville in deciding exactly what they needed to take with them. His mood had changed. If he really had got that coveted promotion, a challenging mission, then soon, surely, that dull internal ache would disappear and he would find his old self-sufficiency again?

'Will you tell me more about the pirates, Cousin Clemence? Please?' The eleven-year-old Grand Duke of Maubourg presented himself in front of Clemence's wicker chair, hair in his eyes, a scrape on his cheek and mud all round the bottoms of his trousers. He seemed to be enjoying his English summer holiday as much as his parents must savour their regular escapes from court life at Maubourg.

His stepfather, her cousin Lord Sebastian Raven-hurst, sprawled on a rug at the duchess's feet, having informed his mother that Freddie had exhausted him. His unsympathetic parent merely dumped his baby daughter on his admirably flat stomach and laughed.

'Don't plague Cousin Clemence,' he said now. 'She wants a rest, too.'

That was true. A morning of exploring the gardens with Lady Standon—Cousin Jessica—who was interested in which exotic species she might import for her glass houses, a close interrogation from Mr Ravenhurst—antiquarian and collector, Cousin Theo—on the use of mahogany in furniture in the West Indies, and a spirited game of bat and ball with Freddie, his stepfather and Lord Dereham—Cousin Ashe—had left her glad to sit down and finally warm enough to shed one of the cashmere shawls she was wrapped in.

Clemence thought she was getting a grip on who was who, who was married to which cousin and what had been happening in their lives lately, but it was making her head spin.

Freddie was still looking hopeful. He had the great brown eyes of his mother, Eva, and, like the grand duchess, was skilled at looking innocent and appealing when it suited him.

'Go and talk to Street,' she suggested with a sudden flash of inspiration. 'He used to be a pirate.'

'No!' The brown eyes grew huge and Freddie turned to gaze in awe at Street, who stood on the edge of the lawn, arms folded, One-Eye sitting at his feet. Clemence was not certain what he thought he was guarding her against, but she found his stolid bulk curiously comforting and Jessica was deeply impressed with the Creole recipes he had introduced to the cook.

'But yes. Although you had better ask your mama

first.' Eva might take a poor view of her only son being sent to play with a pirate.

'You could take the boat out on the lake,' Eva said serenely, fanning herself against the heat of what everyone assured Clemence was a hot September day.

'But—'

'Freddie swims very well,' his doting mama assured her. 'But no cutlasses!' she called after her son as Freddie took to his heels.

It occurred to Clemence that she should have asked her hostess first before introducing a pirate into the household. 'I should have told you all about Street sooner,' she confessed. 'I hope no one minds? Only he saved my life, and he is quite reformed.' She crossed her fingers.

'I thought Captain Stanier had done that.' Jessica sat up, pushing her wide-brimmed hat back from her face.

'He did, several times. But Street saved me from being shot in the galley when there was the battle with the navy.' She woke up every night, shuddering with terror at the memory of those moments when she had been convinced she was going to die, hearing the explosion of the shot, seeing the eyes of the man and his extended arm as he took aim.

Oddly the nightmares had only begun since Nathan had left, almost as though the knowledge of his nearness had kept them at bay. She wondered, when she braced herself to think about it, whether it was the fact that Nathan had not been there when it happened that made it so frightening in retrospect. Last night had been the worst yet. She had woken to find herself drenched with sweat, Eliza's arms around her, trying to shake her out of the nightmare.

'We have some naval guests arriving soon,' Jessica

continued as they all watched Street settling to the oars with Freddie in the bows, his arms clasped round One-Eye's neck. 'Perhaps we had better forget Street's former employment while they are here.'

'Navy in the plural, my dear?' Gareth, Lord Standon, passed her a glass of lemonade. 'I thought it was just George Hoste we were expecting today. Oh, and that idiot Polkington and his sisters.'

'He might be an idiot—he is certainly the world's worst gossip—but I feel sorry for the girls.'

'You should have invited some more bachelors, in that case.' Gareth lay back in his chair. 'There is Harris coming this afternoon and the curate will be at dinner, but we've three young ladies to be entertained.'

'I certainly don't need any bachelors,' Clemence said hastily.

'Nonsense, all unmarried girls need bachelors to practise on. That was what was missing from my life and look what happened to me as a result,' Jessica observed, exchanging a smile with her husband that curled Clemence's toes in her slippers. 'Anyway,' she continued. 'Hoste is unwed, although he is a lost cause—far too indolent for marriage—but the other two may be single for all I know.'

'Surely you know who you invited, dear,' the duchess observed.

'Hoste is in the middle of some urgent navy business and asked if he could bring them,' Jessica said vaguely. 'Oh, look! The hound has jumped in after the ducks. And Freddie has fallen overboard. And there goes Street.'

Quite who was rescuing who, it was difficult to tell. The lake was not deep, but it was muddy and full of weed and the boy and the man were laughing too hard to swim properly and One-Eye was enjoying himself trying to catch ducks, and the rowing boat had over-turned and by the time an elegant carriage with a crest on the door drew up the butler was forced to escort the occupants to the lakeside and a scene of chaos.

The entire house party was gathered by the water, shouting encouragement as Street waded to the bank, Freddie over one shoulder and pond weed draped like a collapsing wig about his ears. One-Eye heaved himself out, his jaws full of a struggling duck, and shook himself violently all over the onlookers.

Amidst shrieks from the ladies he gave a muffled bark and galloped off. Clemence turned with the others to see Andrewes leading three naval officers down the slope towards them. Tail wagging frantically, One-Eye bounded up to the one on the right and deposited the duck at his feet. The bird flapped off, quacking hysterically.

I am going to faint, Clemence thought as her vision darkened and her head began to spin. It couldn't be Nathan—she was hallucinating.

'Clemence?' It was Cousin Bel, Lady Dereham. She slipped a hand under her arm. 'Are you all right, my dear?'

'Yes, just a moment's dizziness. So foolish—I think I must have turned too quickly, made my head spin.' *It is Nathan. He isn't looking this way, he hasn't seen me.* Was it possible to escape? But there was nowhere to go, no ship in harbour. She saw now that the other officer was Captain Melville, and the tall man who was kissing Jessica on both cheeks must be Lord Hoste.

There was no escape, but at least she could hide away until she had regained some composure. The Ravenhursts *en masse*, even without the drama of a soaking wet child and an uncontrollable dog, were more than adequate cover.

Clemence smiled at Bel, skirted round behind Theo and his wife, Elinor, who were in animated conversation with Eden Ravenhurst and his pretty new wife, Lady Maude, and slid thankfully into the cover of the shrubbery. It was not until she reached the sanctuary of the terrace and risked a backwards glance that she saw that Nathan had turned and was looking up the slope directly at her. She jumped over the sill of the long window and ran through the dining hall as though McTiernan and Cutler were at her heels.

'I was just admiring this prospect of the house,' Nathan said to his hostess in apology for his distraction. 'Charming.' Clemence had vanished, leaving him with the haunting image of her white face. She did not want to see him, then—hardly surprising, given that she had heard his dismissive words to her aunt.

It had taken him until Guildford to emerge from the animated discussion he was having with Melville about the risks and benefits of setting up a spying network across the islands and to realise that the road was looking worryingly familiar.

'Where are we going, my lord? In the hurry to get ready, it did not occur to me to ask.'

'Hmm?' Lord Hoste emerged from his perusal of the *Gentleman's Magazine*. 'Standon's place, near Romsey. Damn good food.'

'Excellent,' Nathan had responded hollowly, earning himself a puzzled stare from Melville. Now James was looking at him with dawning comprehension as he was introduced to one Ravenhurst after the other.

'Where's Miss Ravenhurst?' he asked, sidling up to Nathan when attention turned to removing the pond

weed from Street and Freddie and sending them back
to the house.

'Gone inside.'

'Don't blame her,' Melville remarked with feeling.
'I should imagine the last thing she wants is to see us
again, reminding her of the whole bloody nightmare.'

There was that, of course, Nathan pondered as they
walked back to the house. Was he simply being a
coxcomb, fancying that Clemence had a *tendre* for him
and was upset on that score, when more likely he was
simply the unpleasant reminder to her of terror and
danger? Whichever it was, he had no wish to cause her
pain. Somehow he had to stay as far from her for this
interminable fortnight as he could.

'Is the company complete, ma'am?' he asked Lady
Standon as they passed into the hall to be shown to
their rooms.

'Only one party to come—and here they are,' Jessica
said cheerfully as the footman threw open the doors to
admit a small, thin man with the air of having a quizzing
glass permanently poised and two plain young women.

'Polkington,' Nathan said. It needed only that—the
witness to the tragic and shocking last days of his
marriage on Corfu, the man with the sharpest nose for
gossip in Europe, here under the same roof as Clemence.
And also, if he could just drag his mind away from his
emotions and think about his career for a moment, in a
position to remind his distinguished superior officer of
the scandalous and illegal duel he had fought.

'You know each other?' Delighted at this seren-
dipitous circumstance Jessica was bringing him
forward as she greeted her guests. 'Mr Polkington! I
do trust the journey went well? Here is Captain

Stanier, whom I believe you know, just arrived also. Miss Polkington, Miss Jane…' She abandoned him for the two young women.

'Stanier.' They exchanged nods. Up came the quizzing glass. 'You are just back from the West Indies, I believe? My correspondents tell me of the most exciting occurrences taking place—pirates, scandals…'

'Your correspondents are most assiduous. I have scarcely got back myself. Pirates, I have to confess to, in plenty. But scandal?' he drawled, sounding bored. Surely, he could not have heard anything about Clemence?

'My dear man, do not alarm yourself. I have just had the most titillating letter from my second cousin in the Governor's staff, but where a lady is concerned my lips are sealed. Especially a lady with such illustrious relatives.' Polkington seemed to be hugging the delicious secret to himself. Nathan remembered his technique— nothing overt, never that, but hints and teasing and an air of mystery that could blow the slightest glance into a full-scale love affair or one angry word into a blood feud.

'You are wise,' Nathan remarked. 'I have never seen a more formidable collection of cousins. I would be most wary of giving offence to any lady in this household.'

Polkington pursed his lips and produced his high-pitched titter. 'Oh, yes, indeed. I believe you are not the only gentleman present given to duelling, Captain Stanier.'

'If looks could kill,' James Melville commented in Nathan's ear as he watched Polkington being ushered upstairs with his sisters, 'that man would be writhing on the floor at your feet. I never thought to see him here. An unpleasant reminder of Corfu.'

'He has got wind of some scandal in Jamaica. I have just pointed out to him the likely consequence of dis-

tressing any lady under the collective protection of the
Ravenhurst menfolk.'

'What? If you didn't run him through first?' His friend
jerked his head towards one of the panelled doors leading
off the hall. 'Standon has handed over the keys of the
library to Hoste. Tompion is setting it up as an office for
us. I would go and freshen up, he's expecting us down
here in half an hour—the man's a glutton for work.' He
grinned. 'Still, if it'll stop you getting into a fight…'

'I don't duel,' Nathan said harshly. 'Not any longer.'

'I was thinking of a clenched fist, myself,' Melville
countered. 'I can't see you waiting for a Ravenhurst to
happen along if Miss Clemence requires your protection.' He strode off and was through the study door
before Nathan could think of an answer. *Damn it*, he
thought, following the footman who was waiting patiently beside his luggage. *Am I that transparent?*

Chapter Twenty

Clemence managed to avoid Nathan for the entire evening. The reception rooms were numerous and interconnecting, so it was as simple matter, by keeping her wits about her, to slip from one to the other, to take refuge behind a bank of hot-house blooms or to dodge out of an open window on to the terrace and in through another, the moment one sighted a golden-brown head of hair or the blue cloth and gold braid of dress uniform.

She had discovered from Jessica why he was there, had to accept he had had no foreknowledge of it, nor could he have avoided it. It felt as though she was in a nightmare, wanting to go to him, forbidden to do so by every instinct of self-preservation. The rooms were crowded by evening guests come for dinner so she had to concentrate on making conversation with a string of strangers and near-strangers as well as keeping an eye out for Nathan.

She had found a secluded sofa and was catching her breath when a thin man she had been introduced to earlier appeared holding two glasses of wine. Pollington? No, Polkington. She made an effort, sat up straighter and smiled.

'Miss Ravenhurst. May I join you?'

'Of course. Thank you.' There was nowhere to put a wine glass, so it seemed churlish to refuse the one he pressed into her hand.

'And how are you finding our English weather after Jamaica?' he enquired.

'A little chilly, sir. I will soon become accustomed.'

'As will the gallant Captain Stanier.'

'And Captain Melville,' she added.

'Of course. You knew them both on the island?'

'A little.' Clemence shrugged negligently and took a sip of wine. 'I came back on Captain Melville's frigate, the *Orion.*'

'So I hear.' Somehow Mr Polkington gave the impression of hearing a great deal. 'So very fortunate that that dreadful business on Corfu did not break Captain Stanier. Such a loss to the service that would have been.'

Don't ask! 'Oh? What a charming gown your sister is wearing.'

'And a tragedy, too.' Mr Polkington sighed. 'Such a pretty young woman, the late Mrs Stanier.'

Clemence took a mouthful of wine and fought temptation. 'I believe so.' She could feel her will-power slipping away. 'I know nothing about it, of course.'

'No? Well, it was a whirlwind romance, of course. Lovely young woman—half-Greek, you know.'

'I didn't,' Clemence murmured.

'Black hair, flashing eyes, figure of Aphrodite. Such a mistake for young officers to marry, I always think. I said so to my friend the Governor at the time, but there—Stanier was swept off his feet, I do believe.'

'Indeed?'

'And such a lively girl, Julietta. No harm in her—I will never believe otherwise—but lively, you know, lively.'

'A flirt?' Clemence suggested, drawn in despite herself.

'That's it in a nutshell.' Polkington smiled benevolently, while his black eyes were fixed on her like a robin that had spotted a worm.

He is trying to provoke a reaction, she thought, schooling her expression to one of polite interest. *He has heard something about us.* 'Oh, Lady Maude is waving to me, will you excuse me, Mr Polkington?'

Lady Maude was nowhere to be seen, but her's had been the first name to come into Clemence's head. She hurried across the room and out into a antechamber, glancing back to make sure Polkington had stayed where he was.

'Ough!'

'Oh, I am so sorry, I wasn't looking— Nathan!'

'Clemence.' He glanced over her shoulder back into the main room. 'Have you been talking to Polkington?'

'He has been talking to me, rather. Odious, insinuating man.'

'He has a cousin in the Governor's household, it would appear. But he is too wary of the Ravenhursts to do more than poke and pry.'

It felt so temptingly good to be close to him again. Clemence allowed herself to be drawn into the anteroom and seated on a sofa. 'A glass of wine?'

'No, thank you. And he hardly mentioned Jamaica to me.' As soon as she said it his lips tightened and she could have kicked herself for her lack of tact.

'So, he was gossiping about me instead?'

This was not how she had imagined being with Nathan again. 'Yes.'

'About Corfu?'

'Yes.'

'Then I had better tell you the truth.'

'It is none of my business,' Clemence interjected.

'No?' Just what did he mean by that cool monosyllable? 'I will tell you anyway. I prefer my friends to know the facts, not to listen to Polkington's gossip. What has he said?'

'That your wife's name was Julietta, that she was half-Greek and very lovely and, er…lively.'

'That is all true, at least.' Nathan leaned back, his long legs crossed, his arm casually along the back of the sofa as they sat turned to face each other. To an onlooker he must seem entirely relaxed, but Clemence knew him too well to be deceived. There was a tautness about his jaw and the smile on his lips did not reach his eyes.

'I thought I was in love with her—so did half the gentlemen on the island. Her father was a prosperous local merchant married to an Englishwoman of some style and education. I proposed one heady, moonlit evening and she accepted me. Her father—no fool—encouraged a rapid wedding and there we were, two virtual strangers learning to live together.'

'And she was not as you had thought?' Clemence asked carefully. She had thought that hearing about his lost love would hurt her, but instead all she felt was sorrow for the newlyweds, so evidently heading for disaster.

'Neither of us was what the other had expected. She thought she was getting a doting, fun-loving and indulgent husband. I thought I was gaining domestic bliss and set about reforming myself—doubtless into a stolid prig. She carried on flirting, perfectly harmlessly, I can see now. I became the heavy husband, forbidding her to enjoy herself, in effect. One night she slipped away to a party I had said we were not going to attend. When I arrived, fuming, she was on the balcony with my friend Lieutenant Fellowes.'

'Oh, Lord.' Clemence realised she had extended a hand to his and drew it back sharply. 'What were they doing?'

'Nothing so very bad. He had plucked a flower and was fixing it at the bosom of her dress which, Julietta being Julietta, was held up more by will-power than by anything else. I hit Adrian, he accused me of slandering my own wife—and the next thing we knew we were facing each other at dawn in a field with a pair of pistols.' Nathan's eyes were unfocused as though he were looking back down the years.

'You didn't kill him, though? You told me you hadn't?'

'I had told you I had duelled? I had forgotten that. I obviously told young Clem altogether too much.' He smiled at her, back from the past, and something warm and vulnerable uncurled inside her and dared to hope for a second. 'I just caught him on the shoulder, a flesh wound—which you may choose to believe, or not, is what I intended. He missed me. And then we looked at each other and realised what a pair of bloody fools we both were and shook hands and went and had breakfast by way of the doctor's house.'

'Thank goodness,' Clemence murmured. 'But wasn't duelling forbidden?'

'Of course. But Adrian insisted to anyone who would listen that it had all been an accident while we were having a shooting competition to try out his new pistols. The authorities might have taken a harder line—no one really believed a word of it—but by then Julietta was dead.'

He made to get to his feet as if suddenly he could not manage to tell this story any longer. Clemence reached out again and this time curled her fingers into his hand. 'No, Nathan, please tell me the rest.' He sat back again.

'She knew about the duel, of course. Whether she thought I would be killed or whether she feared my anger if I survived, I have no idea. I was not very understanding when I left her that morning. But she rode, by herself, to her father's estate in the countryside and on the way there was an accident of some kind. They found her in the road, the horse by her side. Her neck was broken.'

'*Oh, no,*' Clemence breathed. 'You loved her and you had not even had the chance to say goodbye to her. And to face that in the midst of the scandal after the duel.' She bit down on her lip to steady the quiver in her voice. 'It must have been hell.'

Her hand was still in his. He sat looking down at it for a while in silence, playing with the seams of her glove. 'No, I didn't love her, I realised that too late. That was almost the worst thing of all, the knowledge that if I had had more sense, more self-control, I would never have got us into that situation. I should have waited, seen it was just infatuation, and she would have been safe.'

'How old were you?' she asked abruptly, startling him into looking up at her.

'Twenty-three. She was nineteen.'

'And you blame yourself, with the wisdom of your current age and experience, for the folly of a young man? I am nineteen, like she was—no, I quite forgot it, but I have had a birthday, I am twenty.' Fancy forgetting a birthday! But she had other things on her mind at the time… 'Women mature more quickly than men in matters of the emotions. She should have known she was not in love with you, too.'

'You think you can tell?' His blue eyes were hard and bitter.

'Oh, yes,' Clemence said, releasing his hand and getting to her feet in a swirl of skirts. 'I know perfectly well when I am in love with a man.' Where the courage to utter the words had come from, she had no idea. They stared at each other as he got slowly to his feet. 'It was a tragedy. I am so sorry it seems to have convinced you that it would be folly to risk your heart again.'

'There you are, Miss Ravenhurst. I am to take you in to dinner.' Captain Melville looked from one face to the other. 'Have I interrupted something?'

'Merely Miss Ravenhurst chiding me for taking lessons from past history,' Nathan said. He seemed rather white, but perhaps it was simply her own perceptions that were awry. She was certainly feeling somewhat light-headed.

'Learning from history? Why, that is an excellent precept, I would have thought, Miss Ravenhurst.'

'It is,' Clemence agreed, laying her hand on his proffered forearm. 'Provided one is certain that the circumstances are exactly the same in both cases.'

How she was going to eat anything with her heart apparently lodged in her throat, she had no idea, she thought, smiling at the gentleman on her left-hand side as Captain Melville seated her. What had come over her? She had as good as told Nathan that she loved him. It must have been the selfish relief of discovering that he did not love his wife, and never had.

Her neighbour was addressing her. Clemence struggled to recall his name. Mr…Wallingford, that was it. The lawyer that Cousin Sebastian had summoned from London to help deal with the Naismiths. They were to have a meeting tomorrow, Sebastian had informed her.

'Yes, I am finding it rather cool in England,' she agreed. It was the standard first question from everyone she met. She could easily manage such a predictable exchange with her mind on something else, and now it was working furiously on the conundrum of Nathan.

He felt something for her, she was certain, although he was most certainly hiding it well. And that was doubtless because of her relatives and her money. There was nothing she could do about disowning the connection with the Ravenhursts, Clemence thought, nor would she want to. She looked up and down the long table and felt the glow of knowing that these people were her blood kin and had accepted her with warmth and uncritical affection.

But she could do something about her money. She slid a sidelong glance at the lawyer—he looked like a man of intelligence and cunning. Just what she needed if she was going to take a huge risk with her future.

What the hell was that about? Nathan tried to watch Clemence while maintaining a flow of polite chit-chat with the lady on his right whose name he had already completely forgotten.

Was he going mad, or had Clemence just as good as told him she was in love with him? What else could she have meant? He spooned soup, laughed at some feeble *on-dit* and took too deep a swallow of wine while he wrestled with the mystery of Clemence's feelings.

He had been so sure that all she had felt for him was

a mild *tendre*, the natural result of having been forced to rely on him for her life and of having been propelled into quite shocking intimacy with him. That they were physically attracted, there could be no doubt, but physical attraction, as he knew only too well, was not the same as love.

She was too young to know her own mind, to understand her emotions; he had believed that—and she had just thrown the notion back in his face. Could it simply be pique because he had refused to marry her and had told her aunt he was not in love with her? No. Not Clemence. She didn't sulk, she wasn't petty and she would not play games like that with him.

The footmen came forward to clear the soup bowls. Nathan sat back in his chair, looked down the table again and caught her gaze, clear and green and open. He swallowed, hard, against the lump in his throat and realised, shocked, that his eyes were moist. She loved him. *She loved him.*

And then he saw Lord Sebastian Ravenhurst, his hooded eyes resting on his cousin's face, and the lump turned to lead. She could love him until the stars fell, but that did not make him any more suitable a husband for the wealthy Miss Ravenhurst, with the whole of society spread out at the toes of her pretty new slippers for her to explore. They might love, and she might deem the world well lost for it, but it was his duty to do the right thing.

'Mr Theo Ravenhurst thinks we might dance after dinner,' the plain brunette on his left remarked. 'Do you dance, Captain Stanier?'

'With reluctance, Miss Polkington.' She pouted. 'Not from lack of admiration of my partners,' he added hastily. 'More to spare them from having their toes crushed.' She giggled and began to chatter about past balls and parties. Nathan ate his duck and contemplated an evening torturing himself by watching Clemence dance.

He could imagine her feet in those bronze kid slippers twinkling beneath the modish quilted hem of her skirt. Perhaps there would be a flash of silk-stockinged ankle. Her shoulders would gleam even more in the candlelight as her skin warmed with the exertion and her small breasts would rise and fall with her breathing.

And he would be in severe need of a cold plunge in the lake in a minute if he didn't control his imagination. Nathan spread his napkin strategically across his lap and attempted to recall the unerotic image of Clem's grubby bare feet protruding from the bottom of flapping canvas trousers. It did not help.

But at least inconvenient arousal, however uncomfortable, did not threaten the pain of unrequited love. He had known he had to accept it for himself, but to believe that might Clemence feel the same way was agony.

By the end of the meal Nathan was convinced he would rather be boarding a heavily defended pirate ship than facing an evening of dancing.

'Do you think Hoste is going to want to work on?' he asked Melville.

'You sound as if you wish he will!' His friend nodded towards the group of guests clustered around Lady Standon. There was his senior officer, joining in with the persuasion to have the long drawing-room carpet rolled up. 'I'm looking forward to an impromptu hop.'

'I'm going to have a strategic sprain,' Nathan said

dourly, making his way to the side of the room and favouring his right foot.

'You have hurt your ankle, Captain?' It was the curate, bright-eyed with sympathy, his hands full of sheet music.

'An old weakness.'

'Could you turn the music for me if you are not to dance?' Taking silence for consent, the other man led the way to the piano. 'I do not dance myself, you understand, but rational exercise in a respectable setting such as this is most acceptable, I feel.'

He prosed on, leaving Nathan stranded by the side of the piano, attempting to ignore Melville's unsympathetic grin. Lady Standon came over.

'Mr Danvers, so good of you to play. I am going to teach the company a new round dance and what we need is a nice strong rhythm—ah, yes, this will do nicely. Strongly marked, mind! But I will walk them through it without music first.'

Lady Standon clapped her hands. 'Please, take a partner and form a big circle, facing in. I am going to teach you *La Pistole*, it is new from France.'

Nathan watched, half an ear on the instructions, while the couples turned to face each other, walked back and then together, linked hands and circled... Clemence was smiling up at Eden Ravenhurst, her theatre-manager cousin, one of the less reputable Ravenhursts. How lovely she looked with him, his height balancing hers, her unconventional looks, piquant in contrast to his conventional handsomeness.

They were all making some gesture with their hands that made her frown, fleetingly, then circling again and beginning again with the partner behind them.

'Ingenious,' Mr Danvers remarked. 'Very simple and they are constantly changing partners. Most amusing.' At Lady Standon's gesture he struck up the music and the couples began their measure.

Clemence had still not regained her smile. Back and forth, join hands and circle, back again. What was there to frown about? Then everyone raised their right hands like children playing at shooting, aimed at their partners and stamped their feet hard. *Bang!* Around the circle, dancers were laughing, clutching their hands to their breasts and circling to face their new partner to start again.

She was no longer in profile, now he could see her full face and she had gone pale. Lord Hoste raised his hand, aimed—*bang!* Clemence broke out of the circle and ran.

Nathan took a dozen long strides to where the commodore was turning to follow her. No one else seemed to see anything amiss. 'Leave her to me, sir,' he snapped and was past and out of the room before the older man could respond.

Clemence had not gone far, only through the small salon and out on to the terrace where she was standing quite still, her back to him. She had her arms crossed tightly and was clasping her elbows as though to hold herself together. Her shoulders were quivering. She did not move as the heels of his shoes struck on the stone flags.

'Sweetheart?' He pulled her against his chest, and she came as rigid as a board, her arms still tightly locked. 'What is it? I'm here.'

'You weren't,' she said, her voice choked. 'You weren't there.'

'You wanted me to dance with you?' This seemed a violent reaction for such a cause and not at all like her.

'No! You weren't there when he was going to shoot

me. I was going to die and then Street shot him in the face and he died instead and I saw—' Her voice choked off into silence.

Appalled, Nathan gathered her tightly into his embrace and held on. She didn't seem to be weeping. After a moment he ventured, 'When?'

'Just before the mast came down.' She gave a little shudder and he felt her shoulders relax. 'I dream about it, you see,' Clemence said into his shirt front. 'Not before, but ever since you left me here. I don't dream about anything else, just that. I think it's because you were there for everything else.'

Nathan rubbed his cheek against the soft curls on her crown. *He hadn't been there.* And now Clemence, his brave Clemence, who had fought McTiernan, climbed from her balcony to freedom, defied her scheming, evil family, was reduced to running away from a romping dance with friends in the safety of the English countryside.

'I'm so sorry,' he murmured. 'So sorry.'

'No.' She shook her head, the curls moving back and forth on the starched folds of his neckcloth. 'You gave me Street. He shot the man and then you came for me. It is my fault I am so foolish.'

'Oh, no, not foolish, sweetheart.' He rocked her against the warmth of her body. 'Just tried beyond your strength.'

She had needed him. His absence gave her nightmares. She had looked him in the eye and told him, with some emphasis, that she knew when she was in love with a man. But she had never been in love or formed an attachment, she had told him that, too. His head was spinning.

'Clemence.' He tipped up her face. She had stopped shuddering and her eyes were dry. 'Clemence…' He wanted to say it—the temptation to say those three words and see the reflection of her feelings in her eyes was almost overwhelming. 'Clemence.' Somehow he managed to clench his teeth and be silent. It was harder than it had been to walk with composure to be flogged, to stand here, silent, when the woman he loved was in his arms, waiting.

And then she smiled faintly and lifted her hand to his cheek, running the back of it down and along his jaw. 'It's all right,' she murmured. 'It will be all right.'

How could it be? He frowned down at her, not at all comforted by the sadness in her candid eyes or the calm resignation in her voice.

'Ahem.' They both turned. Lord Hoste was standing, a cloak over his arm, regarding them somewhat quizzically from the window. 'You aunt feared you may be finding the night air chill, Miss Ravenhurst.' He held out the cloak and she went out of Nathan's arms towards him.

'Thank you, my lord.' Clemence allowed him to drape it around her shoulders and then, without a backward glance, stepped over the low sill and was gone.

'Snuff?' Lord Hoste produced an enamel box and flicked it open with his thumbnail. 'I think this might be an opportune time for a quiet talk, Stanier.'

Chapter Twenty-One

'That young man is in love with you,' the duchess remarked, taking a sip of chocolate.

They were seated in the first-floor bow-window embrasure of the duchess's apartment, having breakfast tête à tête and somewhat later than the rest of the guests. Clemence was heavy-eyed after a troubled night's sleep. The nightmare had not come, but her dreams had seemed full of Nathan. 'He is?' she managed, wincing at the inadequacy of the response.

Her aunt regarded her severely over the rim of the cup. 'Do not be coy with me, Clemence.'

'I *think* he is. But he doesn't think he is good enough for me.'

'You could do better,' the duchess remarked dispassionately. In a shaft of morning sunlight the three naval officers, Tompion the secretary on their heels, paced back and forth along the Rose Garden terrace, hands behind backs, as though on the poop deck.

'Only in worldly ways,' Clemence retorted, then subsided at her aunt's smile.

'Indeed. Don't you want a title?' Clemence shook her head. 'Or a great deal of money?'

'I have quite a lot of money, that's the problem—or a big part of it. He doesn't wish to figure as a fortune hunter. I had an idea about that.' The duchess's eyebrows rose. 'I don't intend giving it away, or gambling it or anything foolish. I am going to speak to Mr Wallingford the lawyer this morning, with Cousin Sebastian. They will advise me.' The energy that speaking about her idea had produced ebbed away again. She shrugged. 'At least I can guard against fortune hunters in the future.' Her eyes followed the three men who had come to an abrupt halt. Captain Melville was shaking Nathan by the hand. 'I wonder what that is about.'

'Doubtless Captain Stanier has had a brilliant idea for dealing with the pirates. He will be back at sea soon, no doubt.'

'No doubt,' Clemence agreed, biting her lip. 'Aunt Amelia. You very kindly invited me for the Season, and I expect it is going to take some months to work matters out and deal with my uncle. But in the spring, I would like to go back to Jamaica.'

'Alone?' The duchess's fine brows rose.

'I will find a companion. I am going to run the business.' She wiped her fingers on her napkin, surprised at how comforting that declaration felt, now she had made it. 'I am enjoying England and London will be a great treat,' she added, politely. 'But Jamaica is my home.' If she had to nurse a broken heart, home was a far better place to do it than a chilly foreign land.

'I see. You believe that despite your scheme for removing your wealth as an obstacle, you will not secure an offer from your gallant captain?'

'No, not now. There was a moment last night—if he had been going to speak, then surely it would have been then. It seemed I tempted fate to believe that somehow it would all come right.' Clemence shrugged again, struggling against gloom again. 'I only really believe it at three in the morning.'

'Compromising yourself will not help,' the duchess mused, earning a startled glance from Clemence. 'There is nothing worse you can do that has not already happened.' Clemence felt herself go scarlet and opened her mouth in protest. 'Well, you know what I mean! Proposing to the man will only have him reiterating all those noble sentiments. You will just have to shock him. I don't suppose Street could turn pirate again and kidnap you for ransom?'

'He wouldn't dare.' Clemence smiled at the thought. 'Eliza would give him the rough edge of her tongue. Oh, look, there they go now, walking the dog.'

'That is one expression for it,' her aunt remarked tartly as the three figures vanished into the deep shade of the shrubbery.

'They will get married soon,' Clemence assured her, making a mental note to speak to Street, very firmly, on the subject.

'So I should hope. Now then, do you intend telling me what sent you flying from the drawing room last night?'

'I do not know whether you would wish to hear, Aunt Amelia. It is something that happened on board the pirate ship. Something very…unpleasant.'

'I have nerves of steel,' the duchess said, pouring herself another cup of chocolate. 'Come along.'

'Very well.' Perhaps talking about it would help chase the nightmare away. 'I told you that Nathan had managed to send the *Sea Scorpion* after the decoy ship and when they came alongside there was a battle with men boarding and hand-to-hand fighting? Nathan had sent me below to free the merchant sailors locked in the hold and when I came up again he was fighting. I found myself with Street. A sailor came in with a pistol, he raised it and aimed it at my head.'

'Oh, my goodness, the dance!'

'Yes. It went off and for a moment I thought I was dead, but he missed me and Street shot him. In the face.'

'Right in front of you,' the duchess said faintly. 'I can imagine what that must have been like, coming on top of fearing that you were about to die yourself. But that fat rascal saved your life.'

'Yes, ma'am. Then, when Nathan left me here, I started to dream about it. Horrible nightmares. Poor Eliza tries to wake me, but she finds it hard.'

'You know, deep in your mind, that you are safe when he is near? Yes, I can see the logic in that, although it never occurred to me that nightmares might have a basis in logic.' She tossed her napkin on to the table, her face sombre. 'Leave speaking to Street about your maid to me. It is not something that an unmarried girl should have to deal with.'

A footman came in. 'Lord Sebastian's compliments, Miss Ravenhurst, and he and Mr Wallingford will await your convenience in the library at ten.'

'Thank you.' Clemence stood up and squared her shoulders. Time to think about those hideous months after her father had died. Time to set the wheels of justice in motion. That at least she could achieve.

Two hours later Sebastian was looking grimly satisfied and Clemence felt drained. Mr Wallingford, who must, she thought wearily, be the human equivalent of a terrier crossed with a mole, tapped his piles of notes into a neat stack and beamed. He had burrowed after every detail and, having found it, dragged it out for inspection and shook it vigorously to see if anything else fell out. He appeared to find the process extremely stimulating.

'Oh, very nice. We have him, we have him. He won't be able to wiggle out of this.'

'But he says he can forge my signature,' Clemence fretted.

'Nothing a smart young lawyer can't deal with— and I have just the man in my offices. He'll have the help of the naval representative out there, I understand—and the Governor will be receiving a communication from the highest level, informing him that he is to throw Naismith to the wolves. In the form—' he smirked '—of my Mr Gorridge.'

'He'll most certainly have that,' Sebastian confirmed. He got up and poured three glasses of madeira, surprising Clemence by handing her one. 'You need it. Now. This scheme of yours about your money—are you certain? You cannot undo it.'

'I know.' Clemence sipped her wine. 'I expect to go back to Jamaica as soon as this is settled and to run the business. I do not wish to attract fortune hunters. This idea is for my own protection as much as anything.'

'You do not expect to marry here in England?' Sebastian asked, his dark gaze resting thoughtfully on her face. 'I thought perhaps that this was to facilitate—'

'No. I do not expect it.' There had been the faint recollection of her dream, like a wisp of smoke when she awoke. A dream of the pool in the forest, of her being in Nathan's arms and gold rings glinting through the water. The ghost of the dream had lingered all morning. Now it faded and left her. There was nothing like the down-to-earth realism of a lawyer to snuff out foolish fantasy and as they had talked she had let go of it as though she had felt Nathan's hand slip from hers.

Nathan had had every opportunity to tell her he loved her last night on the terrace, she told herself, and he had not. Now she felt certain that he never would. She hated his honour for keeping them apart. She admired him for possessing it. With it, they could never be together— without it, he would not be the man she loved.

Clemence saw virtually nothing of Nathan all day. Either the weather was warmer than it had been, or she was becoming used to the English climate, Clemence thought, as Jessica made the unusual suggestion of an alfresco dinner.

Rugs were spread on the grass below the terrace, tables and chairs brought out and dotted about and Cook and her minions began to set long tables as a buffet.

Lady Maude appointed herself chief floral arranger and bore Clemence off, armed with baskets and small shears to raid the long borders. 'Are you going to marry Captain Stanier?' she enquired, handing Clemence some foliage sprays.

'I— No.' Clemence was taken aback by the frontal attack. 'Why would you imagine I should?'

Maude chuckled. 'I am not very long married. I see the way he looks at you and the way you look at him and the way you both carefully don't look at the same time.'

'Oh.' Clemence looked warily at Maude as she sat down in an arbour and patted the seat next to her.

'And?'

'I love him. I think he may—does—love me. But…'

'You're a Ravenhurst. Probably a rich one. He is *just* a career naval officer.' Maude threw up her hands. 'Men and their honour! Eden is illegitimate. Did you know that?'

'I gathered,' Clemence said carefully.

'As much pride as a porcupine has prickles, that man. I had to take drastic action in the end and tell him if he couldn't see the difference between pride and honour then I didn't want to marry him anyway.'

'Goodness.'

'I threw him out of my bedroom—' She saw Clemence's dropped jaw and grinned. 'I was ill in bed, he was pacing the corridor outside,' she explained.

'Well, I thought I had an idea to deal with the money, but I still can't see how I am going to attack that conviction he has that I am destined for better things just because I am a Ravenhurst. I hoped, just for a few moments, last night. But he did not speak.'

'Hmm. Well, I have to say, that your Captain Stanier may not be a Ravenhurst, but he is certainly worth fighting for.'

'If I can only find weapons it is fair to fight with,' Clemence murmured, half to herself.

'You will, and the Ravenhursts will help, you'll see. Now, let's get these flowers back.'

Clemence surprised herself by enjoying the meal. Her cousin Elinor, a redoubtable bluestocking, kept her laughing with tall tales of the adventures that had marked her courtship with Theo Ravenhurst. 'You should write sensation novels for the Minerva Press,' Clemence said after a lurid description of being chained up in a rat-infested dungeon with Theo and a jug of poison for company.

'Every word of it is true.' Theo came back with a platter of fruit and lowered himself onto the rug between the two women. 'Word of a Ravenhurst. I had a dull and blameless life until I fell in with this woman.'

'Liar.' It was Sebastian, Nathan at his side. Clemence felt her colour rising and made rather a business of making room on the rug. 'Theo, you should know, Cousin Clemence, is the scapegrace of the family. We are deeply grateful to Elinor for his reform.'

'I may have reformed him,' Elinor said with a twinkle, 'but he has absolutely corrupted me as far as spending money on clothes is concerned. I used to be completely unconcerned about gowns,' she explained to Clemence. 'If a sack had been decent covering, I would have been satisfied with that. But now! I am so looking forward to shopping with you in town.'

'You may be disappointed,' Sebastian observed, peeling an apple. 'Clemence is intending to return to Jamaica after the Season.'

'What?' Nathan, who had been lounging almost out of her sight behind Sebastian, sat up with a jerk. 'Going back to Jamaica?'

'Yes. I intend to run the business.' For some reason her lips felt stiff.

'Oh, well done!' Elinor clapped her hands. 'How enterprising of you. But what if you become betrothed during the Season?'

'I have no expectation of doing so,' Clemence made herself say. 'Nor any desire, either.'

'I used to think that,' Elinor said comfortably. 'I was quite resigned to my studies and being a support to

Mama with hers. And then along came Theo—and here we are.' She smiled, no doubt intending to be encouraging. 'You wait and see. I am sure there is someone just right for you.'

'Possibly Miss Ravenhurst believes she has already met that person and they are unsuitable,' Nathan suggested. He passed the plate with the apple Sebastian had peeled and sliced to the ladies, his hand quite steady.

'How perceptive of you, Captain Stanier,' Clemence said, taking a piece of fruit and biting into it. 'I have and, although I think him perfectly suitable, the gentleman in question has scruples that it appears he is unwilling to overcome.'

'Then he does not love you enough, I fear,' said Theo sympathetically.

'It may be that, of course,' Clemence agreed, selecting another slice. 'I tell myself I would be better off forgetting him, but I have no idea how one goes about that.'

'Painfully,' Nathan said, getting to his feet and walking away.

'Oh!' Elinor put down her glass and stared after him. 'It's him? I am so sorry, I had no idea. I am quite ready to sink, of all the tactless…'

'That's both of us,' Theo said, scrubbing his hand back through his hair. 'Sorry.'

'It's all right,' Clemence said with a sigh. 'Actually, it is quite a relief to talk about it.'

'Er—Sebastian and I will go,' Theo said, beginning to rise.

'No, please, if it doesn't embarrass you. I would rather like a masculine point of view.' Theo subsided. 'Nathan was going to marry me, because I had been compromised. That was before he realised he loved me,

I think. But when he found out who I was, and realised that the family was more than sufficient to protect me from scandal, he withdrew.'

'Why?' Elinor wrapped her arms round her bent knees, propped her chin on top and regarded Clemence earnestly, as though she was one of her Greek inscriptions.

'The scandal in Minorca when his wife died and he fought a duel,' Clemence explained. 'Then, my money—he has only what he earns as a captain.'

'How much is that?' Theo asked. He rolled over on to his stomach and propped his chin in his hands.

'About £450 a year,' Clemence said. Theo winced. 'I asked Captain Melville. Then there's prize money—which could be about the same, could be thousands—but that is complete chance. And, on top of the duel and the money, he thinks I should be looking for an earl or something and marrying *properly*, as befits a Ravenhurst. He thinks that the world is my oyster and that if he married me, it would be wrong.'

'Idiot.' Elinor.

'Very proper sentiments.' Sebastian.

'Both those,' Theo observed. 'The family is all right though, isn't it, Seb?'

'Oh, yes.' Her cousin nodded. 'I have had Captain Stanier investigated from his bank account to the contents of his handkerchief drawer.'

'You've what?' Clemence glared.

'You're a Ravenhurst.' Theo grinned. 'No one breathes on you without Sebastian knowing.'

'Pity I didn't think to extend that to Jamaica when your father died,' Sebastian remarked. 'You were compromised, no getting around that. Do you want me to become the head of the family in Charles's absence and demand that he does the decent thing?'

The thought of Sebastian, or his half-brother the duke, demanding that Nathan marry her, made her blood run cold. 'No! Please, don't do that. Nathan *is* doing the decent thing, according to his conscience.'

'I am baffled,' Elinor admitted. 'I don't suppose Eva could create him Admiral of the Maubourg fleet, could she?'

'Maubourg, you idiot,' her loving husband reminded her, 'has no coast, no navy and a lake with rowing boats.'

'Drat.'

'Who is an idiot?' It was Eva, languidly graceful as ever. She sank down on to the rug and smiled at her family. 'Theo?' Her cousin grinned, balled up a napkin and threw it at her.

Clemence couldn't help smiling. They were all so happy, all so convinced that love would find a way because, for them, it had. She unfurled the old French fan Nathan had given her and looked at the fat little Cupids flying around delivering their prizes of love to the waiting girls. Far from being Clémence with her paragon of a lover, it seemed she was Isis, the one whose lot was to have no lover at all. *Adieu toute espérance*, she read. Farewell all hope.

'Miss Clemence?' Eliza folded her silk shawl away in tissue and turned, biting her lower lip.

'Yes?' It wasn't like Eliza to be so hesitant.

'We were wondering—Fred and me—if we could have a talk with you.'

'Now? At this hour?' The house party had lingered long into the evening on the lawn, the servants lighting citronella candles to keep the insects at bay, and now she was tired.

'Her Grace had a word.' Eliza shifted her feet. 'Its made him a bit edgy, if you see what I mean.'

'Not really, but I suppose I can talk to him now. Is he waiting in the sitting room?'

The single ladies had a room close to their chambers. Sighing for the peace and solitude of her bed, Clemence followed the maid along the corridor. Street was standing in the middle of the boudoir, eyeing the spindly chairs nervously. One-Eye, who knew perfectly well he was not allowed upstairs, was attempting to hide behind a footstool.

'Bad dog,' Clemence said automatically and he wriggled over on his belly, tongue lolling. 'Well, Street?'

'Her Grace said I ought to be making an honest woman of Eliza and I suppose I ought,' he admitted, shuffling his feet.

'What does Eliza think about it?'

'I'll take him,' the maid said grudgingly. Clemence looked from one to the other. The expressions on their faces said it all—the reluctant words meant nothing.

'That's all very well,' she said briskly, sitting down. 'But how are you going to support her?'

'I mean to open an inn,' the big man said. 'A proper country one on a post road with food they'll remember and good ale.'

'That sounds a good plan,' Clemence agreed. But Street was off in a world of his own. 'I'm sure you and Eliza will be very happy.'

'I used to dream about that, you know,' he confided. 'I'd stand there in my galley, stirring the pots and I'd think, *What you wants, Fred Street, is a cosy inn with a big fire in the winter.* Seems a miracle that you were in that very same galley, Miss Clemence. And I thought you was just a scruffy lad! Do you remember that galley?'

'Yes, of course—'

'Wasn't much, but it was mine. In good order, I kept it, didn't I?'

'Yes, well, I'll—'

'All gone now, down to Davy Jones's locker.' He sighed gustily. 'I'll never forget it, that last day. I'll wager you won't, either, Miss Clemence.'

'No, and—'

'I told Eliza, I did, how you almost got killed. He was a mean-looking devil, that sailor with the pistol. I thought you was a goner, Miss Clemence, I did really. He was pointing that thing at you, and I couldn't get to my gun in time.'

Under her hand, One-Eye gave a startled *yip* and Clemence forced her fingers open.

'Miracle he missed you, miracle. And then I shot him. Nasty mess that, extraordinary what a bullet in the head—'

'Fred! That's enough.'

Clemence blinked; Eliza was shaking her elbow. 'Are you all right, Miss Clemence? Fred shouldn't have talked about that, how you almost got killed. It'll bring it all back, that will.'

'We will discuss this in the morning. But I wish you both to be very happy.' Swallowing, Clemence made her way back to her room. The floor seemed to be pitching like the deck of the ship under her feet. Behind her she heard Eliza berating One-Eye.

'Leave him, he can stay with me.' The thought of company felt good. She did not want to ask Eliza to sleep in her room; she strongly suspected she wanted to creep off and join Street in whichever attic fastness he had been allocated. Now all she had to do was to manage to forget the images Street had conjured up, not think about Nathan at all and she might have a good night's sleep. Pigs, Clemence concluded with resignation, might fly.

Chapter Twenty-Two

The urgent knocking on his door had Nathan out of bed and reaching for his sword before he opened his eyes. Then he realised where he was, dragged on the silk dressing gown that was thrown over the foot of the bed and opened the door.

'Street? What the hell are you doing here? What's the time?'

'Two, Cap'n.' The big man, incongruous in flowing nightshirt and bare feet, stood clutching a chamber stick. 'Eliza said to get you, it's Miss Clemence, sir.'

'Tell me,' Nathan snapped, his stomach sinking in a sudden swoop of fear.

'It's a nightmare, Eliza says. She can usually wake her up, but this time she can't and she's frightened.'

Nathan began to stride down the corridor. 'Send Eliza to wake the duchess.'

'She says it is you she needs, Cap'n. Miss Clemence is calling for you something pitiful.'

The room, when he reached it, was lit by four branches of candles. Eliza was leaning over the bed, shaking Clemence, who was tossing and turning, her face flushed and feverish, her hair damp. The bedclothes had been thrown back by her thrashing limbs and her nightgown was twisted around her knees. The old hound was standing on the other side, whining anxiously.

'Nathan? Please, where's Nathan?' Clemence was muttering, her voice hoarse.

'Oh, thank God, sir. She can't call out any more, her poor throat.' Eliza straightened up and as she released her hold on Clemence's shoulders, she began to toss and turn.

'Clemence?' Eliza stepped aside and he took her place. 'Clemence? Hush, I'm here now.' She seized his hand, her eyes still tight shut. Behind him the door clicked. Nathan glanced back—Street and Eliza had gone. Puzzled, but too worried about Clemence to pursue it, he got on to the bed, gathered her into his arms and began to rock her gently, talking all the time.

'I'm here, it's Nathan, you're in England, in bed. One-Eye's here, too, you're safe, no one will hurt you. I'm holding you. My love, I've got you safe.' The painful pleasure of saying it—*my love*—hit him in the gut and he tightened his hold. 'Clemence, my love, wake up, sweetheart, wake up.'

Nothing mattered now, not his honour, not his scruples, nothing, so long as she woke and felt safe. He slid down the bed, pulling her against the length of him, drowning in the scent and feel of her. 'Shh, Clemence. I'm here, I love you, you're safe.'

I love you. Nathan's voice penetrated the smoke and the screams and the noise and suddenly they had vanished and the light against her screwed-up eyelids was different and she was being held tightly against what felt and smelled wonderfully like Nathan's body.

'Nathan?'

'Open your eyes.'

Obedient, she did so and found she was in bed and that Nathan's head was on the pillow beside her, turned so he could look into her eyes.

'There, you are safe back. It was a nightmare, Clemence. Not real.' He was stroking her hair, smiling at her.

'Have I been ill?' She felt weak, as though in the aftermath of a fever. 'My throat hurts.'

'It was a very bad dream. Eliza could not wake you. You had shouted until your voice cracked and thrashed around until you were almost exhausted. Here, can you sit up?'

He helped her until she could sit up next to him, their backs propped against pillows, then held out a glass. 'This smells like barley water, it was on the nightstand. Try to drink.'

She sipped and her spinning head settled and the nightmare evaporated and all that was left was the man next to her on the big bed, smiling at her, his eyes anxious.

'When I woke up, you were saying—'

'I was saying I loved you. I thought I should not tell you, but I find I am too selfish not to let you know how I feel, even if it changes nothing. I should not be here, not now you are awake. I'll ask Eliza to call the duchess.' He began to turn, to get up.

'No!' She fastened her fingers on his wrist. 'Things have changed, everything has changed.'

'Not really.' But he lay back against the pillows, his shoulder carefully not touching hers.

'We know how we feel about each other,' she said.

'Shh! Let me finish. I know you are not in love with Julietta, perhaps never were. You know I am going back to Jamaica and have no intention of settling in England, finding a husband here.'

'It seems I misjudged you. You know your own mind after all if you really mean that,' he said, his fingers toying with the fringed sash of his dressing gown. 'Then you will go back to Jamaica to your inheritance, a wealthy woman.'

'I will go back to an income of one thousand pounds a year, for life,' Clemence said concisely. Her head was clear now. She had one chance—by a miracle that dreadful nightmare had given her this opportunity.

'One thousand? Surely your uncle cannot have squandered your inheritance? The lawyers will get it back for you.'

'They will get it back and they will invest it in the trust fund Mr Wallingford has set up for me. There will be money to invest in the business, maintain the properties, make sure all the staff are kept on. I will have my allowance.'

'And the rest?' Nathan's blue eyes were dark under frowning brows.

'In trust for my children, should I have any, and some lucky young Ravenhurst cousins if I do not. It had become apparent to me,' Clemence continued as Nathan appeared to be struck dumb, 'that my money might be putting off honest men and could attract fortune hunters.'

'Why one thousand pounds?' he asked. There was, surely, a faint relaxing of that frown?

'I asked Captain Melville how much a captain in the navy might hope to be paid and then I doubled it because

I thought, from what he said, that even the most indolent or unlucky might expect that much prize money in a year.'

'A captain in the navy,' he echoed. The frown had gone. The corners of his eyes were beginning to crinkle.

'Such as yourself.' A tiny, warm flame of hope was beginning to fan itself into flickering life inside her.

'Oh, dear. I am afraid, my clever Clemence, that you have miscalculated.' The flame went out with a sizzle. 'You will keep this confidential at the moment, but I will return to sea as a vice-commodore.'

'A promotion? To vice-commodore? Nathan!' And somehow she was in his arms, her own tight around his neck, and they were no longer sitting up, but were full length on the bed. 'That is wonderful!'

'I am moderately pleased,' he agreed with a grin.

'You can support a wife possessing moderate means herself, in that case?'

'Is that a proposal, Miss Ravenhurst?'

'It most certainly is, Vice-Commodore Stanier.'

He rolled on to his back, taking her with him to lie cradled against his shoulder. 'I had become so used to the idea that I could not, must not, wed you that it seems almost impossible. I am not sure I believe it now. Clemence, you are *certain* you do not want the life the Ravenhursts can give you here?'

'Certain. Now, say *yes*,' she prompted, wriggling up on her elbows so she could look into his face.

'Yes, Miss Ravenhurst. I am honoured to accept your very flattering proposal of marriage.'

'Oh.' She dropped her head so her face was buried in the soft blue silk over his right breast. 'Oh, thank goodness.' The relief rolled over her in waves as she lay there, absorbing the warmth and strength of his body.

'Might I hope for a kiss?' Nathan asked.

Suddenly very shy she mumbled, 'Yes.' And found herself rolling again, this time on to her back.

Nathan leaned on one elbow and looked down at her. 'I have dreamed of this moment. I love you very much, Clemence. I realised it as I was denying it to your aunt, knowing you were listening. It was the hardest thing I have done, crushing that feeling just as I became aware of it, knowing I was wounding you as I did so.'

'Kiss it better.' She looked up at him, awed and a little anxious. He was very close and very big and all hers. All hers. 'I love you, too.'

She had thought, when she had dreamt of this moment, that his kiss would be familiar. But it was not like the times before when their lips had met. It was not the sudden flare of physical attraction, the heat of temper or the deliberate incitement that those kisses had been.

Nathan's mouth on hers was sure, firm, very gentle. And it was quite evident that this was a beginning, a claiming, that she was now his and he would take what she could offer him, lead her, teach her until what she could offer and ask went far beyond her imagination and experience now.

Her lips parted for him and he took possession of the heat and the soft intimacy of her mouth with lips and teeth and tongue until she was moaning and writhing against him, her fingers tight on his shoulders, her body arching, seeking. His hands stayed still, cupping her shoulders, his body held away from hers, his control absolute until he finally broke the kiss, leaving her gasping. And she saw the heat and the desire in his face.

'Clemence,' he said huskily, running his hand down

the curve of her cheek. 'My beautiful Clemence.' As he sat up and looked down at the bed, his expression changed to one of rueful amusement.

Clemence sat up, too. 'Oh, my goodness. This bed looks as though we've been making love on it for hours. Did I really do that in my nightmare?'

Nathan nodded. 'I'll help you straighten it. You can't sleep on such rumpled sheets.'

'I don't want to sleep at all,' she murmured, sliding her hand into the front of his robe.

'Clemence, I am trying to be a gentleman.' His breath caught as her exploring fingertips slid over his nipple.

'No one is going to believe that who sees this bed,' she pointed out, fascinated by the effect on his breathing of running her nails down his ribs and towards his stomach. She found his navel and twirled a finger into it and he groaned.

'*Clemence!* Will you make an honest man of me very soon if I let you seduce me?'

'Just as soon as it can be arranged,' Clemence promised, attacking the sash. It was not very tightly tied and he did not appear to be wearing anything under it. Suddenly diffident, she drew her hand back.

'Sure?' She nodded. 'Scared?'

'No. Shy.' She could feel her smile wobbling, just a little.

'There is no need. Just trust me. We have been naked together before—remember the forest pool.' Nathan shrugged out of the robe and it fell on to the sheets behind him like shimmering water. 'Remember the green of the trees and the cool of the water.' His hands were on her crumpled nightgown. She shifted to help him and then it was over her head and thrown to the floor and his hands were skimming down over her breasts, the curve of her waist, to come to rest on her hip.

'Remember how the water felt, Clemence,' he murmured, bending his head to her as his hands stroked. With a shiver she curled against him, partly to hide herself from his hot blue eyes, partly to touch as much of him as she could. He was aroused; she could feel him pressed hot and hard against her belly. Instinctively she moved against him and was rewarded by the way his hands stilled, tightening around her.

Nathan eased her on to her back, firmly moving her hands away when she tried to cover herself, smiling at her until she smiled back, reassured. She began to relax. This was not frightening at all, this was— 'Nathan!' she gasped as his fingers slid into the hidden folds her hands had been shielding just a moment ago, folds that she was startled to realise were wet, hot and, 'Oh, oh, Nathan…'

'Are you sure?' he murmured, shifting his body over hers.

'Sure?' His hand was still *there*, making it almost impossible to think and then he slid one finger inside and she arched up against his palm, gasping.

'Yes, yes, I'm sure. Oh, Nathan, please….' Her body seemed to know what to do, her legs opening to cradle him. Then she felt the pressure and was not so certain.

'Look at me,' he said softly as she tensed. 'Look into my eyes, Clemence. We are going on this journey together. I have you safe.'

'Safe?' She found she could smile, her eyes widening as he rocked against her, filled her, and, just when she thought this was impossible, completed her with a thrust that took her through a flash of pain into the blissful realisation that they were one.

His face went out of focus and then came back. He was watching her, his eyes dark, his face taut with strain. 'Sweetheart? Did I hurt you?'

'Mmm.' She nodded. 'It didn't matter. Oh, I do love you.' She wriggled, trying to get used to the feeling and fascinated to discover the effect that had on Nathan. She had muscles inside as well, she realised, experimenting, and watching his jaw clench and his eyelids become heavy.

'Clemence, my love. If you do that I am going to have to move.' She did it again and he smiled and moved and she forgot everything, lost everything, in this new power driving through her.

She shifted and found she could match the rhythm, watched his face with a kind of awe as he took them deeper and deeper into whirlpool of sensation and then realised that her body was straining towards something, tightening around him, and she was gasping, desperate for something she didn't know, couldn't name and his hand slid between them again and touched her, *perfectly*, and there should have been rockets and cannons and fireworks to go with the stars and the swirling blackness, but there was Nathan's voice, joined with hers and a slow, slow tumble into peace.

'I love you.'

'I love you, too.' Clemence, wrapped in Nathan's silk robe, snuggled closer against his body, letting her fingers explore up and down his ribs.

'What a good thing you had that nightmare.' He was playing with her curls, the brush of his fingers sending delicious shivers down her spine. 'But I thought you said you had it when I wasn't around.'

'It was Street, I think. I had to speak to him and Eliza just before I went to bed and for some reason he wouldn't stop talking about the incident.'

'Last night? Why did you have to talk to them then?'

'Aunt Amelia had spoken to Street about marrying Eliza and—'

'Urgh!' Nathan sat up abruptly and clutched for his ankle. 'That damned dog has just licked me.' Clemence sat up, too. There was One-Eye, tongue lolling, watching them from beside the bed. 'How did that get in here?'

'He must have been with Eliza.'

'No.' Nathan shook his head. 'He sleeps in Street's room. Which means that either she heard you crying out from there, which is impossible, or both she and Street were down here. Which means they knew you were going to dream.'

'And she fetched you, which is a scandalous thing to do.'

'And it is very odd,' Nathan added grimly, 'but those loud cries did not attract the attention of a single one of the ladies sleeping nearby. The Ravenhursts, my love, have been plotting.'

'Dinner last night—Jessica deliberately made it informal. And Theo and Elinor and Sebastian made sure you knew I was going back to Jamaica. Aunt Amelia stopped me talking to Street about his intentions and said she would do it—she must have told him to remind me so vividly that I dreamed!'

Clemence stared at him, appalled. 'Nathan, I am so sorry—my dreadful family.' His mouth was twitching. 'You aren't angry?'

'Angry? Tomorrow I am going to kiss every one of your damned Ravenhursts, Lord Sebastian and the duchess included. They nearly tore us apart, simply by existing, now they've brought us together. And now, my love, I intend to kiss you and spend the next hour making sure you forget which continent you are on, let alone that you have a legion of interfering cousins.'

'Again?' Clemence gasped, as his hands on her body became deliciously wicked.

'And again and again and again for the rest of our lives, my love. One thing you learn as a naval officer is to take every opportunity when on leave.' His voice became muffled as he slid down, trailing kisses over the curve of her hip bone.

'Oh, yes, my love. Please, every opportunity…' And Clemence closed her eyes and surrendered to Nathan and to love.

Afterword

In 1817, when this book is set, the heyday of the Caribbean buccaneers was long since over. But there still remained a dangerous number of pirates, free-booters and the maritime equivalent of footpads to harass the rich trade of the islands, and the government invested considerable resources on suppressing their activities. Red Matthew McTiernan and his crew are a composite of some of these unromantic and dangerous characters.

The book I found most useful in researching THE PIRATICAL MISS RAVENHURST was *Lady Nugent's Journal of Her Residence in Jamaica from 1801 to 1805* (Institute of Jamaica 4th ed. 1966), and I have followed Lady Nugent's return voyage on *HMS Theseus* for *Orion's* route and timings almost exactly.

The fan that Nathan finds in Weymouth and gives to Clemence is real, and I found it in a country auction when I was already writing the book. It seemed such a spooky coincidence that not only was I writing about a heroine called Clemence, but that the virtues of the man destined for her on the fan so exactly matched Nathan's, that I could not resist including it.

I am indebted to Historical Romance author Joanna Maitland for the translation of the difficult eighteenth-century French verses.

The dance *La Pistole*—speed-dating for the *ton* as it struck me at the time—I learned at the Victoria & Albert Museum's wonderful Regency Evening in June 2007.

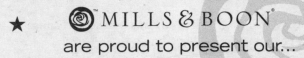

are proud to present our...

Book of the Month

★

Expecting Miracle Twins
by Barbara Hannay

Mattie Carey has put her dreams of finding
Mr. Right aside to be her best friend's surrogate.
Then the gorgeous Jake Devlin steps into her life...

Enjoy double the Mills & Boon® Romance
in this great value 2-in-1!

Expecting Miracle Twins by Barbara Hannay and
Claimed: Secret Son by Marion Lennox

Available 4th September 2009

*Tell us what you think about
Expecting Miracle Twins
at millsandboon.co.uk/community*

millsandboon.co.uk Community

Join Us!

The Community is the perfect place to meet and chat to kindred spirits who love books and reading as much as you do, but it's also the place to:

- **Get the inside scoop from authors about their latest books**
- **Learn how to write a romance book with advice from our editors**
- **Help us to continue publishing the best in women's fiction**
- **Share your thoughts on the books we publish**
- **Befriend other users**

Forums: Interact with each other as well as authors, editors and a whole host of other users worldwide.

Blogs: Every registered community member has their own blog to tell the world what they're up to and what's on their mind.

Book Challenge: We're aiming to read 5,000 books and have joined forces with The Reading Agency in our inaugural Book Challenge.

Profile Page: Showcase yourself and keep a record of your recent community activity.

Social Networking: We've added buttons at the end of every post to share via digg, Facebook, Google, Yahoo, technorati and de.licio.us.

www.millsandboon.co.uk

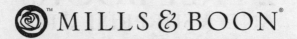

2 FREE BOOKS
AND A SURPRISE GIFT

We would like to take this opportunity to thank you for reading this
Mills & Boon® book by offering you the chance to take TWO more
specially selected books from the Historical series absolutely FREE!
We're also making this offer to introduce you to the benefits of the
Mills & Boon® Book Club™—

- **FREE home delivery**
- **FREE gifts and competitions**
- **FREE monthly Newsletter**
- **Exclusive Mills & Boon Book Club offers**
- **Books available before they're in the shops**

Accepting these FREE books and gift places you under no obligation to buy, you may cancel at any time, even after receiving your free
books. Simply complete your details below and return the entire page
to the address below. You don't even need a stamp!

YES Please send me 2 free Historical books and a surprise gift. I
understand that unless you hear from me, I will receive 4 superb new
books every month for just £3.79 each, postage and packing free. I
am under no obligation to purchase any books and may cancel my
subscription at any time. The free books and gift will be mine to keep
in any case.

Ms/Mrs/Miss/Mr_____ Initials _____

Surname _____

Address _____

_____

_____ Postcode _____

Send this whole page to: Mills & Boon Book Club, Free Book Offer,
FREEPOST NAT 10298, Richmond, TW9 1BR

Offer valid in UK only and is not available to current Mills & Boon Book Club subscribers to this series.
Overseas and Eire please write for details.. We reserve the right to refuse an application and
applicants must be aged 18 years or over. Only one application per household. Terms and prices subject to
change without notice. Offer expires 30th November 2009. As a result of this application, you may receive
offers from Harlequin Mills & Boon and other carefully selected companies. If you would prefer not to
share in this opportunity please write to The Data Manager, PO Box 676, Richmond, TW9 1WU.